LUNACY

CHRIS COPPEL

CRANTHORPE
—MILLNER—
PUBLISHERS

First published by Cranthorpe Millner Publishers (2023)

ISBN 978-1-80378-075-7 (Paperback)

www.cranthorpemillner.com

Cranthorpe Millner Publishers

CHAPTER 1
(1932)

Cassandra had no idea that she was about to die.

She was awakened from her laudanum-induced sleep by two orderlies. She could tell it was either very late or very early as the darkness outside her cramped room was utterly black and showed no sign of residual dusk or impending dawn. They dragged her from her bed and forced her down three flights of stairs into the dark basement. She'd been taken there before when the staff didn't want her or the other inmates to be seen. This time something was different about the underground room. As she was led to the bottom of the stone stairs, she could feel her feet and ankles submerge into a thick, greasy liquid.

It smelled of petroleum, but the odour was far more intense and all-pervasive. Judging by the crying and shouting for help, she knew there had to be dozens of other patients down there with her.

Cassandra couldn't understand why they'd all been led into the dark space. She knew it couldn't be as a punishment as she hadn't done anything wrong. She was also shocked by the disrespectful way the orderlies had manhandled her. Usually, the patients were carefully led into the space so there were no injuries that could later lead to some sort of an investigation.

Cassandra had been shut in the basement before and had learned not to panic as she would doubtless be released as soon as the staff saw fit. She knew from experience that panicking only made the darkness and anxiety even worse.

She made her way through the blackness to the nearest wall and leaned against it as she forced herself to calm her breathing, something else she had taught herself during her eight years of incarceration at the facility.

Cassandra did not consider herself to be crazy. In fact, she had always thought of herself as almost mundanely level-headed. Despite that, her husband had arranged for her stay at Sunny Meadows after her second 'suicide attempt'.

Normally, such treatment would have been the best recourse for someone bent on ending their life, but Cassandra had never once tried to kill herself. Both occasions had, in fact, been attempts by her husband to murder her. Despite pleading her case to local police and doctors, her husband, the honourable senator from Northern Virginia, had persuaded them that though she seemed a little troubled and despondent of late, he was shocked that she would try to end her own life.

Despite Cassandra's pleas, the police had been persuaded by her husband to let him ensure her well-being and not put her through the anguish of a police interrogation or medical examinations. He had successfully convinced all involved, except Cassandra, that her mental state was due to a couple of undisclosed miscarriages over the prior eighteen months. Had they bothered to question her at all, she could have told them that he was lying, and that her husband had not had intercourse with her for over two years ever since starting his affair with Martha Whitten, a young widow living in nearby Warrenton.

After two failed attempts on her life, her husband was afraid to try to kill her for a third time, so he decided on a completely different approach. On the pretext of looking for exactly the right care facility for his troubled wife, he had learned of Sunny Meadows, a centre for mental care located far from prying eyes, next to a small lake in Manassas in Northern Virginia.

The facility was highly praised by everyone he spoke to and offered a unique service for concerned relatives of the unstable and insane. For a sizeable 'donation' plus a monthly patient maintenance fee, the facility would take in almost anybody and ensure that they received the best psychiatric care available, whether they needed it or not.

Cassandra stood silently in the utter blackness and wondered how much longer it would be until she was released from her confinement in the dark space. She had no way of keeping track of time but was certain that more of it had elapsed than was normal.

She began to worry when she found that breathing had become more difficult. The stench of oil had grown stronger, and it was getting harder to get the oxygen her lungs desperately needed.

Suddenly, a yellowish light became visible behind a small open hatch in the centre of what she knew to be the building's boiler. At the same time, the heat within the space became more intense. As she looked towards the iron beast with its one flickering yellow eye, the air around the opening ignited, sending flames reaching towards the dark liquid that covered the floor.

The room exploded with fire and black smoke.

As the flames reached her, Cassandra's last thought, rather than fear, was that she was finally being set free.

CHAPTER 2
(Present day)

When he first saw the ad for General Manager of Audio-Visual Support at the Global Initiative Bank, Mike Ellis hadn't even heard of the place. After working in the post-production end of the film business for almost twenty years, his first reaction was that there was no way he was ever going to work in banking.

Once he Googled them and saw that they were basically the United Nations for funding and development, he became slightly more interested, but even with the knowledge that they weren't a mere bank, Mike still had some doubts as to whether it was somewhere he wanted to work. Despite becoming a successful Technical Operations Executive, he still needed work to be exciting, and nothing he'd learned about the GIB seemed to fit that mould.

The other aspect that made him wary of the whole prospect was that the position wasn't working directly for the GIB. Instead, he would be employed by a company that was contracted to provide and manage the audio-visual support team. Having only ever worked as a direct employee, Mike wasn't at all sure that he liked the dynamics of being little more than a contractor.

After discussing the opportunity with his wife, Lisa, she persuaded him to at least interview for the position. That way, she suggested, he'd know exactly what he was declining to accept.

Lisa often gave him straightforward advice that made him, even at forty-two years old, feel like he was a kid with ADHD.

"What about the fact that the job is in DC?" Mike asked. "Do you really want to live on the east coast?"

"I don't know, babe," she answered. "I've never been there. How would I know until I've at least seen the place?"

Lisa was right of course. Living in California his entire life, Mike had a very narrow view of the world, or even America for that matter. Before Lisa had hitched her proverbial horse to Mike's wagon, she had at least travelled to Europe when she was in her teens. Mike had hardly ever left California except for a couple of boozy trips to Tijuana and of course, Las Vegas.

"What about Kevin?" Mike asked. "How's he going to feel about having to move to a new school?"

"He's five, honey. He's still in pre-school. There must be some great ones in DC, and you just know he'll make friends within the first few minutes."

"What if their curriculum is different than here?" he asked, clutching at one last straw.

Lisa replied, grinning, "I'm pretty sure that the finger painting and naptime protocols are going to be surprisingly similar."

The battle lost, Mike emailed the HR contact at People Force, the company that held the GIB contract.

He ended up speaking to their operations director for over an hour and thought that the conversation had gone well. It felt more like a couple of friends talking, rather than an initial phone interview.

Mike didn't hear anything for over a week, then out of the blue, he got a call from Rick Greenberg, the company president. Rick explained that while they were intrigued by his experience in film and video post-production, they weren't sure that his background was a good fit for running an enterprise-level audio-visual operation.

Mike was stunned at their reluctance to recognise his abilities, especially as he secretly felt that AV was a poor relation to the post-production environment within the film and television studios. More importantly, he wasn't sure he liked the idea of moving his family thousands of miles to work in some stuffy government building.

Mike was about to thank Rick for his time, assuming that the matter was closed, when Rick asked if he was available to fly up to San Jose to meet with him the following day. Apparently, Rick was en route to see some clients in Northern California before flying off to Japan for a series of sales presentations. The only time he had available was a one-hour window before his flight left San Jose airport.

Mike flew out of Burbank at eleven o'clock the next morning and was shaking hands with Rick Greenberg one hour and fifteen minutes later. Rick looked to be in his fifties, had an intentional five-day beard growth and was wearing jeans, cowboy boots, and a black silk shirt. There was no question that he was going for a very specific look. Mike just wasn't completely sure what it was.

Rick led him to a franchise deli restaurant, where they had an in-depth but rushed conversation as they wolfed down fatty pastrami on rye.

"Here's the thing," Rick said as he wiped a smear of mustard off his bristly chin. "You've got some serious chops when it comes to operations and administrative management. The thing is that our general managers are required to be hands-on in case they have to step in during an event or a meeting. You don't have that experience."

"No, I don't," Mike agreed. "However, if what I've surmised so far is correct, you've been through three general managers in the last eighteen months, so maybe your search criteria is a little off. You have a support team of twenty-two technicians and engineers at the GIB, correct?"

"Yes."

"I think your problem is that you have plenty of hands-on technologists," Mike continued. "What you don't have is a real manager. Someone who knows how to distribute the workforce and mentor everyone into becoming one cohesive, high-functioning team. I am sure that you know that technicians and engineers are wired, if you'll excuse the pun, in a completely different way than senior managers. Filling that position with someone who can't possibly focus on the responsibilities of budgeting, staffing, educating and coordinating, to say nothing of handholding and schmoozing your client, is doomed from the start."

Rick placed his remaining piece of sandwich on his plate and sat back in the faux leather banquette. He looked directly into Mike's eyes without saying a word for a good twenty seconds.

Outwardly, Mike smiled confidently back at him. Inwardly he was kicking himself for having been so outspoken. He'd basically told the president of a successful technical staffing company that he didn't know what he was doing.

"I will be back in DC in thirteen days," Rick said. "I'll have HR liaise with you in the meantime to set up an onsite interview at our offices and at the bank. You up for that?"

"Absolutely," Mike replied, even as a tiny voice shouted deep within his head for him to run the other way.

Two weeks later, Mike flew out of LAX.

It was the longest flight of his life, and he was highly relieved when, five hours later, the plane touched down at Dulles International.

Once in the arrival terminal, Mike was pleased to see a driver holding up an iPad with his name on it. He'd expected People Force to maybe have an employee pick him up, instead he got a Lincoln town car with a chauffeur.

The journey from Dulles into DC was a surprise to him. For some reason, he'd expected wall to wall urban blight, but instead was impressed to see large tracks of open land separated by clusters of ultra-modern office buildings and apartment complexes.

For almost the entire drive, they ran parallel to one of the city's metro lines. As it was starting to get dark, Mike could make out sardined commuters making their way back home to what he imagined would be another alcohol-infused evening watching reality TV.

The town car crossed the Potomac on the Theodore Roosevelt Bridge then looped back and drove under the overhang of the Kennedy Center. Once past the massive concrete slab that seemed to be suspended only a few feet above the car, Mike got his first glimpse of the iconic Watergate complex. From all the pictures and videos he'd seen of the storied development, he'd expected it to look dated and uninviting. Instead, with dusk having given way to night, the quintet of curved concrete structures looked elegant, perched only a few feet from the river. Golden light bled from terraced windows, giving the curved buildings an otherworldly appearance.

They stayed on Rock Creek Parkway until the driver joined Connecticut Avenue then headed north towards Bethesda. After a few miles, he pulled into the parking area of a non-descript office block. People Force took up the entire third floor. It was past six and most of the employees had gone home. As Mike entered the reception area a glass door opened at the far end and a tall woman in a formal two-piece suit offered him her hand.

"I'm Linda Heflin," she said. "We spoke on the phone."

"Pleasure," Mike replied, as he tried not to show his surprise. There had been something so efficient and business-like about Linda on the phone that he'd wrongly assumed that she was going to look much older than she seemed in person.

Mike had a brief meeting with the senior management of People Force, after which they took him to a local Italian restaurant where everyone seemed to eat and drink to joyous excess. Normally in an interview situation, Mike would have abstained from drinking, but he could sense within the first few minutes that such behaviour could easily give the impression of his being a non-conformist, or worse, aloof. It was clear that the People Force crew liked to make the most of an evening out and he should at least do the same.

Mike was picked up from his hotel at eight forty-five the next morning and was driven to the visitor/security entrance of the bank. Upon entering, he had to go through an airport-like screening, including having belongings x-rayed, including his shoes and belt.

Rick was waiting for him on the other side of the barrier and gave him a quick tour of the building. Mike was speechless. The structure, which he learned was one of five GIB buildings located in the centre of DC, was immense. It took up almost an entire block. In the centre was a twelve-storey atrium with pale, pink, marble flooring. Rick explained that apart from just being dramatic, it was used for live events, including concerts and speeches from the world's movers and shakers.

It was at that moment that Mike understood that AV at the GIB was a massive undertaking and was both cutting edge and exceedingly well funded. They toured dozens of hi-tech meeting rooms that reminded Mike of movie sets where Bond villains would be planning global chaos.

Instead of his original feelings that the job was potentially beneath him, Mike started having grave doubts as to whether he was up for the challenge. He was starting to realise why they'd been looking for someone with serious technology chops. Suddenly, the big salary made sense.

By the time Mike boarded his six o'clock flight back to LAX, he was a mass of conflicting thoughts, all vying for attention within his tired brain. He was, if he cared to admit it, terrified by the breadth and scope of the responsibilities that came with the job. There was also the small problem that he was unfamiliar with much of the technology he would be overseeing. It wouldn't be the first time that he'd taken such a leap. The problem was that this cliff seemed one hell of a lot higher than others he'd scaled.

By the time he landed in LA, Mike had convinced himself that he wasn't the right person for the job.

CHAPTER 3

It took over two weeks before they got back to him with the news that the position was his and that he had six weeks to get himself and his family to DC.

Once the contract was signed, Lisa managed to persuade the owners of Clarkwell and Mason Publishing that she could work remotely from the east coast. After booking the movers and the travel, she even managed to find a two-bedroom, partially furnished apartment in DC, only eight blocks from the GIB headquarters.

Despite her stoic management of their move, inside Lisa was a mess. She was sick of moving and wanted nothing more than to plant stakes far enough into the ground that any additional relocating would be impossible to even consider.

*

Lisa had been a bright and inquisitive child who loved reading books and writing her own short stories. They lived on Knapp Street in Northridge, thirty miles from downtown Los Angeles. Their three-bedroom, ranch-style house may not have been the newest or biggest on their block, but Lisa thought it was the cutest one by far. With its faux Hawaiian roof and brightly painted shutters, she always felt that it looked like a place where happy people lived.

She wasn't wrong. Her parents, Jay and Rachel, were in fact very happy. Her dad was a successful make-up artist, who at that time was working on the hit sitcom *Amigos*. Lisa's mother worked from home making small-batch, gourmet chocolate chip cookies that she sold at the weekly farmer's market. The profits were hardly going to make them rich, but sampling new recipes was a treat for the whole family.

At twelve, Lisa had no interest in boys and preferred to sit quietly reading a good book. Some of her friends were already into one boy or another, but Lisa couldn't understand why they wanted to go out with anyone that noisy, brash, and even occasionally smelly. Lisa loved being able to simply stand back and enjoy the show.

Despite what some kids considered to be her superior attitude, some of the boys were already noticing Lisa. With her long, coppery-red hair, her green *eyes, athletic build, and a face that looked uncannily like a young Jodie Foster, boys were starting to show a lot of interest.*

One day, her dad got home a little early from a shoot in the hills of Calabasas. He was in a good mood and felt like taking his two best girls out for dinner. That could only mean one thing. He was craving Southern barbeque. It was a fifteen-minute drive up the hill into Simi Valley where Smoky Joe's Fine Eats was wedged between a nail salon and a discount tyre store.

What folks didn't know was that Joe (there really was a Joe) intentionally kept the place looking foreboding and grim. He didn't want his little restaurant to become a destination for elite hipsters, the Sunday brunch crowd, or any non-devotee of real Southern barbeque.

The moment Lisa and her parents walked in, Joe came out from the kitchen and gave them all such a big hug, you'd think they hadn't seen each other for years even though at most it might have been two weeks. For whatever reason, Lisa didn't mind the attention. Joe always smelled of woodsmoke, hot oil, and Old Spice.

Her dad said that Joe had to be a hundred if he was a day. His voice was low and mellow and had a sing-song quality to it. His skin was as black as was humanly possible and his shaved head shined even under the dim restaurant lights.

Joe led them to the only vacant table in the place.

"What are my best customers gonna have today?" he asked, with a twinkle in his old eyes.

"You tell us, Joe," her dad replied. "What's good?"

"If there was anything on my menu that wasn't grade A good, it damn well wouldn't be on my menu!" Joe said with a grin. "Now if yousa asking what is extra special today, that'd be a whole different thing."

"Tell us about those," Rachel said.

"If you've a hankering for something smoky with a kick like a frisky mule, then you need to try the brisket. Three days a marinatin', and one day of smokin'. Yes'm. Them's good eats. Now if you want something a little more subdued, I just pulled some racks of Texas short ribs out of the smoke house. If I do say so myself, they would have been prize winners back when I used to care about such hooey."

"Why don't you bring us enough of the ribs and the brisket so that we'll have plenty to take home for dinner tomorrow as well," her dad ordered.

"Usual sides?" Joe checked. "Beans, fries, and greens?"

"And don't forget the corn bread," Lisa reminded him.

"As if I would do such a thing. Barbeque without corn bread is like chicken without a waffle," Joe stated as he headed back into the kitchen.

The food was as spectacular as always and Joe made sure that they always left loaded down with enough extra to see them through at least two more meals. None of them complained.

When they got home, they watched a new episode of her dad's show, then Lisa kissed them both goodnight before heading to her room to finish off some homework.

As she was leaving the room, her dad called after her. "It's days like these when I feel like we might just keep you around."

"Thanks, Dad," she said as she shook her head and ran up the stairs. "You'd better decide soon," she called from the landing. "I've got two offers from other parents that both sound promising."

Lisa grinned as she made her way to her bedroom. Unlike her friends who seemed to like living among clutter and vividly coloured posters, Lisa had gone minimal. She'd painted her walls bright white, added framed posters of works by Dali, Monet, and her one and only nod to modern culture, a poster of the movie Pulp Fiction, *just because she thought that Uma Thurman looked intensely cool.*

Lisa brushed her teeth, washed her face then snuggled under her white down comforter.

She was asleep in seconds having no idea that in a few hours, her life would be irrevocably changed.

CHAPTER 4

The first jolt, though violent, wasn't enough to fully awaken Lisa. She thought she'd dreamed it and was about to descend back into a deep sleep when the bulk of the earthquake hit. It was terrifying, and her sleep-addled brain couldn't initially understand what was happening. Her room was pitch dark and her bed was literally jumping in place. She managed to get to her feet but immediately found it impossible to stand. She fell to the floor as the shaking increased. Her bedroom window shattered one second before she felt the house tilt sideways. Worse than the shaking and shifting of the structure was the noise. It sounded like one long, never-ending explosion.

It did of course end, but not before giving the house one final massive, unforgiving shake. Lisa heard glass, bricks, and wood grinding and collapsing just outside her room.

Then there was a moment of eerie silence before

every car alarm in a thirty-mile radius went off at once.

There was no power. Instead, there was a distinct smell of gas and the sound of running water coming from both inside and outside the house. Lisa's window and its frame were gone entirely, and she could see their street through the gaping hole in her bedroom wall. The overhead powerlines were arcing, sending sparks high into the air, illuminating the strange scene. Water was streaming down the road. It looked like a river. Lisa had no idea that it was the result of thousands of water heaters that had been torn from their plumbed-in locations, sending millions of gallons of water spewing out of the severed pipes.

Lisa managed to stand but could hardly see anything within the darkened house. She felt along the hallway wall for where her dad had installed an emergency flashlight. It was supposed to have come on whenever power was cut, but judging by the darkness, Lisa assumed it had failed. She found where the cradle was screwed into the wall, but the flashlight was gone. Then she noticed a thin bead of light under her bathroom door. She tried to open it, but it was jammed shut. For a moment, she even thought that someone had locked it from the inside.

She tried again to push it open. It moved an inch, but no more. Lisa, who by then was starting to go into mental shock, threw herself at the door. It only opened another few inches, but it was enough for her to see the emergency flashlight lying on the bathmat. Somehow during the shaking and pounding, it had been forced out of its cradle and bounced into the bathroom before the door slammed shut and jammed. She was so relieved that she started to cry.

With access to light, she began to move towards her parents' bedroom.

"Mom… Dad?" she shouted over her crying.

Their door was closed but the entire frame and wall was sloping down on the right. Because the hinges had been ripped from the frame, it fell into the room after one hard shove.

The sight that greeted her was impossible to compute. Her parents' cheerful bedroom with its ludicrous four poster bed was nothing more than a pile of rubble. The bed had been flattened and Lisa could distinctly see faux wood roof shingles mixed in with rafters, tar paper, and fiberglass insulation from the attic.

She ran to the pile of debris, placing the flashlight on a collapsed beam, and started to claw at the mass, hoping to find her parents alive under the rubble. Lisa managed to shift some of the peripheral debris but couldn't move any of the bigger pieces. With tears streaming down her dust-covered face, she heard a moan.

She stopped moving and held her ear to the pile. She heard the sound again, only it wasn't coming from the bedroom. It was emanating from the en-suite bathroom. Lisa looked through the misshapen door frame and assumed that the sound either couldn't have come from there or it wasn't a human making the noise.

The ceiling had partially collapsed on top of the sink and toilet, causing water to leak out from under the rubble. The glass-enclosed shower had shattered, and a huge rafter was hanging down into it from above.

Lisa was about to turn away when she heard the moaning again. It was louder and was coming from within the room. She approached where the bath had been, but there seemed to be nothing but broken bricks and shingles.

"Hello!" Lisa screamed.

For a moment there was no response, but then, coming from under the pile of roof and wall parts, was another moan.

Lisa balanced the light on the rubble pile where the sink had been and began to dig.

Within minutes, she'd cleared an area, then stopped. She wasn't sure what she was looking at. Where the bath should have been was a long rectangular piece of scarred wood. It took her a second to realise that she was looking at the bathroom door that was lying flat about two feet off the floor.

Lisa grabbed one end of it and pulled it towards her. It was heavy, but fear and hope had given Lisa new strength. The door slid towards her. Suddenly, her end dropped to the ground, revealing the missing bathtub. In it was her mother. She had a bad gash on her forehead and her Pollo Hermanos t-shirt was ripped and covered in blood stains and mud, but she was alive, even if unconscious.

Lisa wanted to drag her mother right out of the tub and the house but knew that if she tried that by herself, she could easily cause her mom even more injury.

Lisa ran out of the house and found a neighbour standing outside his untouched home looking scared and confused.

"Mister Kingston," she cried. "Please help me."

He looked back at her with a glazed look.

"Mister Kingston, it's me, Lisa, from 1207. My mom's hurt. I need help."

Something in her words caused the right set of synapses to fire within him.

"Lisa!" he stammered. "Of course. Let me get some light."

He ran into the house and emerged moments later with a flashlight, his wife, and their teenage son.

Once in Lisa's house, they were able to lift Rachel and place her gingerly on top of the bathroom door and use it like a gurney. They had to tilt it carefully to get through the misshapen door frame, but finally made it out of the partially collapsed house and out onto the front lawn.

"You stay here," Kingston shouted. "I'm going to get my truck. We'll have to drive her to a hospital. There's no phones or power in the whole valley. Might have to try for Santa Monica or Pasadena. I'll put a call out on the CB radio and find out which one is open and which route is passable."

"My dad," Lisa cried. "He's still inside."

"Where?" Mr Kingston's wife asked.

"The bedroom next to where we found my mom."

Mrs Kingston and her son ran back in to see if they could find him as Mr Kingston headed off to get his truck. Lisa was left alone on the front lawn kneeling next to her mother.

She'd never felt so scared and lost in her entire life.

She heard a racket next door and saw Mr Kingston wrestling with his garage door. With the power being off for most of the valley, his garage door opener was about as much use as a tail on a teacup.

Just as the two Kingstons emerged from her destroyed home, Lisa heard Mr Kingston's Ford pick-up roar to life.

"Did you find him?" Lisa asked the two.

Mrs Kingston stepped over to her and took her hand.

"I'm so sorry, Lisa," she said as she pulled her in for a hug.

"He's okay," Lisa insisted. "You don't understand. He never gets hurt. Let me go back in and he'll be fine."

Mrs Kingston held her tightly.

"He's gone, dear. There's nothing to see inside."

For a brief second, Lisa misunderstood the older woman and thought she meant that her father had gone out somewhere. That he'd somehow managed to escape the house before it collapsed. Then she saw the blood on Mrs Kingston's hands.

Mr Kingston's bright red Ford F-150 drove right up on the lawn and pulled up next to the makeshift stretcher.

After gently laying Rachel in the back of the truck, they covered her in blankets then climbed in alongside to make sure she stayed as stable as possible. As they pulled away from Lisa's happy home, a power line dropped from an overhead pole and swung right onto the top of the collapsed roof. For a second, the snake-like cable sparked as it whipped from side to side, then it found the gas leak caused by the cooker when it had rocked itself across the kitchen floor, severing the hook-up at the wall.

There was a muffled FRUMP, then the happy house at 1207 Knapp Street ceased to exist.

They were able to get Rachel to the UCLA emergency room some twenty-five miles away. She was immediately triaged and wheeled to surgery with two broken ribs, a broken right wrist, a compound fracture of her right tibia, a skull fracture, and a bad concussion.

Lisa sent the Kingstons home and promised that she would be fine. After a couple of hours, a doctor found her in the crowded waiting room and told her that her mother was in post-op and would make a full recovery. Lisa was allowed to stand outside the darkened post-op area and look in at her sleeping mother.

At eleven o'clock that same morning, Rachel was moved to a semi-private room, where, with Lisa holding her hand, a policeman informed them that Jay hadn't made it. Rachel didn't seem that surprised. Maybe the fact that her husband wasn't standing by her hospital bed was enough of a clue that he'd never left their house.

Rachel's recovery was slow, but the long-term prognosis looked good. Lisa was able to stay with family friends in Westwood, less than half a mile from the hospital.

Three weeks after the earthquake, Lisa, along with a surprisingly large number of mourners, met at Forest Lawn cemetery overlooking the Warner Bros Studio to honour the life of her father. Lisa had expected to cry inconsolably through the entire ceremony, but in the chapel, she'd been completely dry-eyed and felt emotionless, as if she was viewing the whole service as a disconnected observer.

It wasn't until they moved graveside under a freakishly hot California sun that the reality of what was going on really hit Lisa. The fact that she was saying goodbye to her dad without her mother at her side made it all the worse.

When they got back to Westwood, Lisa snuck away from the wake and somehow found herself on the UCLA campus. She had of course heard of the university but had never visited the campus or its park-like grounds. Why would she? She was a die-hard valley girl and the campus nestled between Bel Air and Westwood was like another world. Grand colonnaded buildings sat among ultra-modern architecture, giving it an air of academic prestige.

Somehow, wandering by herself though the campus as the others ate and drank back at the house gave her a sense of peaceful acceptance that she would have thought impossible only a few hours earlier.

Over the next month, between visiting times at the hospital, Lisa spent endless hours exploring the university grounds. Her favourite discovery was tucked away at the north-east end of the sprawling campus. It was there that the film and theatre school taught acting, directing, and everything in-between. The centre of the school looked exactly like a mini film studio complete with sound stages and production buildings.

Lisa had never even considered the fact that one could go to such a prestigious university and learn how to make movies. She had always assumed that she would end up going go to Northridge University and get a BA in creative writing.

Looking at the list of courses at the UCLA school peaked a newfound longing to be a part of something a little more special.

On the last day of her mother's hospitalization, Lisa toured the school one last time, then shelved all the impossible thoughts about being able to one day attend it. Even with the California resident's reduced rate, the tuition alone would come close to $18,000 a year.

Once Rachel was released from hospital, she and Lisa moved into a one-bedroom service apartment in the Elmdale Apartments complex in Toluca Lake. It was fully furnished and was what people referred to as an extended stay residence. Elmdale would advertise that it was for visiting executives who wanted a home away from home while in LA. The fact was, their primary source of revenue came from newly single divorcees who wanted a no-stress place to live while they decided what to do with their shattered lives.

Lisa and Rachel certainly qualified for the shattered part. Beyond the loss of a husband and father, their financial situation was a mess, to say the least. Jay had had life insurance; plenty of it. The problem was that the insurance company refused to pay, citing the 'act of God' exemption clause.

For a few weeks after that unexpected piece of news, Rachel spoke to countless people about fighting the company. Unfortunately, they all concurred that the clause was clear as day and was repeated numerous times on the policy. Death and home destruction as a result of an act of God were not covered. The 6.8 earthquake was not an accident or a man-made phenomenon.

They had some savings and thankfully owned the lot where their house had once stood but selling property in Northridge immediately after one of the biggest quakes in LA County history wasn't going to be viable for quite some time. Rachel decided that the only rational thing to do was to get a job.

Prior to Lisa's birth, Rachel had worked as the assistant director of a huge property management company at their Sherman Oaks location. After much persuasion from Jay, Rachel had decided to become a stay-at-home mom. As Jay had been bringing in plenty of money, her income hadn't been that vital.

Now, without Jay's salary, it was essential.

The next day, Rachel bought a copy of the LA Times from the complex's general store, and with a cup of coffee in one hand and a red pen in the other, began looking through the classifieds.

She was on her second cup of coffee when one particular ad caught her attention. It was for a property management position. It didn't give the name of the company, just the candidate's education and experience requirements.

Rachel had everything they seemed to want.

With Lisa watching and giving her a thumbs-up from the kitchen, Rachel dialled the number.

"Elmdale Apartments Corporate Office," a perky voice said. "How may I direct your call?"

*

Rachel interviewed at Elmdale's corporate headquarters in Encino. She of course knew of the Elmdale apartment complexes scattered throughout the San Fernando Valley, especially as they were currently living in one of their units but had never known that they were a huge international corporation. They had complexes across the US, Europe, and even Asia.

The position Rachel was applying for was to manage

one particular site. They were a little cagey about which one until close to the end of the interview.

The young woman from HR was immaculately dressed in a dark grey pants suit with a black silk blouse underneath. Her shoulder-length, ironed, auburn hair was feathered back from her ebony forehead, offering an unrestricted view of her slate grey eyes.

"Obviously, you are more than qualified for this position," Cyndra stated. "I think I may have a slightly more interesting option for you, if you are interested."

"Are you saying I didn't get the job?" Rachel asked, trying to keep the disappointment from her voice.

"We would be more than happy to offer you the position you applied for, but hear me out for a second. In six months, our Southern California regional director is moving up to manage the entire west coast operation. From what I can see from your background, I think you would be the perfect fit to take his old position."

"Thank you for saying that, but I don't know anything about your internal workings. I wouldn't know where to start."

Cyndra gave her a big smile. "I was thinking... what if you started in the site manager position you applied for, and over the next six months learned everything you could about us and our operation? Obviously, the advancement would be entirely contingent of how you do at the site, but then again, if you turn out not to be a good fit for that job, we'd be letting you go anyway. You don't have to answer me this minute. Go home and think about it."

"Is this a good time to ask which site I'd initially be working at?"

"That's the wonderful part," Cyndra said. "You'd be managing the complex you're living in right now."

Rachel was lost for words.

"I know," Cyndra grinned. "Almost meant to be, isn't it?"

Two days later Rachel accepted the job, but only after wrangling a two-bedroom unit instead of the one-bedroom unit they were currently in. Because the apartment came with the position, she saved having to pay rent and utilities.

The only downside of living at the Elmdale property was that Lisa had to move school from Northridge to Burbank. Then again, Arcadia High had been three blocks from their old house and two from the mall. It had suffered extensive damage from the quake and had been red flagged, so it wasn't as if she could return there anyway.

Starting at a new school was stressful enough but having to do so midway through the year was agonizing. The other kids were already familiar with the classes and teachers and would have already formed *into their cliques and friendships. Usually, very little fazed Lisa, but on the Sunday before her first day, she was terrified. Her whole persona was built on being able to blend into the background and observe. Now she was going to stick out like a sore thumb. At high school, late starters were automatically subject to harsh, individual scrutiny.*

Normally the bus would have picked her up on Toluca Lake Blvd, but for her first day, her mother offered to drive her to school. Lisa sat in complete silence as they drove past the Warner Bros Studio then took a right onto Riverside. After what Lisa considered to be far too short of a drive, she put on her best indifferent face, then joined the throng of students as they fed into the charmless 1950s school building.

Lisa reported to the administration office and was told to wait in an adjacent classroom with the other new arrivals. When she walked into the room, she was stunned. The staging classroom was full. There had to have been forty kids in there. What really amazed her was that she already knew at least a third of them. Because almost all the students from Northridge had been rehoused with their families since their homes were either yellow or red tagged, this was the first chance she'd had in ages to reconnect.

It seemed that after almost six weeks of being off school, the kids were being parsed out across the

Eastern Valley to whatever facility could take them in. Burbank, being one of the larger ones, took the biggest share.

After hugs and exchanges of sagas, the first transplant was called to the admin office. It took until lunchtime before everyone in that group was processed and given their schedules. Lisa soon learned that out of the twelve hundred students at Burbank High, one hundred and forty-two of them came from Northridge. She wasn't the only newbie by a long shot. Within less than a week, she was able to settle fully into her new school without any of the trauma she'd been expecting.

*

Rachel excelled at managing Elmdale's Toluca Lake complex. The experience was an eye opener. She'd had no idea of the turnover that went on at that type of apartment operation. There were nine hundred units in all, and every month an average of one hundred and twenty-five tenants gave their notice.

That meant that on any given day, there could be any number of units vacated. That required an immediate inspection, which almost always led to paint needing to be touched up, furniture being swapped or replaced, and anything that wasn't working being fixed. After that, industrial cleaners scoured the unit so that it could be shown to prospective, new short-term renters.

Rachel had to supervise every aspect of that process. Each unit had to be returned to Elmdale's high standards and then be re-rented as fast as possible. Even one day's delay in making a property available would impact the complex's bottom line. Rachel enjoyed the daily challenges and to everyone's delight, proved to be great at the job.

As promised, just shy of six months later, she was promoted to the director position. Rachel's primary task was to seek out the locations that were underperforming and fix whatever needed fixing so that their revenues were in line with corporate expectations.

What Rachel hadn't realised was that she was expected to physically live in each targeted site for anywhere from three to six months until the problems had been resolved. Because her area of responsibility stretched two hundred and fifteen miles from San Diego to Santa Barbara and her next posting could be anywhere within that area, Lisa's schooling became an issue.

Rachel stressed for two days, trying to summon the courage to tell her daughter that they were about to become little more than roaming nomads. Finally, seeking safety in numbers, she took Lisa out for dinner to her new favourite Mexican restaurant only one block *from their apartment.*

Before they'd even ordered, Rachel dropped her bombshell, then mentally cringed awaiting her daughter's explosion.

"Where would we go first?" Lisa asked cheerfully as she scooped a prodigious quantity of salsa onto her tortilla chip.

Rachel was floored. She'd expected the initial reaction to be one of anger, then guilt, then would come the big sulk. Instead, Lisa didn't seem the least bit upset.

"The first site would be the Elmdale complex in San Diego," Rachel said.

"San Diego!" Lisa managed to say through a mouthful of chip and dip. "That is so completely cool. Please tell me it's somewhere close to the water."

For the next five years, they moved on average every four and a half months. Some locations were too good to be true, others not so much. Lisa somehow adapted well to starting at a new school roughly three times a year. It wasn't until she had fulfilled her fantasy of being accepted to the writing program at UCLA's film and theatre school that she felt the loss of not having a real home close to the university; one that she could return to at the end of each day.

Lisa had to live in one of the on-campus dorms, and as much as she'd been dreading that part of the experience, by her second year, she was loving the fact that she didn't need to pack up and move every few months. The funny old building at the extreme south end of the campus started to feel like a real home.

After attending her first writing class, she felt as if her entire world had shifted. In one three-hour lecture, she knew more about the practical side of screenwriting than she'd ever known existed. Her euphoric feeling was short-lived as she made her way to her second class. She'd had to choose two production courses to make up her units and cinematography was one of them. The problem was that she knew nothing about cameras or, for that matter, even taking pictures. She was the only person she knew who couldn't even take a decent photo on an instamatic camera. Still, she kept telling herself she was there to learn, and besides, maybe the course would end up being fun.

CHAPTER 5

Mike fidgeted the entire flight from Los Angeles to DC.

It was as if he had somehow taken on all of Kevin's more irksome traits, while his son remained calm and relaxed for the whole trip. At one point, Lisa had to whisper for Mike to sit still and stop whining.

They landed on time as a light snowfall began to season the tarmac and surrounding landscape. Lisa, in the hopes of reducing the moving stress, had booked them into a hotel for the first week until their belongings arrived from LA.

Their slightly unkempt hotel was right off Washington Circle in an area called Foggy Bottom. When Kevin heard the name of the destination when Lisa confirmed it to the Uber driver, he got a serious case of the giggles.

"Mommy... I've got a foggy bottom," he said, before giggling even more.

Lisa hoped it would end there, but just as Kevin

seemed about to wind down, Mike entered the fray.

"You know… when I was in Tijuana this one time, I ate a bad burrito and had foggy bottom for a week."

Lisa could clearly see the driver's eyes as he studied the giggling man and child in his rear-view mirror. He did not seem remotely amused.

Once they'd reached the hotel and got Samantha settled, the three ventured outside with the intention of having a nice long walk to explore the area.

They'd forgotten about the snow. Thankfully, it wasn't coming down that hard. The issue was that it was blowing horizontally, making the wind-chill feel like something you'd expect to find in the Arctic.

They had packed their warm sweaters and jackets, but being die-hard Californians, these were only ever expected to hold back temperatures that were well above freezing point. They quickly learned that DC in the winter was something else entirely. They'd only travelled one block when they turned onto Pennsylvania Avenue and found that the wind seemed to be using the iconic street as a thoroughfare to travel across the city.

They reversed course, stopped at a tiny mom-and-pop convenience store, and bought a few essentials such as soft drinks for Kevin and a bottle of wine for themselves. Once back in their room, they ordered Domino's Pizza and spent the rest of the night watching

Simpson's re-runs. It felt just like home.

First thing the next morning, they headed for the nearest department store to stock up on winter clothing. By the time they stepped back onto the street, the weather had already changed and by mid-morning the temperature had risen into the sixties.

After a snack lunch, the three made their way from the hotel to what would be their new home. Thanks to its central location, they were able to walk to the new apartment, which was on 23rd Street, only a few blocks from the Potomac River.

Their unit was halfway down a hotel-like corridor that didn't appear to have seen much modernising or redecorating since the early eighties. Lisa was starting to worry that her miracle find had been too good to be true. Mike opened the front door of the unit and she felt her heart sink.

The online photos had made the place look like a swanky Manhattan penthouse. The real thing, however, looked dark, low ceilinged and devoid of any character whatsoever. The furniture looked decades old but was at least clean and serviceable, even if the colours were even more drab than the room itself.

Lisa looked at Mike and saw the disappointment on his face. They were both clearly thinking the same thing: 'How the hell do we get out of this?'

Kevin, oblivious to his parents' despair, walked

across the room to where beige floor to ceiling curtains ran from wall to wall. He found the pull cord and, once on his tiptoes, yanked it downwards.

With a series of squeaks and squeals, the window curtains parted, letting in dazzling sunshine. Beyond the sliding doors was a balcony that looked across the large area of parkland with a couple of government buildings dotted within it. Beyond that, they could just see the Potomac as it curved towards Regan International Airport in the distance.

Suddenly the apartment gave them hope. It certainly wasn't what they expected but with the view and the natural light, Lisa knew they could make a go of it.

While they were busily taking some measurements of the rooms, Kevin suddenly sat down. He looked pale and a little unsteady.

"Kev, are you okay?" Lisa asked.

He slowly shook his head.

"Is it a bad one?" she asked.

He nodded.

Kevin had started getting migraines a few years earlier. His doctor couldn't find anything wrong, and an MRI showed nothing anomalous. It was therefore felt that they might be tension driven. Though they told the doctors that they couldn't think of what could be stressing their son, Mike and Lisa both had a pretty good idea. They had moved house twice over the past three years so that Mike could be within reasonable commuting distance to each new job as he climbed the corporate ladder. Though they themselves weren't that affected by the change of scenery, they knew that it could have easily been a stressor for Kevin.

They got back to their hotel and Lisa administered one of Kevin's disposable nose sprays that had been prescribed by his Los Angeles doctor. An hour later, Kevin was back watching cartoons and seemed none the worse for wear. The incident reminded them both that they needed to register with a local doctor for themselves and a paediatrician for Kevin.

*

Five days later, on yet another unseasonably balmy day, they met their movers at the new apartment. In what was to become a regular occurrence, the service elevator was out of order and the two men had to use the passenger elevator to get their belongings up to the fourth floor.

It took the men over four hours to get everything out of their truck and into the unit.

The one good distraction that day was when a boy close to Kevin's age appeared in their doorway and asked, with a complete lack of inhibition, "What are you guys doing?"

The boy, Peter, lived five floors above them and was off school because of a boiler failure. After a brief exchange, he invited Kevin to play upstairs. Lisa walked up with them, met Peter's grandfather, and felt completely safe in letting Kevin stay away from the controlled chaos of their move-in.

After unpacking enough boxes to get a feel for what was going to go where, and retrieving Kevin from his unscheduled playdate, they called it a night. Exhausted but excited at the prospect of formally moving in the next day, they splurged and ate at a retro diner only a short walk from their hotel.

The restaurant was buzzing, and the food was great, but all Mike could feel was dread for what the next day would hold.

Mike hated starting a new job.

When he'd been a lowly assistant working at Warner Bros, the first day had been a blast. There'd been no worries about responsibilities or employee acceptance, he'd simply become part of the team and got on with it. Once Mike had entered the executive tier, first days were a whole different animal. Mike had learned early on that the higher the position, the higher the stress level.

CHAPTER 6

Mike left early for work, and as he headed down Pennsylvania Avenue, he stopped at the Edward R Murrow Park. It was little more than a small triangle of dying grass with benches occupied by the homeless who were camped out for the day. What had caught his eye was a minor skirmish taking place only a few feet away from where Mike was standing.

An enormous crow and a black squirrel, something Mike had never heard of, were fighting over the remains of a dead fish. There was something so completely Edgar Allan Poe-esque about the visual that Mike just stood there gaping until some of the homeless took him for a soft touch and began to approach him like a zombie horde.

Mike got to GIB at nine sharp and after going through an airport-like x-ray and metal detector, was escorted down a labyrinth of narrow corridors until he was deposited in a small, windowless waiting area with three other confused-looking newbies. His name was called almost an hour later. The entire process took over three hours. The bureaucratic nightmare finally ended with him being presented with his photo ID badge, which had someone else's picture on it. After a further fifteen minutes of banishment to the nasty little waiting room, he was handed the correct badge by an officious woman the size of a Fiat 500.

By the time he found his way to the sub-basement lair of the AV group, almost every member of his team was elsewhere, managing meetings, events and productions. Thankfully, Wayne Givens, his operations manager, was in his office and was expecting him.

Mike had hoped to be able to have a nice chat with his number two and go over the basics that he felt he needed to know. Wayne however, advised him that he was scheduled to have lunch with Martin Keep, the bank's head of AV operations, and that Mike was already fifteen minutes late for that appointment.

Wayne led Mike through several cubicle farms until he knocked on a non-descript door halfway down a poorly lit hallway. It opened and Martin gave Mike what appeared to be a sincerely warm smile.

"So, this is the poor sucker they conned into working for me, huh?" Martin said as he winked at Wayne.

Martin was about the same age as Mike, tall and just a little gangly. He had prematurely thinning hair and looked uncannily like the late David Bowie.

"Come in," he gestured to Mike.

Wayne knew that he wasn't included in the invite and drifted away unnoticed. Even though Martin was a senior manager within the bank, his office was tiny. There was just room for a desk and return, one bookcase, one filing cabinet, and two small guest chairs.

Martin must have picked up on Mike's thoughts.

"Not exactly an executive suite, is it?" he said rhetorically. "The Global Initiative Bank doesn't go out of its way to overindulge their employees."

Mike had to turn sideways to slide between the desk and the first chair just to get seated.

"I'm sorry I missed meeting you when you were here the first time." Martin said. "This must all seem a little overwhelming."

"It does," Mike agreed. "I'm stunned at the size of the place."

"Welcome to DC. The entire city was designed to impress foreign officials and thus humble them into submission."

"Well, it worked on me," Mike replied.

The two discussed Martin's and the bank's expectations. In the middle of explaining to Mike about the protocols for supporting the board room, Martin stopped mid-sentence.

"You hungry?" Martin asked.

"Starving," Mike replied honestly, having skipped breakfast due to nerves.

Martin led him down to an even lower basement level, which was starting to mess with Mike's usually dormant claustrophobia. All such concerns vanished when they walked into the commissary.

There had to have been at least a dozen food stations, all preparing different foods from around the world. The dessert section alone looked like a display from a five-star hotel brunch. Being completely overawed at the choice of food, Mike followed Martin's lead and went for Vietnamese chicken with wok fried veggies.

After paying what Mike felt was a bargain for the meal, they found a table for two in a dining area that could have easily sat over five hundred people.

After a few minutes of silent eating, Martin continued with the pep talk.

"My philosophy is that we are paid to make sure that all events and meetings have full AV support. That's simple. What makes what we do special is that we don't tolerate mistakes. Or should I say that I don't tolerate mistakes. I've been in this business my whole career and I know as well as you that technology can fail. The bank knows that as well. If a room goes down mid-meeting because a system component crashes, they are understanding so long as we can rectify the situation immediately. Whether that means bringing in a mobile AV cart or shifting the meeting to another space, they don't care. They just want to carry on as if nothing happened."

"That sounds fair," Mike answered.

"However," Martin continued. "If the meeting is disrupted because of an error by one of the technicians, they will want blood. If a particular room develops a hiccup of some sort and engineering doesn't resolve the problem before the next meeting... they will want blood. Are you getting the vibe here?"

"Very much so," Mike replied. "Basically, don't take my eye off the ball for a second."

"Exactly. You are going to find that most bank staffers are decent human beings, but some, especially those from other cultures, are very, very demanding. They are the ones that you have to watch out for. If they demand a service we don't provide, let me know immediately so I can intervene. If there's a problem with a client during a meeting, let me know. I never want to get a call from my superiors about something I'm completely unaware of. When that happens, there's no way I can cover for you."

"Understood." Mike really did understand. He'd learned that lesson at the studios. When the shit started to rain down, if he wasn't forewarned about an issue, there was nothing he could do to pre-defuse the situation.

Mike felt good about his first session with Martin. There was no doubt that the guy was going to be a hard taskmaster, then again, that was Mike's reputation as well.

*

While Mike was being onboarded within the GIB, Lisa had the daunting challenge of dropping Kevin off for his first day at a new pre-school. She had managed to get him into a highly rated Quaker-run establishment that was walking distance from their apartment. Though they'd visited Apple Tree a few days earlier, and Kevin had seemed very positive about the prospect of going there, his happy demeanour vanished the moment they crossed P Street and approached the front entrance. His walking speed dropped to half and his grip on his mother's hand suddenly had the strength of a vice.

Lisa stopped just before the entry steps and knelt down to be at eye level with her son.

"What's going on, Kev?" she asked gently.

"I don't want you and Daddy to leave me," he suddenly howled. His voice was loud enough for several passers-by to turn and look at the poor child.

"We're not leaving you. I'm just dropping you off at pre-school just like I did in Studio City. You used to love to go to Happy Days every morning."

"I don't mean here... now," Kevin managed to say between sniffles. "I mean later. When we move to the bad place."

"Honey," Lisa said as she enveloped him in a hug. "We've already done our move. That's what the trip in the big airplane was all about. Tonight, we move into the apartment which you helped unpack yesterday. The place with the balcony and the great view."

"That's our home?" he asked meekly.

"Yes. That's our home."

Kevin seemed to immediately relax.

"I take it you like the apartment?" Lisa asked, relieved.

Kevin nodded.

"Well, that's a relief."

Lisa walked him up the steps and rang the security buzzer. Almost immediately, a cheerful woman in a paint-covered smock opened the door and grinned down at Kevin.

"So, this is the famous Kevin Ellis!" she crooned. "Boy oh boy, how we've been looking forward to you getting here. We are about to start painting class but didn't want to begin without you. Are ready to get all messy?"

Kevin grinned up at the large lady. "I like painting."

The woman held out her hand. Kevin didn't hesitate for a second. He took it and let her lead him into the building.

Just before he walked around a hallway corner, he turned and looked back at Lisa.

"There was a dead lady in our new home," he said cheerily, before vanishing from view.

CHAPTER 7

"Did someone die in our apartment?" Lisa said as she walked into the tiny rental office on the ground floor of their building.

The rental agent, Mitsi Gant, looked up in shock at Lisa's unexpected arrival and outburst. Mitzi was in her fifties but looked a decade younger, despite her greying hair and almost prudish clothing.

"Why don't you have a seat and you can tell me the problem?" Mitzi suggested.

Lisa composed herself and sat facing the agent. Having stressed over what Kevin had said the entire way back to the apartment, she realised that she may have been a tad abrupt and dramatic with her accusatory entrance.

"Sorry about that. Let me start again," Lisa said with forced calm. "Would you be able to tell me if a woman has died in our apartment?"

"Mrs Ellis, we have over eight hundred units and

have been leasing those for over fifty years. I can pretty much guarantee that people have died in many of the units within the complex."

Lisa hadn't been expecting such a blunt, though logical response.

Mitzi opened a file on her computer and entered their apartment number.

"Actually, there was one death reported in your unit. A Mrs Wincolm passed on February 24th, 1987."

Lisa hesitated to ask the next question.

"Was it violent?" she finally said.

"Was what violent?" Mitzi asked.

"Her death. Did she die violently?"

Mitzi gave the other woman a nervous glance then looked back at her screen.

"Actually, no. She was ninety-one years old and passed quietly in her sleep."

"Oh," Lisa said, surprised. "I'm impressed that you have that sort of information to hand."

"We have to keep such records for the DC Department of Health and Safety. Believe it or not, there's a mean average of resident deaths that we have to stay within or below to ensure they don't take an unhealthy interest in the building."

"I suppose that makes sense," Lisa replied. "Was Mrs Wincolm the only one?"

"That's what the records say. Were you expecting to

hear something else?" Mitzi asked. "You seem disappointed."

"I know this will sound strange, but just before dropping my son at pre-school, he announced that a woman had died in our unit."

Lisa wasn't sure what reaction to expect from the agent, but certainly never thought that howling laughter was one of the options.

"I'm sorry... I really am," Mitzi snorted. "You must have had some scary thoughts going through your head."

"I was a little worried," Lisa replied cautiously.

"Your boy... Kevin?"

Lisa nodded.

"He's become friends with Peter Goldstein from unit 907, hasn't he?"

Lisa looked puzzled. "Yes, but..."

"Let me explain," Mitzi interrupted. "The Goldstein family has lived in the building for over thirty years. Peter's parents both work at the IFC and his grandparents live in the next-door unit. His grandfather used to be a historian and worked at the Brooker Institute, if I'm remembering correctly. Anyway, after a couple of years of retirement, he decided that he wanted to write an in-depth history of the Potomac Apartments."

"These apartments?" Lisa asked.

"You don't have to look quite so surprised. You'd be amazed at just how many famous and notorious people have lived here over the past fifty years. Anyway, part of his research was about who died in the buildings, including when and how they passed away."

"That's a bit morbid," Lisa commented.

"Death always seems to interest people."

"I guess."

"The grandparents look after Peter whenever his parents need a sitter. I don't know if you've noticed, but the boy is a bit of a handful. From what I hear, the only way his grandfather found to keep him from running wild was by telling him stories about the various units, especially about who died in them. The poor kid was initially so scared that he just sat there and took it all in. The funny thing is that Peter seems to have one of those minds where he can remember everything he's told. Poor kid has only just turned six, and all he wants to talk about are the dead people from all the units. I'm sure that the first words out of Peter's mouth when he met your son was to tell him about poor old Mrs Wincolm."

*

After lunch with Martin and having a much better understanding of the scope of his responsibilities, Mike returned to the AV area and for the first time sat in his office and contemplated the enormity of the challenge ahead of him.

As the days passed, Mike found his rhythm and began to understand what went where, and when. He realised very early how skilled his technicians really were and that, as an extra stress, the bank staff were quick to blame the AV team for everything from poor meeting attendance to slow coffee service.

Within six months, Mike had gained the full respect of his team and had the department running both efficiently and productively.

He finally began to relax and actually enjoy the work, blissfully unaware of the two events that were about to change his life.

CHAPTER 8

The first piece of news came at the end of the weekly audio-visual planning meeting. After Martin thanked Mike and his team for their good work, he asked Mike to stay behind for a moment.

Once they were alone, Martin closed the door and proudly advised that he was being promoted to Director of Technical Operations.

Mike knew that Martin had been hoping for the promotion for years and felt a strange sense of something akin to pride that Martin's hard work was finally being rewarded.

Martin explained that he would still be overseeing all AV operations but from a more senior vantage point. The bank would therefore be hiring someone to take the reins of his current position. For a moment, Mike thought that he was in consideration for the job. That thought evaporated instantly after Martin's next words.

"The annoying thing is that you would be the perfect person to take over from me."

"Why is that annoying?" Mike asked.

"The bank doesn't permit in-house contractors to transfer to staff positions within a department they're currently working in."

"Why?"

"There were instances where conflicts resulted, and at one point things got nasty. Now it's simply not permitted, which as far as I'm concerned is a case of complete overkill. If I ever have the authority to do so, I'll change that edict immediately."

"Do you have any candidates in mind?" Mike managed to ask without letting his disappointment show.

"I put a few names forward to HR, but they will almost certainly have a list of their own."

"I'm surprised that HR would be that up on who's available from our industry."

Martin took a long while to answer.

"The bank doesn't always hire people who have the exact skills for the job. They often shoehorn people into positions who have almost no experience just so they can meet their international diversity quotas. My hope is that with this position being so obviously technical, they will ensure that the candidate at least comes from the same universe."

As Mike walked home, early summer humidity enveloped him. To make matters worse, he felt a knot growing in his stomach. Even after Martin's assurance that the bank would not be stupid enough to put a technophobe in the position of running a complex technical support operation, he still felt an inexplicable foreboding.

Mike hadn't even closed the front door to their apartment when Lisa handed him a glass of champagne.

"I have some amazing news," she said, her green eyes sparkling with excitement. "I've come to a monumental decision that will affect all of us."

"I love living within an autocratic unit," he joked and clinked glasses. "So, what is this news?"

"We're going to have a baby," she announced.

Mike immediately grabbed her glass away from her.

"Are you nuts?" he said, shocked. "You know you can't drink alcohol if you're…"

"I'm not pregnant," she replied as she regained control of her champagne. "But I've decided that I do want another child, but first I want us to have our own home."

"We have a home," Mike said, gesturing to the cramped living room.

"This is a small rental apartment in the middle of a highly transitory city," Lisa replied.

"Transitory?" Mike questioned.

"Absolutely. This city was designed to be nothing more than temporary housing for politicians and members of the military. This place may have an incredible history, but in case you haven't noticed, it doesn't have much of a soul."

"Nice speech," Mike sighed. "So, what's your big plan?"

"You assume I have a plan?"

"You always do."

Lisa grinned. "My plan is that you plant a baby inside me, and we move out of the city."

"That was scarily concise."

"It's a very simple plan," she responded.

"The first part will doubtless be enjoyable. It's the second part that worries me. The thought of trying to find a rental within the beltway is going to be a bitch. Maybe we could find a bigger rental in the same complex?" Mike suggested.

"That's why we're not going to rent," she announced. "We are going to become actual homeowners. We've discussed this a thousand times. Between us, we are getting killed on taxes because we don't have any real deductions. We need to buy this time. Not rent."

"We can't afford anything bigger than this place anywhere close to DC, and if we did somehow find somewhere, it would almost certainly be in an area you wouldn't like," Mike stated.

"Yes, but if we were to go out a ways, we could afford a real home – something in the 2500 square foot range, or even bigger. What's more, we could probably find something new. Wouldn't that be cool, to be the first people ever to live in our new home?"

"That all sounds great... for you. You work from home," Mike argued. "I would end up getting stuck with a mammoth commute every day."

"It wouldn't be that bad," she said. "If we, for example, lived out beyond Vienna, say in Gainesville, you'd have an easy drive to the metro station, then a straight shot to the Foggy Bottom station."

"It sounds to me like you've been doing a lot of research into this," Mike said, amused.

"Come on. Wouldn't you like to come home to a brand-new house with its own little plot of land and never hear traffic again?" Lisa pitched. "Imagine what the weekends would be like. Instead of us being stuck in the city, we'd wake up on Saturday and be in the middle of the countryside."

"What about when we wake up on Sunday?"

"Don't be so negative," she replied. "Just think, you could barbeque again. You'd like that."

"Apparently, I don't need to think. You seem to have done that for both of us already."

"I'll tell you what," Lisa said as she looked into his eyes. "How about us having a little road trip this Saturday and check out a few places?"

"Let me guess," Mike laughed. "You just happen to have a list of which places we'll be visiting, don't you?"

Lisa shrugged with feigned innocence.

"Why am I not surprised," Mike said. "Does Kevin know yet?"

"No. I thought I should tell you the plan first, then if you agreed, we could both tell him. He's upstairs playing with Peter."

"Do I have a choice in this matter?" Mike asked, smiling.

"Of course not, my darling."

"How do you think Kev will take it?" Mike asked.

"I think he'll be delighted," Lisa replied. "He's always asking when he can live in a house with a backyard."

"Even with him having to change schools?"

"He has to anyway. He's about to be too old for kindergarten. Besides, in case you hadn't noticed, we somehow made a pretty well-adjusted kid."

Lisa took Mike by the hand and led him to the old sofa then plopped down next to him.

"We can't live here with two children. You do know that don't you?" Lisa said. "Especially when one's a baby who will probably scream like a banshee throughout the night."

"That wasn't very maternal."

"I wasn't taking about the new-born, I was referring to you," Lisa said, grinning.

"Is this the point when I accept your plan, or should I pretend I still have a choice?"

"Now would be as good a time as any," Lisa replied.

*

They left DC just after nine on Saturday morning. It was hazy and humid as was often the case in the city from late May through September. They stayed on 66 until the Gainesville exit, then Lisa instructed Mike to head towards Warrenton. Once they'd doubled back under the highway, she told him to take the next left on Linton Hall Road. After a further mile, they turned right onto Glenkirk. Before long they began to see signs advertising new home developments.

Lisa knew exactly which one she wanted to see. Only a few hundred yards past the Glenkirk Dam was a development called Lake View Estates. They drove up to a rock wall with a wrought iron security gate. Mike pushed a button labelled 'SALES' on a new-looking keypad.

The gate silently swung open.

CHAPTER 9

What appeared to be recently laid macadam curved through a copse of mature red maple trees before a discreet sign for the sales office appeared on the right side of the road. They followed the arrow and arrived at a picture-perfect family home. It was a large, two-storey, gabled house. The pale cream-coloured brick frontage was accented with dark oak shutters and a stone entry. A three-car garage door had a vintage look and had been painted a bright matte white. The overall effect was grand while at the same time appearing comfortable and inviting.

The entire inside of the house was the sales office. Every wall space and floor area displayed a different texture, material, or colour scheme.

A portly man in his mid-fifties approached them with a smile on his face and a See's toffee pop in his right hand. He bent over in front of Kevin and held out the treat.

"I hope it's okay if I indulge the little man?" he asked.

"Bit late to do much about it now," Mike said, smiling, as Kevin's hand reached up for the candy.

"I always feel that when the little folk get a good feeling about a place, it helps the parents decide what to do."

"Sounds like a good strategy," Lisa said. "What do we get?"

"You both get the chance to find the home of your dreams," he parried back. "Hi, folks. My name is Walter Hill." Walter extended his hand. "And you are?"

After the introductions, Walter led them to a sloping display that had to have been twenty feet long and fifteen feet wide. It was a model of the entire development showing which lots were available and which were already spoken for.

"How long does it take from choosing a lot and model to being able to actually move in?" Lisa asked.

"At the moment, we are quoting twelve to eighteen months," Walter advised. "But sometimes they get finished a tad earlier."

"That won't work for us," Mike said. "I just found out that my wife wants to be pregnant so we're kind of on a tight schedule."

"Really?" Lisa said, rolling her eyes.

"That's a new one," Walter replied.

"We had no idea that it took so long to build a house," Lisa added.

"Normally it doesn't, but since the protests and the lockdowns, folks seem to want the security of a brand-new home."

"I guess we'll have to buy a re-sale somewhere," Mike said, disappointed.

"Actually, I may have an alternative," Walter said. "Let me show you one particular model to see if you like it. If you think it's something you'd be happy to live in, I might be able to cut the wait time in half."

"Wouldn't it be better to tell us how you can do that before showing it to us?" Mike asked.

"What would be the point in getting your hopes up about something you end up not liking?" Walter said.

"I agree," Lisa jumped in. "Let's see the model."

Walter led the trio past two model homes on abutting lots, then stopped in front of almost an exact clone of the one being used as the sales office. The only difference seemed to be that it only had a two-car garage and the brickwork was pale grey instead of beige, otherwise it was identical.

"Do you like the outside?" Walter asked.

"It's beautiful," Lisa said.

"Don't tell the salesman that," Mike said, joking. "We have to seem lukewarm about it so that we can knock the price down."

"All prices are fixed so you can be as enthusiastic as you want," Walter explained.

"I like it," Kevin said between licks of his toffee pop.

The others laughed.

"Let's have a look inside, shall we," Walter suggested.

The house was gorgeous. The interior colours and finishes were stunning. It also happened to be one of the featured properties that Lisa had saved online to add to her folder of fantasy homes.

"Okay," Mike said. "We're interested. Now what?"

"Now we go for a little drive. You stay here and have a poke around for a minute while I get the cart from the office."

After only a few minutes of said 'poking around', they heard what sounded like a toy car horn coming from out front. They found Walter sitting in a four-seater golf cart emblazoned with the developer's logo. They climbed in then headed into the main part of the estate.

"This car's funny," Kevin said.

"It certainly is," Lisa agreed, not wanting to try and explain what a golf cart was.

They rounded a gentle, tree-lined bend and saw a lake in the distance. Four side streets fed off the one they were on. They all had tree names like Cedar Rd, Maple Pl, etc. About a third of the lots had completed homes. Ten more that were dotted throughout the estate were in various stages of construction.

They continued towards the lake.

"That's Lake Manassas that you can see ahead," Walter advised. "It's beautiful, isn't it?"

It was beautiful. As they got closer, they could see that the grey-blue water was still as glass. Trees from the opposite bank were reflected perfectly in the mirror-like water. Less than a hundred feet from the lake, Walter turned onto a packed dirt drive. Fifty feet further on was a partially constructed house. The lot it was on sloped gently from the construction site down to the water. Because of the configuration of the shoreline, the house was on its own small finger of land and had no close neighbours.

"What do you think?" Walter asked.

"Are you kidding?" Mike said. "This is your option for us? It's got to be the most expensive lot in the development."

"Actually, it's not," he replied. "Most people who move here have children and don't like the fact that the house is so close to the water."

"That's a good point," Lisa said.

"What we were going to do for the original buyers was to – at our cost, mind you – put in decorative safety fencing around the entire property line. You'd get to have your say about material, colour and so forth, but your kids would be just as safe as in any other house in the estate, and you'd have a home right on the shoreline."

"And this is going to be the same as the model we just looked at?" Mike asked.

"Sure is," Walter replied. "You can still change the colour scheme and fixtures and such if you wish, but the original buyers wanted exactly what they saw in that model house."

"So do we," Lisa replied.

"Let me walk you around the property then we can go back to the office and have a little chat."

As they began to walk towards where the front door would eventually be, Kevin stopped and refused to go any farther.

"What's wrong, little man?" Mike asked.

"My head feels funny," he replied as his bottom lip quivered.

"It was fine a moment ago," Lisa said as she knelt next to him.

"I don't want to go in the house," he whispered.

"Why? Is it 'cause it's unfinished?" she asked.

Kevin shrugged. "It looks bad."

"It's not bad. It's just because it hasn't been built all the way yet," Lisa explained. "When it's all done it will look just like that house we were in a few minutes ago."

"I don't want to go inside," Kevin insisted.

Lisa knew not to force him into doing anything out of his comfort zone. Instead, she settled him on the back seat of the golf cart and gave him her iPad mini so he could play one of his games. He immediately seemed to relax.

"How's the head?" Lisa asked.

"All better," he replied as he activated his favourite puzzle app.

"Don't leave the funny car, okay?" she said. "I will be able to see you from anywhere in the house, so if you need me just wave."

Kevin nodded his understanding.

Walter took them through the framed front door and showed them where the various rooms were. The staircase was already in place, so they were able to check out both floors. Neither Lisa nor Mike had ever stepped foot in a home under construction. They had no idea how strange and discombobulating it felt to walk through an entire house with no actual walls. They were framed, but until wiring, plumbing, vents, insolation, and drywall were in place, you could see right through all the studs and rafters to the outside.

Lisa and Mike found that trying to work out what each space was going to be was almost impossible. Thankfully, Walter was able to help them visualise every room and explain which way they were oriented and what went where.

"Before we go back to the office, may we walk through the model again?" Lisa asked. "While this place is fresh in my mind, I want to see what it will look like once everything is finished."

"Of course, we can," Walter said. "Before we do, let's step in here," he gestured to a door frame. "And have a look at the master bedroom."

The first thing they noticed was that it was big enough for a sitting area; something that Lisa had always dreamed of having. The second thing was the view. One entire side of the room was framed to have floor to ceiling windows looking directly onto the lake. As Mike and Lisa stared down at the water, as if on cue, a pair of wild geese soared over the house and flew only inches above the water.

Something suddenly made a huge splashing sound from part of the shoreline they couldn't see.

Lisa had a microsecond of irrational panic. She spun around and looked down at the golf cart. Something made her think that Kevin wasn't going to be there. Shadows from the nearby trees had thrown a dark swath across the vehicle and it took her a moment before she could make out that Kevin was still in the back, playing with the iPad.

When the birds had flown over the house, Mike had looked up at the sky and something had caught his attention. One of the attic floor joists seemed to be broken in half. While one part was still securely in place, the other was nowhere to be seen.

"Is that normal?" Mike asked as he pointed out the anomaly to Walter.

"That one piece of broken wood is why this house has become available," he replied.

"That sounds ominous," Lisa remarked.

"It's not. I'll explain everything when we get to the office."

Lisa gave him one of her best questioning stares.

"There's nothing wrong with the house and the damaged area will be replaced," Walter said, feeling that her glare needed some sort of a response.

On the way back to the sales office, Walter detoured and showed them the entire development. From the comfort of the golf cart, he pointed out the different streets, the club house, the swimming pool, and even two tennis courts.

"This place has it all," Mike commented.

"That it does." Walter nodded.

Once they reached the office, Walter showed them to an area that in an actual house would have been the den or family room; instead, it had been turned into a play area for younger children. There were various toys and puzzles, and even a flat screen TV switched to a cartoon channel.

"This is unusual," Lisa said.

"We find that the parents are able to focus more on the details when their kids are occupied elsewhere. We set this up so that the little ones are visible but not underfoot."

Once Kevin was settled, Walter led them to his office.

"Can I get you something to drink... water, coffee?"

They both declined and sat in the guest chairs facing his desk.

"Let me start by confirming that you are both interested in the Dakota model and that you are happy with the position of the lot I showed you?"

"That's why we're here," Mike replied.

"Good," Walter began. "First let me explain that damage you saw. Two weeks ago, a builder was traversing the attic on one of the joists. For some reason, it broke, and the man fell to the master bedroom floor below."

Lisa gasped. "He died, didn't he?"

"No. He did not," Walter assured her. "He did break both legs and damaged his back, but he is going to make a full recovery. We are mandated to inform any buyer of any serious injury or... worse, that occurs during the construction of their home. Some people find that such things detract from the entire experience and either want to change lots or cancel the purchase altogether.

"Is that what happened in this case?" Lisa asked.

"Yes. And while we are very understanding of such eventualities, we are still, at the end of the day, in the business of selling homes. Our contract stipulates that if buyers wish to pull out of any purchase once construction has begun, we will honour that request so long as another buyer can be located who will basically take over the original contract. Obviously, the original buyers will expect compensation to cover whatever monies they have already paid, but they understand that it will most likely not be the full amount."

"This sounds interesting," Lisa said, turning to face Mike.

Walter continued. "If you were to buy that model on that lot at today's inflated prices, it would run you close to $675,000, maybe even $700,000 with all the upgrades they ordered. Because the original buyers put down their deposit fourteen months ago, the selling price back then was $542,000. They have already put down the fifty percent deposit, or $271,000 as specified in the contract, prior to the start of construction. I am almost certain that they would consider settling for a $250,000 buyout or even less, in effect giving you the ability to get the house for way below market price. Plus... it's far enough along for it to be completed in under six months."

"We don't have $250,000 in cash. We only have the

twenty percent down payment we thought we'd need," Mike advised.

"You won't have to come up with that much yourself," Walter explained. "You will sign a normal new home construction purchase contract and as long as you have good credit, you'll only need to put down twenty percent of the total, so around $108,000. The bank will then release funds to us as required in the construction contract. We will coordinate the pay back to the original buyers and you will have a brand-new home in about four to five months."

"Why would the buyers walk away just because someone got hurt on the job?" Lisa asked. "I don't mean to sound harsh, but people get hurt on construction sites all the time. Why did this instance freak them out?"

"Unfortunately, the poor man fell while the buyers were checking up on the status of the construction. They were actually in the room when the accident happened."

"How awful," Mike said.

"I guess I can understand it now." Lisa nodded. "That would have probably upset me as well. I don't know that I would have given up my house because of it, but then again, I'm not a big believer in bad joojoo or whatever."

"That's good to know," Walter replied. "Shall I start

going through the contract and outline the construction stages?"

Mike and Lisa looked at each other.

Lisa nodded.

CHAPTER 10

That night, as Lisa lay fast asleep alongside him, Mike reflected on the magnitude of what they had just done. They'd signed a contract for a house. Not just any house either. They were going to live in a brand-new home on the edge of a picturesque lake, tucked away in some of the most breathtaking countryside in Northern Virginia. Mike felt his eyes mist over at the thought of finally being able to make a real home for his family for the first time in his life.

*

Mike's parents had been real estate flippers. They would buy a tired, older home in a decent part of Los Angeles then, while living in it, give the house a complete facelift. It normally took about six months work plus two to three months to sell it. Unfortunately, they never seemed to want to follow the usual financial model of adding any profit made from each sale to purchase something a little more expensive, eventually owning a home worth some serious money. Instead, they used to make about a fifteen percent profit off each sale and live off that while doing up the next house prior to putting it on the market. With inflation and rising property costs, they were slowly painting themselves into a very unprofitable corner.

Because of his parents' nomadic existence, Mike was never allowed the luxury of living in one place for more than nine months at a time. His home, and more especially, his bedroom, was either under renovation or staged for viewing. The only time he could ever bring out his toys and games was after the house had gone into escrow.

By the time Mike had reached his teens, he was able to discern the fact that each house they moved to seemed to be just a tiny bit smaller, and the area, just a tiny bit less appealing. This never-ending cycle also had an impact on Mike's schooling because each new house was usually in a different school district.

The entire experience had instilled in him a sense of being perpetually unsettled. He had no strong friendship base, he never had a good familiarity with his current neighbourhood, and worst of all, he had no memories of a real home.

His parents' master plan, if indeed they ever had

one, began to unravel in 1994 when they found themselves in a newly refurbished house in North Hollywood just as the entire real estate market went down the toilet after the Northridge earthquake. They couldn't give the house away. It wasn't until 1996 that they finally found a buyer, but only after accepting close to a twenty percent price reduction.

His father had hoped that with the market still being shaky, they'd be able to pick up something underpriced and manage to recoup their loss. The problem was that investors had been grabbing the bargains a full year before that. Somehow, LA house prices emerged from the slump a few ticks higher than before the quake. What money his parents had at that point only bought a home in a far less desirable area where quick face lifts did not necessarily equate to a quick profit.

When Mike left home to go to UCLA's film school as an undergraduate on a full scholarship, his parents were holed up in a tired 1950s house in Pacoima. All thoughts of living on the profits from real estate were gone. Both had taken low-paying jobs until they could work out what to do next with their lives.

Because of the distance from the house to the university, the commute would have been brutal and expensive. Thankfully, the 'full-ride' scholarship to the directors' program covered on-campus meals and accommodation, meaning Mike rarely had to trek all the way across the San Fernando Valley.

The strangest thing for Mike was that living on the UCLA campus for two years while studying how to shoot, direct, and edit movies was the most stable period of his life. Most students, when they left home and had to live miles from their family and friends, felt lost and untethered. Mike felt the exact opposite. His on-campus dorm was the closest thing to a stable environment that he'd ever had.

Halfway through his first quarter at the film school, Mike decided to dump his editing class and change over to cinematography.

Though Mike was nervous about taking on a new course, he reasoned that even if it wasn't all that he hoped it would be, it would at least help him maintain the required number of units. On his first day on the cinematography stage, he had to keep reminding himself that taking a new course wasn't that big a deal. It wasn't as if one class was going to change his life.

Mike walked onto the cinematography sound stage even though he was almost an hour early for class. He thought he was the only person there and began snooping behind the set flats and lighting rigs. It was his first time on a film set, even if it was one only used for instruction rather than broadcast.

After walking through a staged living room, he stepped through a pair of French doors onto what he *thought was a sunny patio. Instead, he found himself in a three-foot deep alcove filled with lighting equipment.*

He smiled to himself at having been fooled into thinking there was an actual outdoor area even if it had looked completely real. As he turned to walk back onto the set, a cute redhead bumped into him as she too headed for what she thought was an outdoor patio.

"Sorry," Mike mumbled.

"There's nothing out here," the girl said, surprised.

"I did the same thing," Mike stuttered as he tried not to stare into her green eyes. "I guess it shows that we're both kinda new to all this."

"I guess it does. Are you in this class?"

"I hope so," Mike answered. "I'm Mike by the way."

"Nice to meet you, Mike. I'm Lisa. Maybe us bumping into each other is like one of those meet-cute movie things."

"What?" Mike asked.

"Boy. You really are new to this," Lisa laughed.

"You also fell for the fake patio thing, remember. We're both new to this."

Lisa gave him a long appraising look.

"Yeah. Maybe we do have that in common."

*

Mike rolled over and spooned against Lisa. His

movement caused Samantha to stir from her sleep and after a brief stretch, she cozied up against the couple. Mike dozed off with the sound of purring behind him, and Lisa's steady, even breathing only inches in front of him.

He lay there imagining them all together at the new house.

He suddenly felt extraordinarily content.

*

The search for Martin's replacement at the bank seemed to go on forever. It took them almost three months to put together a short list of three candidates. Martin bent bank rules and showed Mike their resumes. Two candidates were from technical backgrounds at similar enterprise operations, and both looked like strong contenders.

Candidate one was Marilee Javid who was currently working at the United Nations in New York, basically doing the equivalent of Mike's job. She sounded perfect. Number two was Tim Palmer who had been working at the International Development Bank in their video conferencing group and had risen from being an AV tech, all the way up to managing the team. He also looked like a good fit. The third candidate was a wild card. Kerry Coates worked at the *Washington Gazette* supervising their video production team, which consisted of three people. She had little technical background and no experience managing a large technical operation.

In addition, according to Martin, the woman had a reputation of being exceedingly hard to work with and many technical vendors would go out of their way to avoid having to deal with her.

Martin assured Mike that he needn't worry considering that she was by far the weakest candidate of the three. Plus, now that human resources had selected the finalists, Martin had been appointed to be part of the interviewing and hiring committee for the position and would have a big say in the results.

A few weeks later, Martin walked each of the candidates though the bank, showing off the rooms, the technology, and the AV support team. Mike was introduced and had a brief chat with each one. Marilee and Tim were open, interested, and respectful. Kerry was not. She knew that Mike wasn't a bank employee and treated him with as much respect as one would for something that crawled out of a piece of cheese.

It was obvious to both Mike and Martin that Kerry saw herself as far superior to a contracted general manager. Neither felt that that boded well for her being the type that could work as a cohesive member of an operational team.

Once the interviews and tours were complete, Martin stopped by Mike's office and plopped down in one of the guest chairs. "So, what did you think?" he asked.

"If I was doing the hiring," Mike responded. "I would go for Marilee. The UN operation is so similar to here and it has the same multi-cultural facet, which is pretty unique. What she was saying about the problems with the new Haiden conference microphone system was right on. She seemed to know her stuff."

"What about Tim?" Martin asked.

"I liked him. I felt he needed maybe a couple more years of seasoning before stepping into a job like yours."

Martin laughed. "Great minds think alike."

Martin started to get to his feet.

"You didn't ask me about Kerry?" Mike said.

"I don't really think there's much of a need, do you? I don't see the bank choosing her. I've never seen anyone wired so tightly. As you well know, this place can be a pressure cooker. Someone like Kerry would snap in five minutes."

"I don't know," Mike said, straight-faced. "There was something about her charm and humility that kinda won me over."

"Don't joke yet," Martin said. "I've seen stranger things happen here."

"Odds?" Mike asked.

"Hundred to one."

"You better be right," Mike said as Martin got up to leave.

"Don't worry too much," Martin added. "They have to let me know before making any offer, and if for some reason they do pick Kerry, I would pull in some favours from a few department heads."

CHAPTER 11

Weekends were spent combing furniture, bedding, and lighting stores. Mike had no idea how Lisa tracked down every single item on her list while still doing her book editing and proofreading, yet she had.

Despite being dragged through half of Fairfax County's shopping precincts, Mike loved to watch his wife go through her new nesting compulsion. Lisa used to be satisfied with him ordering a complete house worth of unassembled furniture that he'd spend weeks assembling.

With only a month before move-in day, everything had been ordered, and delivery was guaranteed for the day after the house became theirs.

Lisa was on cloud nine.

They both felt that they'd done everything they could possibly do to make the move-in as stress free as possible. The only slight issue was that Kevin seemed to still be apprehensive about the house. Even once the structure was weather safe and the rooms looked like rooms, he still went quiet every time they walked into it.

On the last visit, Lisa had sat on the floor in what was to be Kevin's bedroom and had looked into his clear blue eyes.

"What's up, Kev?" she asked. "This is going to be a beautiful house when it's finished. Plus, once we're in, we won't have to move anymore. Doesn't that sound good?"

"I guess so," he mumbled. "What about Apple Tree? Can I still go there?"

"No, honey, but that's not because of the house. You got too old for Apple Tree. You get to go to a grade school out here. You're going to be in the first grade. Isn't that cool? You're a big kid now."

"I am?"

"Sure, you are," Lisa insisted. "Just as soon as we move in, I'm going to take you to the mall and buy you lots of big kid clothes."

"You are?" he said, managing a smile.

"Do you feel better about the house now?"

"I guess... a little... it's just that..." Kevin said as he drew shapes on the dusty floor with the tip of his shoe. "Can't we live somewhere that no one has died in?"

Lisa tried to not show her surprise at his question while at the same time inwardly cursing his friend Peter for putting such thoughts in his head.

"That's why this house is so special," she explained. "It's never been lived in by anybody. We will be the first people living here... ever. That means that nobody has died here."

"Then who is the man who lives up there?" Kevin asked as he pointed upwards.

"You mean, in heaven?" Lisa asked.

"No. Up there on top of your bedroom. That's where he fell from."

Before leaving the estate, Lisa pulled the car up outside the sales office. She told Mike to stay with Kevin and that she would only be a few minutes. She hadn't been able to tell Mike what their son had said while at the house and wanted a quick word with Walter without alarming either him or Kevin.

"I just want to check on a paint colour," she lied as she got out of the car.

Walter was in his office with a young couple who looked to be poised to buy one of the homes. He looked up and smiled warmly when he saw who it was.

"Mrs Ellis. What a pleasure. Folks, this is Lisa Ellis. She and her husband will be moving into their home in just a few weeks."

"May I have a quick word?" Lisa asked.

"I'm a little tied up here at the moment, how's about I give you a call when..."

"Now, please," she interrupted. Her harsh tone made it clear that she was not going to be easily brushed off.

Once she and Walter were out of earshot of the couple, Lisa turned to face him.

"You lied to us," she stated bluntly.

"I've done no such thing," Walter replied, flustered. "Lied about what? I've been selling real estate for over twenty years, and I make it a rule to never..."

"The builder who fell from the broken joist... he died, didn't he? You told us that he was going to get better, and he died."

"Now just a minute here, Lisa... Mrs Ellis. When we spoke about the poor man, he was in hospital and expected to recover. I got word about a month or so later that he died of a brain embolism as a result of the fall."

"You told us that he'd broken his legs and hurt his back," Lisa replied.

"He did," Walter stated. "Apparently, the injury caused a blood clot to form, and it found its way up into his brain. One minute he was sitting up talking to the nurse, the next, he was gone. I probably should have told you, but you all seemed so darn happy. I didn't want to drag a rain cloud into an otherwise wonderful time. To be perfectly honest with you, I never thought for one second that you'd ever hear about it, so I decided to keep it to myself. After all, it's not like he died on the property."

"You should know that I am very unhappy about this. I get what you were trying to do, but to not tell us that he passed away was wrong. Just plain wrong."

"I understand," Walter replied solemnly. "I'll tell you what I'm gonna to do to try to make it up to you. As you know, once the house is complete and you take possession, we will landscape the front garden, but the rest is up to the homeowner. Would it help if I offered to have our landscaper do the whole dang thing? Front, back, and sides. I can show you some designs of what I think would look good and you could just choose the one you like."

"And you'd pick up the cost?" she asked, trying not to show her surprise.

"Every last penny. Once the landscaping is done, I can also arrange for the fencing we talked about to be installed."

When Lisa got back in the car, Mike asked if everything was okay as she looked a little rattled.

"You know how we've been stressing about how we were going to be able to afford to do all the landscaping?"

"How could I forget."

"I just got Walter to pick up the entire tab. All of it. The backyard and the sides."

"Why the heck would he do that?" Mike asked.

"My guess was so he wouldn't get sued."

Mike cringed. "You can tell me what really happened later. I get the feeling there's a backstory to all this."

"Oh yeah, there is." She nodded.

Once back in their apartment, Lisa waited until Mike was involved with a work email before going into Kevin's room and sitting next to him on his bed. He was playing with his toy dinosaurs and was having his T-Rex jump onto a hapless Triceratops that had been peacefully grazing atop Kevin's Muppet-themed comforter.

"What ya doin'?" Lisa asked in a feigned, casual tone.

"Just showing all the other dinosaurs that my T-Rex is the baddest monster of them all."

"You know back at the new house when you asked me about the man in the attic?" she asked.

"What's an attic?"

"That's the area under the roof at the top of the house."

Kevin stopped his playing and nodded slowly as if assimilating the new word into his ever-growing vocabulary.

"You mean where the man fell down?" he asked.

"Yes... him," Lisa said, smiling in the hopes of

keeping the topic light and fluffy. "How did you know about him?"

"I don't really know him," Kevin answered.

"I understand that, but... I guess what I'm asking is, do you see him?"

"Sure. Don't you?"

"Does he speak to you?" she questioned as an icy shiver crawled up her spine.

"A little. He sounds funny when he talks."

"What does he say?"

"Not much," Kevin said as his T-Rex attacked another, even smaller dinosaur. "He told me that his name was Papa."

Lisa wound up the conversation by discussing the few dinosaur facts that she knew, then left him to his game. She went into their bedroom and closed the door so that Mike wouldn't hear and called Walter's cell phone.

"Why, Mrs Ellis," he answered, surprised. "It's a little after business hours. Is there a problem?"

"What was the name of the man who died in the house?" she asked bluntly.

"Well, I'm not sure that I should..."

"Please just give me his name. I need to know. In fact, just the first name will do."

"I don't suppose there's any harm in that," he voiced. "His name was Sebastian. He was from Puerto

Rico, I believe."

"You're sure that was his name?" Lisa asked.

"Absolutely. I have, or rather had, all his work documents on file in the office."

"Thank you," Lisa said, relieved that Kevin wasn't interacting with the dead builder after all and that his vivid imagination had probably been influenced by his young friend from the ninth floor.

"I'm sorry to have bothered you," Lisa said, happy that she'd solved the creepy mystery.

"Never a bother talking to one of our buyers," he recited as if by rote.

"Have a nice evening," Lisa replied.

She was just about to disconnect the call when Walter spoke again.

"I just thought of something. I doubt it will make much of a difference to you, but all the other workers called him something else. Apparently, every moment of downtime that Sebastian had at the site, he would pull out this old paperback and read it to himself. He thought it would help his English."

"What paperback?" Lisa asked.

"It was *The Old Man and the Sea.* The guy read it all the way through then started over again. I heard that he'd read it more than a hundred times. That's why his co-workers gave him the nickname."

"Papa?" Lisa said, her voice shaky.

"Yup," Walter replied. "Papa Hemmingway himself."

CHAPTER 12

Four days later, Mike got a text from Martin asking him to join him at a Starbucks close to work. Martin had never asked to meet him anywhere but within the confines of the bank campus during business hours. Mike couldn't think of any reason for such a clandestine meeting and hoped there wasn't a problem.

"This can't be good," Mike said as he sat across from Martin.

"It isn't. They offered the job to Kerry Coates."

"But why?" Mike stuttered. "I thought you could veto something like that?"

"So did I. What I hadn't counted on was that Gary Schneider is a close friend of Kerry."

"The executive director of the Support Services Group?" Mike gasped.

Martin nodded.

"When you say close friend... how close are we

talking about?" Mike asked.

"I think they're just friends now, but from what I could glean from one of my sources in the executive suite, they were once an item."

"I'm sensing an itsy bit of a conflict of interest here," Mike stated. "How is that even possible nowadays?"

"It's possible because the executive director is one of the highest-ranking department heads at the bank and can hire anyone he wants. If he was still screwing her, it could be considered a problem, but their little dalliance was years ago and both parties are now happily married to their respective spouses, so for some reason, HR is willing to look the other way."

"I thought you had someone high up that could jump in if this happened."

"I did," Martin sighed.

"So?"

"Garry Schneider was my ace in the hole."

"Oh, shit."

"Yeah," Martin answered. "That pretty much sums it up."

"So, what do we do now?"

"We hope like hell that she's nothing like the rumours we've heard about her."

"And if she is that bad?" Mike asked.

"We either learn to live with it or dust off our resumes."

"When is she supposed to start?"

"She has to give the *Washington Gazette* sixty days' notice, so I assume it will be right after that," Martin replied.

"We'll be in the new house by then," Mike mentioned.

"That's what you need to focus on, not this mess. It's a big step buying your first home. Try not to worry about Ms Coates until we know that there's something to actually worry about."

*

Lisa sat by the phone waiting to hear from the title office. The deed was scheduled to record sometime that morning, and she had strict instructions to call Mike the moment it happened.

The call came through a few minutes past ten. The house was theirs. Lisa was so overjoyed when she heard that the deed had been recorded that it took her a moment to remember that she had to tell Mike the great news.

Within minutes of getting her call, Mike was standing at the L Street entrance of the bank, waiting for Lisa to pick him up so they could collect the keys and walk through their new home.

They reached Gainesville in record time, and as they

approached their new home, the clouds that had been obscuring the sky for most of the morning suddenly parted, allowing a narrow beam of sunlight to shine directly onto the house. The timing couldn't have been better. It made the place look almost magical.

They walked through every room, inspecting the finish as well as less obvious nooks and crannies. They ended the inspection in the master bedroom. After poking around all the cupboards, they stood looking out at the lake.

Mike took Lisa's hand and held it tight. As if by telepathy, they both knew what the other was thinking. Within seconds they were on the floor, 'christening' their home. As they made love, Lisa thought she saw, in her peripheral vision, a shadow pass across the ceiling. She wanted to see what had caused it, but feeling Mike gently push deeper within her, she was carried away by a far more urgent craving.

As they lay in each other's arms on their brand-new Berber carpet, Mike smiled.

"I think that may have been the best homecoming we've ever had."

"Maybe that's because this time it really is a home," Lisa suggested.

She suddenly remembered the shadow and glanced up to where she thought she'd seen it. There was nothing but matte white ceiling. It dawned on her that with all the trees that surrounded them, odd shadows were bound to appear on occasion.

That thought relaxed her until she realised that if the sun was shining straight down, how could a shadow have appeared on the ceiling, inside the house?

Her moment of calm evaporated.

On the drive back to DC, Mike picked up on the fact that Lisa had gone strangely quiet.

"You okay?"

"I'm fine," she fibbed. "I'm just thinking about tomorrow and all the deliveries. It's going to be chaotic as hell."

"Of course, it is," he agreed. "No one ever said that moving was fun. I'm just glad that we booked the movers on a different day than the deliveries. Can you imagine if we'd tried to do all of that at the same time?"

"At least we would have been fully moved in by tomorrow night. This way, we've spread the misery over forty-eight hours."

"Are you sure that's what's bothering you? The logistics of moving usually gets your tail wagging."

Lisa almost told him about the shadow, especially after Kevin's comments about the dead builder, but decided that she didn't want to spoil his excitement over things that were bound to have a logical explanation.

"Yup," she said. "It's just the move-in."

"It'll be fine," Mike assured her. "Turning a place into a home in a matter of days is your specialty."

"I know, but for some reason everything about this move just seems so much more important."

Mike patted her knee.

"Is that because this may be the last one?" he suggested.

Lisa knew that Mike meant it in a positive way, but saying it could be their last one almost sounded ominous.

"That was a weird thing to say."

"Well, I certainly didn't mean it that way," Mike replied. "I just meant that this is going to be the home we dreamed of. Whatever else happens in our life, it will always be our safe, happy place."

CHAPTER 13

"Please be careful!" Mike shouted at the delivery men, who, for the second time in less than ten minutes, had managed to scrape the furniture they were carrying against the brand-new walls, leaving visible marks on the new paint.

Mike walked into the kitchen and found Lisa sticking post-it notes on drawers and cabinets showing what was to go where. The kitchen was her domain, and she was very fussy about the placement of every pan, bowl, and spice container. Then again, as the primary chef in the house, she was justifiably entitled.

"Can you please have a word with those clowns from Maddox Furniture? They're destroying the walls," Mike begged.

"That hallway is awkward if you're trying to manoeuvre something long into the living room. Why don't you open the living room doors that go to where the patio will be? That way they'll have a ton more room to get things in."

Mike gave her a confused look.

"What?" she asked.

"How do you always do that?" Mike asked.

"I don't know. I feel like my brain's really in the zone at the moment. It's like I'm developing move-in superpowers."

"Maybe that's because you're thinking for two," he said as he patted her flat stomach.

"Stop saying things like that. There's no way to know yet," Lisa replied.

"While we're on the subject," Mike said. "I don't want to see you trying to lug things around tomorrow, either during the move or once everything's in the house. That's what I'm here for."

"I've been wondering," she joked.

"Seriously, you tell me where you want each box and I'll move it for you," Mike countered.

Lisa was about to respond when the distinct sound of something hitting a wall came from the other room.

"You'd better get those patio doors open before they do some real damage," Lisa reminded him.

By midday, all the deliveries had arrived, and the house was starting to look like a real home. The pale grey sofa and loveseat looked amazing against the taupe-coloured walls and dark wood flooring. The dining set that had looked too small in the showroom fit perfectly in situ.

Everything they'd bought just seemed to work. Even the faux weathered bedside tables that looked inconsequential in the store, looked stunning on either side of their brand-new super king-sized bed.

As Lisa walked from room to room dusting and polishing each piece, Mike, armed with a ratchetted lug wrench and industrial-sized screwdriver, was tightening every bolt and screw on the dining chairs and anything else that had required assembly by the delivery teams.

They were about to stop for the day when the house was suddenly filled with the piercing screech of a smoke detector. The two ran around frantically trying to locate the source of the noise but couldn't seem to find it.

Finally, Mike found the detector mounted above a door in the hallway. As he approached it, the noise level doubled to the point of pain. He had to open the door to get their short step ladder in place so he could reach the unit and physically disconnect the detector from the mains to get it to stop its wailing.

Lisa appeared and gave Mike a thumbs-up at having defeated the deafening noise maker. Unfortunately, he wasn't in the mood for accolades as he could smell something burning coming from beyond the open door.

Mike walked through the doorway and could make out a staircase that descended through a haze of smoke. A faint light flickered somewhere below.

"We seem to have a basement," Lisa stated as she stood next to Mike on the small landing.

"I'm going to see where that smoke is coming from."

"Shouldn't we call someone? The fire department maybe?" Lisa suggested, even though she couldn't see or smell the smoke that Mike was referring to.

"And have them drag hoses across our brand-new floor?" Mike replied. "It's probably nothing."

Lisa stayed at the top of the stone stairs as Mike slowly made his way down through the smoke. As he reached the bottom, it seemed to diminish then disappear entirely, leaving behind only an acrid smell of burned wood.

It was the first time that Mike had seen the basement and he was delighted and surprised, not just that they had one, but also at how big it was. It seemed to stretch the entire length of the house. The only negative was that the ceiling was low, probably no more than seven feet high. As Mike paced the room to get an approximate measurement, it dawned on him that the smell of smoke had gone, leaving behind a neutral odour of mustiness and cold concrete.

Lisa joined him at the bottom of the stairs as they sniffed the air, trying to find a trace of the smoke that

Mike had smelled earlier.

There was none.

"Well, that was weird," Mike stated.

"Everything is new," Lisa reminded him as she headed back upstairs. "There's bound to be some lingering construction smell. If we notice it again, we'll call Walter."

Mike was about to walk back up into the hallway when something caught his eye. In the centre of the basement was a tiny black mark on the otherwise blemish-free concrete. He touched it with his finger. It felt warm and ash-like, and his finger came back black and sooty.

"Honey, come down here and see this."

"No time. We need to get back to town so we can pick up Kevin. This is his last day and we promised to be there early."

Mike turned and looked up at her.

"This is something you'll want to see," he insisted.

Lisa tsked, then trotted down the stairs. She stood over him, looking down.

"What am I supposed to be seeing?" she asked.

Mike rolled his eyes and pointed to the floor.

There was no sign of the soot. Mike stared at his finger and saw that it was clean.

There was no trace of the ash.

*

"You seem very quiet," Lisa said as they navigated highway 66 towards DC. "Are you still stressing about that smoke detector?"

"It wasn't the detector that freaked me out, it was what I saw down there."

"I'm sorry, babe, I was there with you and didn't see a thing," Lisa reminded him.

"I know, but I did," Mike insisted. "I even touched the stuff."

He held the finger where he'd seen the soot under her nose.

"You can still smell it."

"Will you please put that thing away," she said, flinching. "I'm trying to drive."

Mike reluctantly withdrew his hand and sat sulking as he stared out the car windscreen.

"I'm not saying you didn't see something, or at least believe that you saw something, but what's more likely: you were overstimulated by the alarm and had a little melt down, or that there was an actual fire? A fire that self-combusted in a concrete basement with nothing flammable anywhere close to it. Let's not spoil the whole move because of something as silly as an overly sensitive smoke detector."

Mike didn't even acknowledge her words.

"Please consider what I'm saying," she almost begged.

Mike sighed and turned to her.

"I'm not an idiot," he stated. "I know that I couldn't have seen what I thought I saw, but it was so real. It was just for a few seconds, but… I don't know what to say. You're probably right about the alarm and me freaking out, but… seeing things? I really hope that that's not going to be a whole new thing for me."

"Of course, it's not. But think about it. We've just bought our first house. We are suddenly committed to making payments and being responsible for the upkeep and the repairs. You are stressed about having to commute to work every day. Then there's the little matter of your new bank supervisor… Penny…"

"Kerry," Mike corrected.

"Whatever," Lisa continued. "You are suddenly under unbelievable stress. It's natural that your mind's going to rebel in some way. That awful noise from the smoke alarm was enough to send anyone a little goofy."

"You didn't see or smell anything strange," Mike pointed out.

"No, but I'm wired better than you are. You had a pretty weird childhood. I'm surprised you aren't stranger than you actually are."

"Thanks a lot," he said, smiling.

Lisa blew him a kiss, believing everything she'd just explained to her husband as the justification for his little hallucination. The problem was that she couldn't help feeling like a fraud. Here she was, convincing her husband that he was seeing things when only one day earlier, she could have sworn that she'd seen an impossible shadow pass across their bedroom ceiling.

They managed to find a place to park on P Street and made it to the pre-school five minutes ahead of schedule. They waited in the Apple Tree hallway until Kevin's last activity came to an end. A couple of his teachers joined them and said how much they were going to miss Kevin.

A door at the end of the hall opened and a stream of five-year-olds filled the corridor. Kevin saw his parents and gave them a big wave as he said his goodbyes to his school friends.

He then ran down the hallway and into Mike and Lisa's arms as they embraced him in a super-hug.

"Eww," Kevin said as he wrinkled his face.

"What's the matter, little man?" Mike asked.

"You smell like Mr Goldstein after he's been on their balcony," Kevin stated.

"What exactly does Mr Goldstein smell like?" Lisa asked, amused.

Kevin took a moment to find the right words.

"He smells like smoke."

CHAPTER 14

Lisa decided that there was no point keeping details of what was going on from Mike. He needed to know exactly where things stood, and she needed for him to know so she could have an open discussion about what she wanted to do next.

As soon as they got Kevin to bed and finished packing the last few things for the next day's move, Lisa planted a big wet kiss on Mike's lips. Before he could get the wrong idea, she told him about the strange shadow, the builder known as Papa and how he'd died as a result of his fall from the rafters.

Mike listened calmly and kept all questions and comments until Lisa had finished.

"Why didn't you tell me about the shadow when you saw it?" Mike asked.

"We were having sex and I certainly didn't want that to stop. As far as Kevin and the dead builder, there never seemed to be a good moment to tell you. That's why I'm doing it now. Besides, I'm still not one hundred percent certain that he's really communicating with anyone. There was also the issue that I didn't want to burden you with such lame problems."

"You didn't want to burden me with the fact that a man died in our house..."

"He didn't die in the house," she interrupted.

"Whatever," Mike continued. "And now our son seems to be able to see him? These are the things we really need to share with one another."

"I know. I'm sorry."

"Let's start with the basics here," he said. "Do you believe that the house is haunted?"

"Absolutely not," she answered forcefully. "If anything, there may be some weird psychic energy that's remained after the accident. I don't know enough about that stuff, but what I do know is that we need to clear it up before it becomes an issue."

"Clear it up?" he asked. "How the hell do we do that? I doubt it's a service we can find on Yelp, do you?"

Lisa gave him her best cheesy smile.

"No way." Mike rolled his eyes.

"Yes, way. There's a number of highly rated psychics who do house cleansing in DC and in Northern Virginia."

"You're saying that you want to hire a psychic to come into our house and have them somehow get rid of this Papa guy?"

"I just want someone to cleanse the house," Lisa replied.

"I never knew that you believed in any of that stuff," Mike said.

"I didn't... I don't. It's just that when our son tells us that he's been talking to a dead guy who reads Hemmingway, it kind of changes your outlook on things."

"If we had known that the builder died, would you have wanted to pull out of the deal?" Mike asked.

"No," Lisa conceded. "I do, however, think that as we have a warranty for every other sodding thing in the house, we should have some legal recourse against a damn ghost."

"Seriously?" Mike asked as he gave her a concerned glance.

"We don't. I checked," Lisa admitted. "In fact, there are a bunch of laws about houses where people have been killed or where there are histories of hauntings, but none of them cover new homes. It seems that the creepy stuff only exists in the used-home marketplace."

"That's comforting," Mike smirked.

"Besides," Lisa added. "I don't want to try and get our money back. We managed to buy the best house in the development for an absolute bargain."

"And it came pre-haunted," Mike added.

"We love the place and that's all there is to it. We'll find the right psychic…"

Lisa noticed Mike's expression.

"I'll… find the right psychic and schedule them to do a cleaning as soon as possible."

"Do you hear yourself?" Mike asked. "You make that sound so normal."

"I'm not saying that I believe there's an actual ghost wandering around our brand-new house, but I do believe in weird energy. Remember when we saw that apartment in West Hollywood? The one with the massive skylight?"

"I remember."

"Do you also remember that we both felt a strange chill inside the place, especially in the living room? It was eighty degrees out yet we both started shivering, yet the realtor never felt a thing."

"Yes, I do recall that particular event."

"Well, I think that we've got something like that in our house, and the best thing to do is simply get rid of it. If we tell Kevin what we're going to do, then announce that Papa has gone, I will bet you that we will have no further problems."

"What about the thing in the basement?" Mike asked. "Is that part of all this?"

"No, my darling. That's just you going off the rails for a moment."

The next day was a model of Washington DC chaos. The moving van arrived exactly on time and was immediately told by an officious police officer that they couldn't park in front of the building without a permit.

Thankfully, the building engineer happened to be walking by and heard the exchange. He led them to the trash and recycling pick-up area next to the service elevator, which by some miracle was actually working that day.

After only ninety minutes, the apartment was cleared of their possessions and was back to looking drab and impersonal. Samantha was in her cat carrier and Kevin was carrying his favourite cuddly panda toy by the ear as they trouped down to the underground garage.

Once in the car, they pulled onto Virginia Avenue and immediately found themselves in bumper-to-bumper traffic. Apparently, the Theodore Roosevelt Bridge was closed for the annual Armed Services Marathon meaning they were completely stuck. The only good thing was that they could see the moving van about a hundred yards ahead, caught up in the same mess. At least they wouldn't get there before them.

After almost forty minutes, the line of overheating cars began to edge forward. Soon, the backup started to thin, and they finally made it across the Roosevelt Bridge.

They passed the moving van just before the Falls Church exit on 66 then sped away so that they could get the house open before the movers arrived. They needn't have rushed. The two men decided that they might as well take their lunch break early and pulled off at Gallows Road, where they knew of a cheap diner with cute waitresses.

At no point did either mover think to call Mike or Lisa, who were waiting at the front door for over an hour.

The two unloaded the van and dumped the boxes in the centre of the living room. Lisa had asked if they could carry them to where each would be unpacked but they refused, citing the fact that they were running late. When they'd closed their van and had Mike sign the receipt document, the men stood motionless as they gave Mike a hopeful look.

"Is there something else?" Mike asked.

"It's usual to give us a tip," the bigger of the two advised.

"Oh, of course," Mike said, theatrically slapping his own forehead. "My tip for you two is to not simply vanish for an hour without letting your clients know. Also, when a customer asks for help putting the boxes in the rooms where they're supposed to go, you might want to actually do that. It might just lead to... I don't know... a tip maybe."

The bigger man looked as if he was going to make a move on Mike, but his partner grabbed his arm.

"It's not worth it," the man said.

After watching them drive off, Lisa turned to her husband.

"Feel better now after telling them off?" she asked.

"Much," he replied.

"I'm so glad," Lisa said as she headed back into the house to start unpacking the boxes.

For the second time that day, Samantha was released from a bathroom. She did one of her anxious belly crawls out into the guest room, then immediately hid under the brand-new bed. Meanwhile, Kevin was still in the master bedroom watching cartoons on the flatscreen TV.

"You okay in here?" Lisa asked as she opened the bedroom door.

"Yeah."

"Do you want lunch yet? I could make you a baloney sandwich?"

"Okay," he answered, distractedly.

"Do you want anything else?" Lisa asked.

"Aren't you going to ask Papa if he wants anything for lunch?"

Lisa felt her innards turn icy cold.

"Is he here now?" Lisa asked.

Kevin nodded.

"Is he here in the room with us?"

Kevin shook his head.

As Lisa started to turn away from him to go back downstairs, Kevin added, "He's looking down at us from up there."

Kevin kept his eyes glued to the TV but pointed up at the bedroom ceiling.

*

Lisa managed to find a highly reviewed spiritualist who lived just outside the town of Culpeper, just under forty miles away. Nigel Deever turned out to be very picky about vetting his clients. He had even asked that Kevin attend the interview (his term) as well, but both parents refused, especially considering that Nigel, instead of coming to them, insisted they drive out to his farmhouse in the middle of nowhere.

Nigel's other foible was that he would not meet any prospective clients on a weekend. That meant that after a long day at the bank, then the commute home, Mike had to immediately turn around and head out again.

After dropping Kevin off with their friends Wayne and Barbara (Wayne was Mike's operations manager), they headed east. Unsurprisingly, Mike was grumpy from the start.

"I don't see why we have to go all the way out to the middle of nowhere to be interviewed so that we can have the honour of paying this idiot a small fortune. Shouldn't we be the ones calling the shots?" he grumbled.

"Are you able to see dead people?" Lisa asked.

"No, of course not."

"Well, he is, so please shut up about what a huge imposition it is for us to go on a nice drive to somewhere we've never been before."

"Do you always have to find the best in every situation?" he shot back.

"I married you, didn't I?" she said, giving him her best winning grin.

The drive took them through a forest of fast-food enterprises and car dealerships on the outskirts of Warrenton before they took a sharp right onto 211. They drove past some seriously expensive-looking farmland then took a left on 229. Signs of modern habitation diminished. Weather-beaten farms with rusted equipment and vehicles peppering their front yards were visible through chain-link fencing and old-growth elm trees.

After eight miles of scenery that looked eerily like the location for the film *Deliverance,* they arrived at the turn-off to Alum Springs Road. After a couple of miles, the paved section ended and was replaced with heavily rutted, packed earth.

They rounded one final bend and saw Nigel's house. At least they assumed it was his as there were no others beyond it. Neither expected his home to look as it did. Being tucked away, far from what, to them, was civilisation, they expected something in the Uni-Bomber style of shack, or maybe even a lone trailer blocked up on stolen bricks. Instead, his abode was a carefully maintained, two-storey farmhouse surrounded by a well-tended lawn and assorted topiary.

They turned onto the gravelled drive and before getting anywhere close to the house itself, two Dobermans came charging towards them. They kept pace with their car, one dog on each side of the vehicle. Once parked, the animals sat on their haunches only inches from the driver and passenger doors.

Mike reached for his cell phone with the intention of calling Nigel to come out and save them from the vicious attackers, but just as he noticed that he had no service, Nigel stepped out the front door.

Just like the house, he was nothing like they'd expected. Both had envisioned an older man, probably dressed in something eccentric and in need of repair.

Nigel was in his early thirties, fit, tanned, and

wearing jeans with a pale green polo shirt. He laughed when he saw his dogs guarding the occupants of the car.

"Nebraska… Lincoln… get away from there," he called out.

Both dogs immediately relaxed and trotted happily over to their master.

"You can get out now," Nigel called to Mike and Lisa.

They reluctantly left the safety of the car, keeping their eyes glued on the two dogs in case Nigel was mistaken and they did decide to attack.

He must have sensed their concern.

"They're not attack dogs. In fact, they weren't keeping you from getting out of your car; they were protecting you. These are the silliest animals you'll find anywhere." Nigel turned to the dogs. "Give the guests a big smile. Come on, big, big smile."

To Mike and Lisa's complete amazement, the Dobermans turned to face them and pulled back their muzzles in something that looked vaguely like a grin. Their white teeth were visible but looked completely benign.

"Did you teach them that?" Lisa asked.

"No… well, I taught them the command, but the actual smile, they taught themselves. I came back from a business trip a few years ago and they greeted me with those silly faces."

"They didn't teach themselves," a voice said from inside the house. "I got bored with Nigel away, so I taught them how to do it."

Tricia Deever walked out the front door, shook her head at the grinning hounds, then stepped up to Mike and Lisa.

"I'm Trish," she said, holding out her hand to Lisa. "I have the dubious honour of being married to Nigel, here."

"Why dubious?" Mike just had to ask.

"We're talking about a man who writes code for the NSA and in his spare time talks to dead people. Why dubious, you ask?"

Lisa laughed.

After all the introductions were complete, Nigel gestured to the front door.

"Let's go inside so you can tell me about your little problem."

Lisa and Mike followed the Deevers and their dogs into the house. The inside looked like something out of *Architectural Digest*. The furniture was clearly expensive, the artwork original, and the colour scheme calming and inviting. The air smelled just slightly of jasmine and wood polish. They were shown to a subtly patterned, overstuffed sofa facing a picture window that afforded views of green pastures surrounded by densely wooded areas that looked as if they'd been there, untouched, for a thousand years.

"Can I get you both something?" Trish asked. "I won't be staying, so this is your only chance."

"We don't mind you hearing this," Lisa said.

"That's not why I'm leaving," Trish replied. "This part of Nigel's life freaks me out. I might be a sensitive, but I'm not a fan of ghosts and ghoulies."

"Neither are we," Mike mentioned. "Hence why we're here."

"Last chance?" Trish said, smiling.

"We're good," Lisa answered.

Once Trish was out of the room and Nigel heard her office door close, he turned to face them, expecting one of them to give him the details.

"How do we start?" Mike asked.

"From the beginning is probably best," Nigel replied. "Just relax and tell me as if you were describing a problem with your fridge or garage door opener. Most people have trouble being upfront and plain speaking when it comes to discussing the supernatural. They shouldn't. Nothing you say will shock me."

Mike looked to Lisa in case she wanted to start, but she simply looked at him to begin.

Mike took a calming breath, then outlined the whole saga. Lisa chirped in a few times to add something or put a different slant on what Mike had said. Despite Lisa's belief that the basement event was only in his head, he included that in the telling of their problem.

"Thank you both for sharing," Nigel said when they'd finished. "I have a few questions for you before we go on. Your son's headaches, when did they start?"

"We don't think that has anything to do with it," Lisa stated. "I only mentioned it because he has had a couple over the last few days."

"Please, just humour me," he requested.

Mike tried to think of the first time.

"When he was three," Lisa answered.

"Where was he at the time?"

"We were all in a hotel room in West Hollywood. We stayed the night, before moving into a new rental apartment."

"How old was the hotel?" Nigel asked. "I don't need an exact age. I just mean was it newer or older?"

"It was older. It was an art deco apartment building that had been turned into a hotel," Mike said, remembering.

"This will be a little harder," Nigel advised. "When did the second headache occur?"

"That's easy," Mike answered. "We were invited to my boss's house in the hills overlooking Glendale. The moment we walked in, Kevin started to cry and said that his head hurt."

"How old would you guess that house was?" Nigel asked.

"Same sort of period as the hotel, so I'd guess… 1920s?" Lisa answered. "Are you suggesting that his headaches have something to do with his being in older buildings?"

"Just from what you've told me, it sounds as though Kevin might be what we call a 'sensitive'. It's possible that he can subconsciously feel the energy from a restless spirit."

"If that's the case," Lisa said. "Why is he suddenly able to actually see and interact with this Papa person when he's never been able to do so before?"

"I think that he may only have the ability at this point to see someone who has departed very recently as their energy is still strong. At the other locations, I believe that his mind was sensing something but didn't know what it was. That in turn would have caused stress, which manifested itself as one of his headaches."

Mike and Lisa stared at Nigel in complete silence. Neither could find the right words.

"You said something about his only having the ability at this point," Mike said. "Does that mean that he will grow out of it?"

"Actually, it's the opposite," Nigel explained. "As he gets older and his brain begins to function at a higher level, there's every likelihood that he will be able to see the spirits of those that are still trapped on our plane;

at least the ones that want to be seen."

"Are you saying that he's going to become a medium or a spiritualist?" Lisa asked.

"Not at all," Nigel replied. "Kevin will choose whatever profession and lifestyle he wants to pursue. Just because he can see earthbound spirits doesn't mean that he has to interact with them."

"That's a relief," Mike blurted out.

"Though," Nigel continued. "If a spirit senses that he can hear and see them, they can be very persuasive in trying to open a line of communication. In all likelihood, they have been waiting years, if not decades or even centuries, to be able to converse with someone... anyone. They will sometimes pester someone who has eyeshine until they are acknowledged. It can be quite a nuisance."

"Eyeshine?" Lisa said.

"That's a term we use for when someone can actually see a spirit. Many people can sense one – the room goes cold, a shadow isn't where it should be, that sort of stuff – but only a lucky few can actually see them in whatever form they are able to take."

Mike and Lisa glanced nervously at each other.

"In any case," Nigel continued. "Kevin does see the deceased builder and seems to be able to communicate with him. Believe it or not, that is a good thing. Most hauntings, as most people refer to them, are entirely one-sided. The spirit is trying everything it can to be heard or seen. Sometimes, if the entity has enough lifeforce left, and is exceptionally anxious or just plain angry, it can move physical things on our plane. At that point, they are referred to as poltergeists."

"We saw the movie," Mike said.

"You don't have any of those worries," Nigel continued, ignoring Mike's lame comment. "If Kevin can see Papa, then I should be able to do the same. If we can communicate in some way, I am certain I can persuade him to move on."

"Does that mean that we have passed the interview?" Lisa asked.

"With flying colours. I'm sorry about having to make you drive all the way out here, but I've learned through experience that almost half of all prospective clients who contact me only do so in order for me to come to their house and either perform a séance or entertain their guests with tales of especially scary hauntings. Some people seem to believe that they can hire a spiritualist almost as a party clown, to amuse them and their guests. By forcing prospective clients to come to me, it proves that they are sincere, plus it also gives me the ability to speak with them in an unfamiliar setting."

"Makes sense," Lisa said.

"May I ask you a personal question?" Mike requested.

"Of course."

"When did you first know that you had the… eyeshine, was it?"

"When I was a child, I used to have nose bleeds quite often. The strange thing was that they would only occur when I was in an unfamiliar location. Usually, an older building or home. The doctor told my parents that there was no medical reason for the bleeds and felt that it was possibly caused either by repeated nose picking or stress."

"And were you a prodigious nose picker?" Lisa asked, grinning.

Nigel laughed.

"I was not. It wasn't until I'd just turned fifteen and my parents had taken me to Merryville to celebrate that I found out the cause. While I was on the Jurassic Monsters ride; just as we were approaching a group of animatronic raptors devouring a carcass beneath a mountain overhang, I saw this girl sitting on a stone ledge, watching our boat approach. She had to have been around seventeen or eighteen and was quite pretty, though impossibly pale with dark shadows under her eyes, and her left arm was missing. I naturally assumed that she was part of the animatronics, but as we got closer, she must have seen me staring at her.

She began to wave with her remaining arm. I looked back at my parents to make sure they were seeing what I was seeing, but they were fascinated by a tetradactyl flying by overhead. I then felt a dribble of blood come out of my nose."

"You poor thing," Lisa interrupted.

"The girl began waving even more frantically as if she understood that our brief connection was about to be severed. We were approaching a tunnel that ran under the overhang, and I knew that once we were in it, I wouldn't be able to see the girl again. Then, just as I started to relax, she stood up on the ledge and jumped down onto our boat. There were dozens of other people on the ride, and I fully expected them all to start screaming. Unfortunately, I was the only one who did. My parents actually thought it funny that the animatronic dinosaurs had managed to scare me."

Nigel took a moment to take a few deep breaths. It was obvious that just retelling the story brought back difficult memories for him.

"As everyone on our boat, except me, giggled and laughed at me, we sailed under the bridge and the girl placed her remaining hand on my arm. It was like an electric shock. I saw her thoughts. It was only for a second, but during that time, I saw her riding in one of the boats as they approached the dinosaur habitat. I could feel that she was either drunk or high and one of her friends dared her to try and grab a piece of fake rock that was lying on the ground only a few feet from the boat. As her friends held her legs, she stretched across the flowing water and grabbed the prize. What she hadn't noticed was that they were fast approaching the tunnel. Her friends tried to pull her back on board, but before they could, her arm became stuck between the boat and the concrete wall and was torn off at the shoulder. Everyone on board tried to help, but I could feel her life slip away as she bled out onto the fiberglass flooring.

"The girl stayed with me, her hand on my arm, right up until we emerged into the light. She then faded away like a wisp of wind-blown smoke. I again looked to the others on our boat, but nobody but me had seen a thing."

"What did you do then?" Mike asked, transfixed.

"I pretended to enjoy the rest of the day, then as soon as we got home, I went online and looked up deaths on amusement park rides in Merryville."

"Did you find anything about the girl?" Lisa asked, her voice sounding a little shaky.

Nigel got to his feet and walked over to a built-in bookcase on the far wall. He gently removed a framed item from the middle shelf and brought it back to Mike and Lisa. They took it from him. It was a newspaper article dated July 3rd, 1995. It told of how Mercy

Handler had died as a result of a horrific accident on Merryville's Jurassic Monsters ride. Her arm had apparently become caught between a boat and a tunnel wall and had been severed from her body. She had died of blood loss and shock before anyone could help her. She had been seventeen at the time and was celebrating with friends before starting at Georgetown University in the fall. There was a photo of Mercy that was taken a few months earlier.

Both Lisa and Mike thought she was beautiful and looked full of life and hope.

CHAPTER 15

Two days later, Nigel stepped foot in the Ellis's Lake View Estates home. He was wearing cargo shorts, a faded *Pet Sematary* T-shirt, and Birkenstock sandals. He couldn't have looked less like a medium if he'd tried.

Nigel graciously declined a cup of tea or coffee and asked if he could walk through the house by himself. He began upstairs and slowly walked from one bedroom to the next. As he entered the master bedroom, he felt the temperature drop. He could immediately sense a presence but found no trace of hostility or anger.

Nigel decided to finish his entire walk-through before focusing on that one room. He doubted there would be any other entities within the brand-new home, but he wanted to follow his usual routine, just in case.

Mike and Lisa were sitting on the bare earth (where one day their back patio would be), to give him the privacy he needed. Nigel walked through every inch of the ground floor and sensed nothing out of the ordinary, until he walked past a door in the downstairs hallway.

Nigel was intrigued. There was a slight vibration coming through the door, but it didn't feel at all like a displaced or trapped spirit. In fact, Nigel didn't know what it was. He tried the handle but found it locked. He felt above the door frame, found the key and opened it. Nigel looked for a light switch before descending into the basement. He couldn't find one, but then noticed that a single bulb suspended in the middle of the room was already on. Nigel first walked the perimeter, keeping as close to the concrete walls as he could without actually touching them. He then moved closer to the middle and repeated his walkaround. Finally, he stopped in the very centre of the basement, closed his eyes, and lowered his head.

The vibration was slightly stronger, but Nigel still couldn't identify what was causing it. If it was spirit-based, he'd never sensed anything like it before. It felt a little like the tingling sensation he'd had once when he'd put his tongue across the top of a nine-volt battery. Whatever it was, Nigel decided not to mention it to Mike and Lisa. There was no point in bringing something to their attention that had no bearing on the primary issue and didn't appear to be of immediate concern. Besides, just because he was able to pick up the sensation didn't mean that anyone else could.

Nigel walked back up the concrete stairs and was about to step out into the hallway when he smelled the faintest whiff of smoke. It was there one second then gone the next.

He was intrigued, especially after Mike had told him about the earlier smell, but with it gone, there was nothing to investigate. Besides, it could perfectly well have come from anywhere. The farmers in the area often burned dry brush and dead leaves in oversized oil drums. He assumed it had to be that and focused his mind on the task at hand, which was to deal with Papa.

Nigel walked back upstairs and stepped into the master bedroom. He closed the door behind him and shut the plantation shutters, darkening the room enough so that he could focus on any sign of a physical presence. It was extraordinarily rare for an entity to be able to show itself. On the few occasions when he'd been blessed with seeing a physical manifestation, the spirits appeared as a gossamer-like haze that free-floated just above knee height.

Nigel sat on the floor with his back against the end of the bed.

"Sebastian," he spoke slowly and softly. "I am here to help you cross over. Please let me know if you can hear me."

His request was met with complete silence;

however, he sensed an increase in electrical energy within the room that raised goosebumps on his bare arms.

"Sebastian," Nigel tried again, this time in his broken Spanish. *"Estoy aqui para ayudarte. Por favor, habla conmigo."*

Again, nothing.

Nigel stayed seated and closed his eyes. He wanted the spirit to begin to feel comfortable with his being in the same room, or at least in the same house.

Nigel cleared his mind of all extraneous thoughts and brain chatter. He timed his breathing and was soon in a light meditative state.

"Who are you?" a heavily accented voice whispered somewhere nearby. "Are you *policia, federales*?"

"I am not," Nigel replied.

"La migra?"

"I am none of those things, Sebastian. You never have to worry about immigration or the police ever again." Nigel spoke in a gentle monotone.

"Estoy muerto?" Sebastian asked.

"Yes, Sebastian. I'm sorry to tell you this, but you are dead."

There was a long silence.

"Would you like to leave this house and move on to where you should be?" Nigel asked.

"Cielo?" Sebastian asked.

"Some people call it heaven. Others call it the glorious light," Nigel replied. "Do you understand glorious light?"

"*Sí*," Sebastian answered. "*Luz glorioso.*"

Nigel simply nodded.

"I must stay... help the *niño*," the spirit whispered.

"The boy has his *padre* and *madre* to take care of him. You need to look after yourself now."

"*El esta en peligro.*" Sebastian's voice became stronger and sounded as if he was much closer. "*Muy mal peligro.*"

"I don't know what *peligro* means," Nigel answered.

There was no response.

"Sebastian, are you still here? Sebastian?"

Nigel was worried that Sebastian no longer wanted to talk to him.

"Sebastian," he tried again. "Please tell me what pel..."

"Danger!" Sebastian voice sounded as if he was only inches from Nigel's face. "Bad danger."

For a brief instant, the room brightened and less than a foot in front of him, Nigel watched as something that looked like a luminous jellyfish twirled once, only a few inches from the floor, then shot upwards and passed through the ceiling.

Nigel just sat there. He had never seen such energy in a spirit before. There was a sense of strength in its ability to take form and achieve movement.

Nigel sat in silence, trying to sense where Sebastian's spirit had gone but felt no presence whatsoever. It was as if Sebastian had simply wanted to warn someone of the *mal peligro* before passing on to the next plane. At least that's what appeared to have just happened. There was no longer any trace of spirit energy in the room or in the house.

Nigel wondered what danger Sebastian was warning them about. Whatever it was, Nigel could think of nothing that could threaten anyone in the new home. Perhaps the poor man was still irrationally fearful of immigration and deportation, even though no government force on this earth would ever threaten him again.

Nigel joined Mike and Lisa outside, and after very little convincing, accepted a cold Heineken.

"How'd it go?" Mike asked.

Before answering, he took a long gulp from the frosty bottle. "I spoke with Sebastian."

They both looked back at him in amazement. Though the whole intention had been for that to happen, somehow hearing him state something so fantastical was something of a shock.

"You actually talked to him?" Lisa asked.

"Yes, I did. Thankfully some of my school Spanish still seems to be buried in my muscle memory."

"I was expecting it to take much longer," Mike commented.

"Just because you've seen someone in a movie spend anguished hours trying to communicate with a spirit doesn't mean it has any actual bearing on the real process. If the spirit wishes to speak, they will. If they are a little reticent, one simply has to let them know that they are in a safe place and they usually open up. Once Sebastian realised that he had passed away, he seemed to understand that it was time for him to move on."

"That was it?" Mike asked. "You just asked him to move on and he said yes?"

"It seems that he was only waiting here so that he could look after Kevin," Nigel explained. "Once I convinced him that Kevin had two parents who were here to do whatever protecting was necessary, he left."

"Did you see him?" Mike tried not to sound too geeky.

"At the very end, Sebastian appeared as a flickering light, then was gone. You shouldn't have any more problems."

"While you were walking the house," Mike spoke offhandedly, having promised Lisa that he wouldn't mention his basement hallucination. "Did you sense any other presence in the house?"

Nigel laughed. "Isn't one enough?"

"Of course, it is," Lisa said while glaring at her husband. "Mike's just making sure that he gets his money's worth."

After a few minutes of small talk, Nigel got to his feet and said his goodbyes. There was something so refreshing about the couple's gratitude over his managing to persuade Sebastian to move on, that he was torn about whether he should mention the spirit's warning about there being a bad force in the house. He was also in two minds about telling them about the vibration he felt in the basement, even if it was only to make them aware of it in the event it became anything more serious.

Nigel decided that they were better off not knowing about things that would probably have no impact on them or their home. He'd learned over the years that by telling clients about even the slightest sensation he may have perceived, it was usually enough to cause them concern and even some degree of anxiety.

No. He would leave them feeling happy in the knowledge that their house was clean and that they could now enjoy it to the fullest.

As he drove away from the house, he looked back in his rear-view mirror and saw the couple waving happily at him. He was about to look away when he thought he saw a dark shadow rise up behind their home. It was only there for a brief second, but it had looked almost like the outline of a building, then it was gone as fast as it had appeared. In its place were the trees that backed the house.

Nigel realised that the light must have caught them in such a way as to cause the momentary *trompe l'oeil*. He laughed at himself. He was the last person who needed to start seeing dark and menacing things that weren't really there.

Especially when dark and menacing were his bread and butter.

CHAPTER 16

A few days later, Mike walked into the bank building and saw Martin storming off in the other direction. He sped after him and caught up just before he could reach one of the elevator lobbies.

"Martin," Mike called. "What's going on?"

"Come with me," Martin almost snapped. "I just got a call from the president's office. They wondered if I was coming to the last-minute planning meeting."

"What planning meeting?" Mike asked as he stepped into the elevator.

"Apparently, they called my office earlier about the meeting, and Kerry took the call."

"Kerry started today?" Mike asked. "Did you know about that?"

"Nope. I thought we had another month before she was due to turn up. Apparently, she just woke up and decided that she'd come into work today."

"But what about her notice period at the *Gazette*?"

"I'm going to check into that, but I'll bet you anything that the moment she gave her notice, they told her she didn't have to come in anymore."

"Sounds to me like they couldn't wait to get rid of her?" Mike asked.

"Ya think?"

"It still doesn't explain why she felt it was okay to be in your office and answer your phone," Mike said.

"No, it doesn't. Security apparently didn't know where the hell to put her as they had no idea she was going to turn up today. It seems that she was making such a scene at the security desk that they decided the best plan was to unlock my office and let her wait in there until I got in."

"Okay, but still... answering your phone?"

"I know. Nice start, huh?" Martin sighed. "Now we have to try and undo a complete mess that she's already managed to create. It seems that the president wants to hold a last-minute virtual town hall with a revolving set of panellists on stage with him. He also wants live video conferencing with all of the bank offices, worldwide."

"Good grief," Mike shook his head. "When does he want to do that?"

"Friday," Martin answered bluntly.

"This Friday?" Mike was stunned. "Where?"

"In the middle of the atrium."

"That's the one space that doesn't have any technology," Mike gasped. "Why did they pick there? They never use that space for town halls."

"From what I've managed to put together, they were going to use the Grand Hall, but Kerry suggested the atrium when she answered my phone."

"But she doesn't have any idea of what we do here, or what the capabilities are for each space," Mike insisted.

"Yet," Martin responded. "She seemed comfortable enough to speak up and offer services we can't provide, in a space we never use for video conferencing and has the worst acoustics in the whole building."

They stepped out onto the eleventh floor and made their way through the warren of executive hallways until they arrived at the president's private suite. The receptionist waved them toward the conference room. When they entered the lavishly decorated space, it was obvious that the meeting had been going for some time judging by the remnants of what looked to have been at least two separate coffee services.

Thankfully, as per normal protocol, the meeting agenda went through each support need one item at a time. AV for some reason was always last. As they were late for the meeting, the only available seats were far from the conference table in a dark corner at the back of the room. Both Mike and Martin immediately noticed that Kerry had managed to get herself a prime seat at the table, right next to the president's executive assistant.

As Miranda, the bank's director of food service, finished outlining the catering support that her department would be providing for the meeting, Martin was about to start the discussion regarding the AV requirements and highlight the negatives to holding the meeting in the atrium. Before he could get his first word out, Kerry introduced herself as having taken over Martin's position and then began to outline what she felt would be needed for the meeting.

As she talked, the faces around the table and the room began to glance over at Martin and Mike with expressions of surprise and concern. Though not technically minded as such, they had all used the AV services within the bank and knew what could and could not be done. After a few more minutes, one of the event organisers thanked Kerry, cutting off her nonsensical ramblings mid-sentence.

"Thank you... Kerry, was it, but I believe that for a meeting of this importance, we would all feel more comfortable if Martin Keep and Mike Ellis spoke on behalf of the AV group. I'm sure you understand."

Kerry did not understand at all. She sat back in her chair as her face turned a dark crimson. Her anger radiated out in waves.

Despite her obvious displeasure, Martin took over and systematically corrected everything Kerry had previously suggested or offered. He was able to have the meeting changed back to the Grand Hall, where the eight wall-mounted cameras as well as the fully installed video conferencing system would help the meeting flow seamlessly.

The last item was the choice of microphones for the participants on stage. Because there would be so many speakers who would, over the course of the meeting, rotate with other participants throughout the day, any thought of using lapel mics as Kerry had suggested was nixed because of the constant requirement of the tech crew having to clip a mic onto each person before they walked onto the stage.

Martin's suggestion was that handheld microphones be provided for all the guest speakers. They were easier to be moved around, could be shared by multiple guests, and AV could provide mic runners to ensure that whoever wanted to speak would have a mic within seconds.

All in attendance agreed with Martin's suggestions. All except one, that is. Kerry waited until Martin had finished then brought up the point that handheld mics were clumsy and cumbersome and that everywhere she had worked, lapel mics were always used.

Martin was about to respond when the organiser spoke.

"I have seen handheld mics used very successfully at countless large-scale meetings here at the bank, but I understand your concern. Mike, what about you? Which do you think would best serve a meeting like this, considering its high-profile nature and VIP guests?"

"I have to agree with Martin that lapel mics just wouldn't work in this case. I understand what Kerry is saying, and she is right in normal circumstances, but for a fast turnover meeting like a global town hall, handheld mics are the only way to go."

After a few additional security notes, the meeting was adjourned. Martin was called over to talk to a few of the attendees on another matter, so Mike headed out of the room with the others. He ended up walking a few paces behind Kerry and couldn't help noticing that her entire body seemed to be hunched over in anger.

There was a short wait for the next elevator, during which time Kerry intentionally ignored Mike. Once everyone piled into the next car, he felt that he should try to defuse the situation.

"I'm sorry about not agreeing with you over the mic question, but we've done a lot of these meetings and..."

Kerry literally pushed aside an elderly staff member so that she could come face to face with Mike.

"Let me make one thing clear to you," she snarled. "From now on, no matter what I say, the only answer I want from you is the word 'yes'."

Mike felt as if he'd been slapped across the face. He had no idea how to react or respond. The other eleven people in the elevator had all heard Kerry's words and were looking at her in complete shock. Two people actually moved farther away from her. The rest of the ride down to the basement level transpired in complete, awkward silence.

Despite the auspicious start, Mike hoped that Kerry would, at some point, understand the operational flow of the bank and start to recognise that things were done in a specific way for good reason.

She never did.

Within a matter of only a few weeks, Mike began dreading going to work. Kerry had managed, in an extraordinarily short time, to alienate most of the bank staff, all the People Force team, and just about every technology support vendor in a hundred-mile radius.

She refused to listen to any advice or to learn the best uses for the technologies and crew. She had even made it clear to Martin that she was now running the AV operation, not him. Despite Martin's decades of knowledge, especially in the audio sector, she chose to do everything her way, which led to countless technical hiccups and way too many meeting failures.

When the internal clients began to formally complain about their AV support problems, Kerry blamed laziness and sloppiness on the part of the People Force technicians. She even went so far as to suggest that they would most likely not be invited to compete in the next RFP (request for proposal) when the current contract expired.

Life within the AV suite became one long effort to avoid Kerry at all costs. To be cornered by her during one of her frequent 'walk-throughs' meant that she was either going to blame the person for some newly perceived screw up, or they would be assigned to one of her 'special projects'. Those were the worst. She would concoct some new approach to supporting a high-viz meeting, only to have it crash and burn because of her misunderstanding of the client needs or her choosing the wrong technology. Ultimately, the technical support team had to shoulder the blame every time.

The biggest problem was that People Force's head office in Arlington did not believe Mike's reporting about Kerry's inability to manage, as well as her complete lack of technical comprehension. They started putting pressure on him to get a better handle on his crew and get them back up to being considered flawless and unreproachable. They also reminded Mike that Kerry was the client and as such had the last word when it came to contract performance and quality adherence.

Basically, they told Mike that they believed he was the problem, not Kerry.

Mike had an emergency off-site lunch with Martin, who he rarely saw since his promotion, to come up with some sort of strategy about how to manage working with Kerry and not let the service quality suffer.

Martin was little help. In fact, in some respects, he was suffering from a very similar problem as Mike. His executive director, Gary Schneider, had called him into his office twice already to tell him that there was concern about the People Force contract and that management was considering an early contract termination in light of their poor performance.

Martin had tried to point out that prior to Kerry's arrival, the People Force team were considered to be the best crew in DC and that the reported problems only began once she came on board.

"Are you suggesting that one new manager can undermine a professional AV crew to the point that they seem to do nothing but screw up?" Gary had asked.

Martin replied that if he were to look back over the past two years' performance evaluations for the crew, they scored above ninety-eight percent every review period. Martin again mentioned that there were no performance issues with the AV contract prior to Kerry's arrival at the bank.

At their last meeting, Gary had leaned back in his chair and looked at Martin with almost fatherly concern.

"I know how hard it's been for you to adapt to senior management. You have always liked to be hands-on when it comes to meetings and event support. Some even felt that you were too much of a micro-manager. At the end of the day, the department ran well, and the client's perception and approval rating of the operation was at an all-time high. The issue now is that you have to let go and let someone new manage the day-to-day operations so that you can focus on more strategic goals and how to achieve them."

Gary took a slow, calming breath.

"This little vendetta you seem to have with Ms Coates is not healthy. I applaud how protective you have always been of the contract team, but if they are underperforming, you defending them is both inappropriate and unprofessional. From what I hear, Ms Coates is doing a great job…"

"Hearing from who?" Martin interrupted. "Her telling you that she has been doing a great job does not make it true. Why don't you ask the meeting support managers about Kerry or check with the clients and see what they think?”

“Why would I destroy all the goodwill that Ms Coates has already garnered by questioning her peers about her performance. That would be just about as unprofessional as it gets. If she tells me that the problem is with the contract team, then I believe her, and, if I may suggest, you should believe her as well. She reports to you, therefore anything that falls under her responsibility is by default your responsibility as well. Learn to trust your managers.”

Martin informed Mike that two days after that last exchange with Gary, he had received a written warning from HR concerning his lack of leadership skills and unwillingness to support a staff member that he was responsible for managing.

“This is a nightmare,” Mike commented.

“Yup, that’s exactly what it’s turning into,” Martin agreed. “I either have to support her while she destroys the entire AV department, which I will ultimately be blamed for, or else I can continue to try and get management to see what’s really going on and most likely lose my job.”

“Those are two wonderful choices,” Mike sighed.

“What about you? What are your plans?”

“Until this lunch, I wasn’t aware that I needed a new plan. I had sort of hoped that between us, we could find a way to get things back into some sort of normality.”

“I wish I could think of some way to do that, but once you’ve invited a vampire into your house, there’s no way to get rid of them till they’ve sucked you dry,” Martin stated as he tore off a corner of his sandwich with his teeth.

Mike couldn’t help noticing that Martin looked almost feral as an errant piece of beef dangled from his lips.

The only remaining problem with their new home was that for some reason, fibre hadn't been run all the way to the house. It terminated in a green, melanite box at the curb but came no closer. It had taken weeks of begging, coercing, and finally threatening before Horizon Cable finally arrived to trench a path into the garage where the house multiplexer was located.

The simple operation turned out to be much harder than the Horizon installers had expected.

The trenching started out normally with the mini backhoe slicing through the ground without issue. The problem started when they were about fifteen feet from the house. The machine suddenly came to a jarring stop, almost toppling over.

After some poking around, and an unscheduled coffee break, the installers informed Lisa that they had come up against what appeared to be solid concrete. She immediately called Walter to ask if he had any clue as to what they'd encountered, but he was as shocked as everyone else to hear that there was anything except untouched soil surrounding the house.

Thankfully, the backhoe had a breaker attachment that was designed to shatter concrete each time it connected with it. As Lisa watched them attach it to the backhoe, she couldn't help thinking that it looked more like a metal beak or some sort of gruesome torture device from the Middle Ages.

Once the breaker was attached, the hoe driver edged it above the exposed part of the concrete obstacle. The beak-like device rose in the air then crashed down into the solid slab, shattering a section into ragged cement chunks.

*

At the same moment as the vicious-looking spike struck the concrete for the first time, three miles away in the first-grade homeroom of the Gainesville Elementary School, Kevin fell to the floor and cried out in pain. One minute he was watching his teacher show how a cube of ice could turn into water and then into steam; the next, he was on the ground clutching his head and screaming for all he was worth.

The school nurse was called and despite his obvious discomfort, couldn't find anything obviously wrong with him. By that point Kevin was not just screaming in pain. His whole body was shaking and spasming. The principal, a petite, dark-haired woman in her late forties, forced herself to sound calm as she called Lisa while the nurse called 911.

Lisa drove as if possessed and arrived at the school building less than five minutes later. She didn't need any directions to find her son. His screams were echoing through the hallway as frightened teachers and students peered through the glass inserts of their closed classroom doors.

Kevin was on his back staring blankly up at the ceiling in the classroom as he continued to thrash about as the paramedics gently held him down.

They managed to examine Kevin, expecting to find one area that was causing the pain. They prodded everywhere, but the intensity of his cries didn't increase or abate.

Kevin's little face was ghostly white and shiny with perspiration.

Lisa knelt next to him and tried to hold his hand, which was near impossible due to his thrashing about.

"What's wrong with him?" she cried.

The lead paramedic shook his head.

"We have no idea," he replied. "Does he have a history of epilepsy or seizures?"

"No. The only thing he ever had wrong with him is

that he occasionally gets migraines."

"Have those ever resulted in an episode like this?"

"God no," Lisa replied. "In fact, if anything, he becomes quiet and withdrawn."

Lisa looked on as the two paramedics continued trying to diagnose the cause of Kevin's condition.

*

The breaker attached to the backhoe was working like a charm. It had, in less than thirty minutes, been able to shatter enough concrete to create a viable trench that was only inches from reaching the house. It certainly wasn't pretty to look at, but it would do. With one final jarring impact, there was space for the plastic conduit to run the entire way from the street to the connection box in the garage. The driver then guided the backhoe onto the street and switched off the diesel engine.

*

Kevin stopped screaming.

One minute his shrieking voice sounded as if it could shatter glass with its intensity; the next, the room was filled with complete silence. Within moments, his body relaxed and the shaking subsided until he was completely still. His breathing returned to normal and his face regained colour.

"What's happened?" Lisa cried, finding the quiet almost scarier than the fit.

The two responders were already taking his vitals and looking puzzled.

"This doesn't make any sense," one of them said. "After what he's just been through, his blood pressure and heart rate should both still be elevated; instead, they're normal. Not just normal but are those of a child at rest."

"What does that mean?" Lisa asked. "Is he going to be okay?"

The lead paramedic got to his feet and eased some of his over-stressed muscles.

"I don't know what to tell you. His vitals are ridiculously normal, and he doesn't seem to be showing any signs of the trauma we all just witnessed."

"So, what do we do now?" Lisa asked.

"Hi, Mommy," Kevin said, his voice hoarse from all the screaming. "What are you doing here?"

"Should he go to the hospital?" Lisa asked.

"I don't see what for," one of the paramedics answered. "They'll do the same tests we just did and send him home. I suggest keeping a close eye on him. If he has another… whatever it was, call 911 immediately."

"Thank you," Lisa said as she helped her son get shakily to his feet.

"Can I watch cartoons when I get home?" Kevin asked, as if nothing had happened.

*

Mike's commute from work was even more depressing than usual. It was one of those late August days in DC when the humidity is so high that you are drenched within seconds of stepping outdoors. By the time Mike reached the Foggy Bottom metro station, (since commuting, all humour over the name had evaporated), his clothes were soaked through. The usual euphoric realisation that he'd managed to get in a compartment with working air conditioning vanished as the overly refrigerated air cut through his damp clothes within seconds, and by the first stop, he was starting to shiver.

Mike used the time it took to get to Vienna to weigh up his options. The fact was, he didn't have many. Only a few weeks earlier, he'd loved his job and felt secure in the knowledge that the bank and People Force were happy with him. On the day that he and Lisa had signed the loan agreement for the house, he'd had zero concerns about the debt and its repayment.

After his earlier lunch with Martin, he wasn't feeling

anything like as optimistic about his future. If People Force wasn't on his side and nobody was in a position to help him at work, he could easily be made the scapegoat for the perceived drop in performance and that would be that. $2600 a month in mortgage and property tax payments and he could end up out of work in the blink of an eye. Thankfully, Lisa brought in enough so they could survive, but things would get tight real fast.

The hardest part was that Mike had decided after Kerry had shown her true colours in the elevator, to not tell Lisa all the gory details of each day's work horrors. She knew that Kerry was difficult, but that was about it. If she was to hear every gory detail on a daily basis, she would only worry, which meant that both of them would start feeding off each other's stress. It was better for Lisa to remain cheerful and level-headed and let him take the brunt of the psychological wounding.

The problem was, now that his employment future was in potential jeopardy, Mike knew that he was going to have to share everything with his wife.

*

Lisa checked her watch and saw that it was almost six. She should be getting her nightly phone call from Mike as he swapped the subway for his car at the Vienna station. She'd tried numerous times to get him to call from the train, but Mike hated when other people carried on hyper-personal phone conversations in a public place, especially one as cramped and claustrophobic as the metro train.

Lisa considered telling him when he did call about Kevin's fit but decided that until he was home with his family, there was no point upsetting him while he was on the road.

Lisa was about to check on the chicken casserole in the oven when her phone rang.

"Just got in the car," Mike said. "I'll be there in forty minutes. Everything good at home?"

"Of course, it is," she responded, maybe a tad too quickly. "How was work?"

"The usual," he replied.

Once they'd disconnected, Lisa checked on Kevin, who was colouring-in a paint-by-numbers drawing of a dinosaur eating leaves off a huge tree.

"You okay, Kev?"

"Uh huh," he mumbled distractedly, as he tried to keep his green crayon from bleeding over the lines.

Satisfied that he seemed unaffected by his earlier seizure, Lisa then went to DEFCOM 2 status for dinner prep. Lisa had never owned a brand-new appliance, let alone an entirely new kitchen. Her only complaint was that the cabinets were nowhere near as large as she was used to and there was nowhere deep enough to store her bigger pieces of china.

With only fifteen minutes to go before Mike got home and saw the unsightly cable trench that led to their house, a newer model Ford F-250 pick-up unexpectedly pulled up in their driveway. Lisa went outside to see what someone was doing showing up unannounced only minutes before dinner time.

Moses Taylor stepped out the truck and gave her his best smile.

"Mrs Ellis," Moses said, as he removed his cap adorned with a logo for some place called Agrid Farms. His hair was pure white and once free of the head covering, puffed back out into a well-groomed afro. The contrast of the ultra-white hair against his ebony skin was startling. "My name is Moses Taylor and I'm going to be doing the landscaping for your property. I know it's late, and I certainly didn't mean to disturb you, but I wanted to have a look at this trench thing that Walter told me about."

"It's hard to miss," Lisa said as she gestured off to the left.

"Yeah. I saw it when I drove in," Moses said as he stepped over to the scarred earth. He stopped at the fifteen-foot section where the concrete had been torn up. He squatted down on his haunches and picked up a chunk of broken cement. He turned the piece in his hand, then raised it to his nose.

"Judging by the colour and the sand they used, I'd say this was from the early 1900s."

"You mean there was a building here?"

"Not necessarily," Moses said, standing back up. "Could have been a foundation for just about anything, or even just a slab of concrete. With the lake just down there, it might have been laid as a place for people to sit and take a gander at all the wildlife. Fact is, it's pretty hard to tell."

"Is it going to be a problem to landscape over it?" she asked.

"Nope. Shouldn't be. We're not planning to put down anything with serious roots anywhere close to the house. As you can see, there's a good foot and a half of soil above whatever it was, plus we'll be laying either sod or planting soil over that, so I think you'll be fine. If we run into any trouble, I have a GPR unit I can send over so that we can work out what's what."

"That's a relief," Lisa replied. "I'm sorry to sound so stupid, but what's a GPR?"

"Nothing stupid about not knowing everything. Stupid is not admitting it," Moses said, grinning. "GPR is short for ground penetrating radar."

"Isn't that what the police use when they're looking for a buried body?"

"It has many uses, and I do believe that that's indeed

one of them."

"Should I be concerned about them having built this house so close to something that no one seems to know about?"

"I wouldn't," Moses said. "This whole area had some big old homes dotted around the place. Most were destroyed during the Civil War, but some lasted well into the 1900s. It'd be pretty hard to dig deep around here and not find some evidence of either the battles or the old properties. I don't think you need to worry in the least."

"Thank you," Lisa said, shaking his hand. "What time does your crew start in the morning?"

"If it's all right with you and yours, seven is our normal start time."

"We're all up way before then."

"Seven it is."

Moses replaced his cap and climbed back into the truck. It was only then that Lisa noticed the logo on the driver's door.

TAYLOR LANDSCAPING INC.
NEW YORK, MARYLAND, VIRGINIA, WASHINGTON DC.

It suddenly hit her that she'd seen Taylor Landscaping equipment and vehicles all over DC. They were a huge company. When Moses had turned up, she had assumed that he was a one-man band and would be using day-hire labour. She reminded herself once again about the pitfalls of unfounded assumptions.

As Moses drove away from the house, Mike passed him and drove up their driveway.

"I always knew it," he said with a grin. "The moment I leave for work, your lover shows up."

"I was bound to get caught at some point," she said, playing along.

"I always imagined that you'd go for a younger man, but I guess sometimes maturity is also a good…" Mike noticed the trench and concrete debris. "What the hell happened here?"

"Don't worry about that. The landscapers have promised that we won't even know the trench was there. I need to talk to you about something else."

Not wanting to have Kevin overhear what she had to tell her husband, Lisa walked Mike towards the lake. They stopped under a huge pine tree that had, over the years, canted over the still water while keeping its roots firmly intrenched under the sandy topsoil.

Lisa told Mike about Kevin's seizure. His immediate reaction was one of fear and concern. Lisa managed to calm him, explaining that the paramedics were certain it wasn't a real seizure at all. Besides, other than the convulsing, he'd exhibited none of the traits of epilepsy or any other causes of a grand mal seizure.

"So, he's okay?" Mike asked, relieved.

"Seems to be. I'm going to call Doctor Kerr tomorrow morning and see what he thinks considering he only just examined him a few months ago."

"Poor kid," Mike said. "What the hell could cause something like that?"

"I have no idea. Hopefully it was a one off."

"Well, while we're talking about bad days, I think I need to fill you in on a few things that have been going on at work."

CHAPTER 18

The next day, Moses was true to his word. At seven o'clock on the dot, his crew arrived together with dump trucks filled with topsoil in one, and decorative rocks and boulders in another. Two flat beds were loaded with plants, trees, shrubs, and rolled up lengths of sod.

The crew got to work immediately. Lisa looked on as the six men began transforming the raw dirt that surrounded the house into the drawings that she and Walter had created.

Lisa had watched countless buildings go up throughout her life but had never seen a professional landscape crew in operation. It was like a ballet, but with trucks, cranes, and bulldozers. She felt like a regular snoop, peering at them through various windows, but she couldn't seem to help herself. It was fascinating to watch.

*

Mike was not having as good a day as his wife. It was Tuesday, which meant that there was a staff meeting for the People Force team. It always started at seven so that most of the crew could attend and still be ready for their work assignments throughout the bank. Mike chaired these meetings and usually enjoyed the exchange of information and the sharing of concerns and technical solutions.

This meeting was different. Despite not being invited, Kerry not only turned up, but took the seat at the head of the table.

Mike's seat.

Mike chose to ignore her intentional slight and carry on with the meeting as usual. It always started with Mike making a few announcements to the group concerning new protocols, upcoming events, or news from People Force's head office. Before Mike could get a word out, Kerry took over the meeting and began pointing out the myriad of flaws and problems that she had with the team's recent performance.

Everyone around the table was aware of each issue and knew them to have either been the result of Kerry ordering the wrong equipment for an event, or something that she herself had perceived as being wrong during her frequent swings through the control rooms and event spaces.

Her first criticism was against Patrick Paine, the lead technician. She reprimanded him in front of the others for having been watching a video in a control room instead of prepping the room for a big meeting later that day.

Mike knew all about that run-in. Patrick was indeed in the control room watching a video. What Kerry refused to accept was that he was watching a video that had been sent by the company that made the new conference microphone system, showing how to troubleshoot the software for the new DX 12 D control unit.

The unit was a demo model that Kerry had insisted the company send to the bank so that she could see if it was right for their needs. The manufacturer had at first refused to send her the unit as it was undergoing pre-release testing and still had countless bugs and interface issues.

Kerry didn't care. She wanted to be the first person to try it out. The fact that it wasn't ready and would doubtless crash during a meeting didn't faze her in the least.

Mike had already tried to explain what Patrick was doing, but as usual, she didn't want to hear his 'lame' excuses. She spent the next forty-five minutes finding fault with each member of the team. Once she'd managed to bring morale to an all-time low, she got to her feet, flipped her hair back, and before leaving the meeting room said, "Go out there and make me proud."

Once she'd gone, every pair of eyes in the room looked to Mike for some sort of answer.

He wished he had one. All he could do was let them know that he knew what a good job they were doing and to just try and stay out of her way.

It wasn't even eight o'clock and Mike felt exhausted and utterly demoralised. He dearly hoped that the day would somehow get better.

It didn't.

When Mike stepped into his office, he was surprised to see Rick Greenberg sitting in one of his guest chairs. It wasn't unheard of for the People Force president to stop by the bank. It was however the first time he'd done so without advising Mike ahead of time.

"Rick," Mike said, trying to act casual. "To what do we owe this honour?"

"Sit down, Mike," Rick said. "We need to have a talk. This feud with Kerry is putting the whole contract in jeopardy. When I hired you, I thought you were one of those people who could take a few punches and keep on fighting. From what I'm hearing, you seem to be trying to derail just about anything that Kerry is trying to accomplish."

Mike simply stared at him. He had no idea what to say.

"I decided that the best thing to do was for me to come down here this morning and meet with her myself, one on one. I'm going to suggest that I assume the role of an intermediary between People Force and her until we can find a way to make this work. You will carry out all your normal duties but won't talk directly to her. I'm going to bunk in this office with you for as long as it takes to find a way to either make this current arrangement function or look into a staffing reshuffle."

"When you say reshuffle...?" Mike asked.

"Find someone else to run this contract," Rick replied bluntly.

"Does Martin know about this?"

"Martin isn't the one who's threatening to cancel this contract. Kerry's the one we need to focus on."

Mike just nodded.

"I would also like to suggest that you take the rest of the week off while I get things put in motion around here. I presume I can rely on Wayne if I need anything?"

"You can, yes."

"It's Tuesday today," Rick continued. "Why don't you come back next Monday, and we'll see where we are."

Mike again nodded.

"Don't you have anything to say?" Rick asked.

"You know what I have to say. I've told you the problem both verbally and in emails, and despite being your general manager, you seem to doubt everything I've said."

Rick shook his head. It was clear that he was disappointed in Mike's words.

"Go home. We'll talk in a week."

CHAPTER 19

Mike's mid-morning commute home was one of the lowest points in his life. It was nice to have the metro carriage to himself, but the complete solitude only added to the feelings of anger, resentment, fear, and insecurity that were feeding on his brain.

He'd never had so much as a mediocre review at any of his jobs. Now, here he was, alone on the metro, having been sent home in disgrace while others would decide whether he should even be kept on.

For some reason, Mike had chosen not to call Lisa from the office and tell her that he was on his way home. He felt embarrassed to have to inform his wife that he'd basically been suspended from work. He wasn't even sure if that was a real thing or not. Being suspended from school was real, but from a job paying six figures, that just sounded wrong.

When the train terminated at the Vienna station, Mike, for the first time since he'd begun commuting, didn't call Lisa to tell her he was getting in the car. There had always been something fun about making that call, letting her know that she had forty-five minutes to prepare for his arrival.

He didn't feel that it was right to tell her on the phone that he was likely out of a job. Bombshells like that were better done in person.

It took Mike twice as long to get out of the parking lot as it was still crammed full of commuter vehicles, not all of which had been parked with much consideration for someone needing to exit the lot in the middle of the day.

The drive along 66 was much easier than usual. The lanes weren't crowded and those with whom he was sharing the road seemed oddly courteous. In a subconscious attempt to delay his inevitable arrival at home, Mike got off 66 and took 29 the rest of the way. It was the scenic route that ran alongside where the Battle of Bull Run had taken place. Mike felt that he needed a little peace and beauty before facing his family.

The drive was mildly cathartic and did have a slight calming effect. By the time he turned in through the Lake View Estates gate, he was feeling almost capable of telling his wife that they were potentially in deep financial doodoo.

As he rounded the last bend and saw their house, he

was stunned by the frenetic goings on around the property. He knew that the landscapers had been planning to make a start but had no idea that the Corps of Engineers had been called in to help, at least that's what it looked like. He could hardly see their home behind the wall of vehicles. He'd only left the house five hours earlier, yet they now had lawn, and a paved walkway now led from the front door to the street. Decorative shade trees were dotted around the property as well as strategically placed boulders, for no real purpose other than they looked nice.

At the back of the house, workers were skimming a new concrete slab where the used brick patio would be.

Mike parked farther down the street, not wanting to disrupt anybody by having them move their vehicle so he could get in the garage. He was halfway up the new walkway when Lisa, having spotted him from the side window, came running out of the house.

"What a great surprise," she said as she threw her arms around him. "My big-shot hubby playing hooky from school."

"Something like that," he said as she kissed his neck. She smelled of jasmine and lemon Pledge. "Let's go inside so I can tell you about my exciting morning."

Lisa seemed so happy; Mike didn't quite know what to do. He knew he had to tell her the real reason he was home so early, but at the same time, didn't want to dampen her enthusiasm for what was happening to the house.

"What do you think of what they've done already? All they have to do is build the railroad tie planters next to the exterior walls then lay the bricks on the patio. Both of those will have to wait till tomorrow."

"I always imagined that the landscaping would take weeks, not a day and a half," he commented.

"Moses, that's the owner of the company I told you about yesterday..."

"The one you're having an affair with," Mike joked.

"That's the one," she said, smiling. "He said that as most of his crew are full-time salaried employees, it's easier to tackle a small job like this with as many hands as possible."

"Well, I'm impressed. We can actually enjoy the outside for a few months before the Siberian winter shows up."

Mike felt proud that he'd managed to act as if everything was hunky dory.

As Lisa stepped into the entry hall, she called back over her shoulder, "You know I can always tell when something's bothering you, don't you?"

Mike sighed as he closed the door behind them.

"Where's Kevin?" Mike asked as soon as they were inside the house.

"He's at school, silly."

"Of course, he is," Mike said. "It's probably best if he doesn't hear what I'm about to tell you."

"Go sit in the dining room. I'll get you a beer."

"Anything stronger?" he asked.

"Not until I've heard what you've got to say."

Mike did as instructed and sat in the dining room.

"Here you go," Lisa said as she reappeared with a tall glass of lager.

She sat next to him and took his hand (the one that wasn't reaching for the beer) and looked him in the eyes.

"You have the floor," she said gently.

Lisa already knew all about Kerry being difficult. The news that she had been undermining everything Mike had been doing at the bank, then had even had the nerve to usurp the Tuesday morning meeting, while not a complete shock, still managed to infuriate her. She was about to comment when he asked her to hold her thought as he hadn't told her the good part yet.

When Mike finished describing the impromptu meeting with Rick Greenberg, including his having been sent home like a naughty child, the colour drained from her face. It took a few minutes before she could speak.

"You know what?" she stated. "This is a good thing. I've known you were miserable for weeks. Now, after what happened today, you should send them an email telling them to go fuck themselves."

"You know I can't do that," Mike replied.

"Why? Any feelings of loyalty to People Force or the bank just went out the window. You no longer owe them a thing. Not anymore. What I can't believe is that Rick has treated you this way. I thought that he and Cathy had become our friends?"

"So did I, but I guess when it comes to business, the mighty dollar trumps friendship every time."

"But he flat out doesn't believe what you've been telling him. I'd understand it if you had turned out to suck at your job, but you were being lauded by the bank and People Force only a few months ago. I remember Rick saying, right there in our DC apartment, that you were one of the best general managers he'd ever seen in the AV circles."

"Apparently none of that counts when someone like Kerry..."

"You mean someone that's a conniving bitch," Lisa interrupted.

"Actually, I think you're understating her charms," he replied. "But yeah... all it takes is one voice, even if that voice is unhinged and vindictive."

"So quit," Lisa insisted. "Right now. Write the email and it's done. The stress will be gone, and you will never have to think about the bank or DC ever again. We'll sell the house, probably at a profit, then go back to LA. As they say in the UK – easy peasy lemon squeezy."

"They don't really say that do they?" Mike said, smiling.

"Absolutely," she advised. "I'll go get your iPad and you can write the email before lunch."

"I can't," he said with a sigh.

"If it's the money, don't worry about it. I can easily cover all our costs until the house sells. At that point we'll be rolling in it."

Mike squeezed her hand.

"Babe... this is your dream house."

"None of that mat..." Lisa began.

"It completely matters. This is what you've been dreaming of all your life, and now we have it. It's ours, and I'm not going to give it up just because of one insane woman where I work."

"That's very noble of you, but your peace of mind is worth way more to me than a stupid house. We can always get another one someday. Your sanity on the other hand..." Lisa did a seesaw motion with her hand. "Not sure that we can get that replaced if you go completely loopy."

"I have no intention of going loopy. I do however intend to stick it out and see where it takes me. I know this is going to sound a little naïve, but I still believe that right eventually wins out. I can't see the bank putting up with her bullshit indefinitely. She's only getting away with it now because she was, and quite possible still is, sleeping with the director of the department. Not even he will protect her if her behaviour starts jeopardising the bank and his job."

"That could take years," Lisa said. "From what you told me about your conversation with Rick, you don't have years. You might not even get to go back at all."

"If that's how it plays out, then fine. I just refuse to walk away from this fight when I know that I've done nothing wrong."

Lisa smiled as she sat silently, staring at him.

"What?" Mike said, a little unnerved by her gaze.

"You just reminded me why I fell in love with you," she replied.

"I thought it was because of my film-star good looks."

"Oh, honey. You really do live in a dream world, don't you," she said, grinning.

"How was Kevin when you dropped him at school?" Mike asked. "Any sign of whatever ailed him yesterday?"

"Not a trace. I was going to take him to see Doctor Kerr after school, but when I called his office this morning, he said that unless Kevin had relapsed or seemed off in any way, he didn't feel that a trip to the doctor was warranted."

"If he thinks that's best. Did the doctor comment on how Keven could show no signs of having had whatever he had?"

"Nope. He just said that as long as he doesn't have another one, there's nothing to worry about."

"Is Kevin worried about what happened?" Mike asked.

"That's the weirdest thing," Lisa said. "He has no memory of it happening at all."

"That is a little strange, isn't it?" Mike asked.

"Yeah," Lisa replied, her voice strained. "Very strange."

CHAPTER 20

Mike was dreaming that he was back in school, only it wasn't his school. It was very modern and stark. All the other children in his class were immaculately turned out except him. He had mud on his shoes, a rip in his trousers, and a ketchup stain on his white shirt.

It was history class and each time the teacher asked if anyone knew the answer, he would squirm in his seat and raise his hand. In each case, the teacher asked Mike for the answer and though he knew he'd got it correct, she shook her head and told him that he really needed to study harder.

One question had been, 'Who was the first President of the United States?' Mike had answered George Washington and was reprimanded. When the class was asked how many states there were in the United States, Mike almost fell out of his chair, trying to get noticed.

"Very well, Mike," the teacher said. "This will be

your last chance. If you get this one wrong, we will have to decide exactly what to do with you."

"It's fifty, Miss Courtney," Mike exclaimed proudly. "There are fifty states."

"Oh, Mike," she said as she shook her head. "You've been given every chance."

"But I'm right. I know I am."

"Class," Miss Courtney said. "Please tell Mike how many states are in the United States."

Every child in the classroom turned to face him. Not one of them had any eyes. What they did have were oversized mouths that all opened at the same time.

"There are fifty-one states," they shouted. "Fifty-one... fifty-one... fifty-one..."

Each time they spoke the number, their mouths opened just a bit wider. Mike could see that they all had black, reptilian tongues that forked at the end.

Mike woke up with such a start that he managed to bash his elbow on the bedside table.

"Shit!" he shouted just as Lisa walked in with a mug of coffee in one hand and the *Washington Post* in the other.

"Charming," Lisa said, shaking her head.

"Sorry. I just had the worst nightmare."

"Not particularly surprising, considering," she said as she placed the mug on the table and a kiss on his forehead.

Mike was about to tell her the gist of the dream when the house shook.

"What the hell?" he started to get out of bed.

"Boy, you have been asleep," Lisa said. "That's the landscapers unloading the railroad ties for the planters. They've been at it for an hour."

Mike relaxed and swung his feet back onto the bed and took a sip of the coffee.

"Yum. Cinnamon. I should stay off work more often."

"I gave you that option last night," she replied.

"So, what are we going to do today?" Mike asked, ignoring her comment.

"I don't know about you, but I was planning to do some editing on the new Gleinman book."

Mike shuddered. "I don't know how you can read his stuff. It's too creepy."

"It's not the same when you are evaluating every word and every bit of punctuation," she replied. "The big question today is what the hell are you going to do so that you are out of my hair?"

"I was planning on taking you for a romantic lunch in Culpeper, followed by a hot air balloon ride, then I thought…"

"Slow down there, stud. This isn't a holiday. I have to work, and must I remind you, we might as well start counting our pennies now. We can have romantic balloon rides and hot air lunches some other time."

"That's not what I said."

"I know that." Lisa shook her head. "I was just making sure that you were listening."

"I was," he answered.

"I know. I'm very impressed. Why don't you really dazzle me and take a shower, then I'll fix you some breakfast before I start work."

"Sounds like a plan," he agreed.

Once he'd emptied his bladder, Mike turned on the hot water in their marble-lined, multi-jet shower. As he looked at the sparkling new cubicle, he felt like he was in a five-star hotel.

When he was satisfied that the water had reached his preferred temperature, Mike slid off his pyjama bottoms (he'd given up wearing the tops twenty years earlier) and stepped into the shower.

After soaping the lower half of his body first, he rinsed and pumped a palm-full of shampoo from a built-in dispenser. He lathered up then, with his eyes clenched shut, stepped under the rain-effect showerhead.

Something was wrong. The water was still hot, but it felt almost gritty. A trickle managed to find its way into his mouth, and Mike almost gagged. The water tasted like burned wood. He tried to spit it out, but because he was still standing under the showerhead, more water found its way into his mouth. He tried to lean away from the spray, but the custom showerhead was designed to give the effect of a warm spring rain, covering every inch of the cubicle.

Mike started to panic. He couldn't seem to remember how to shut off the water. The four chrome knobs had to be turned off in a particular order. He opened his eyes to see what he was doing but immediately felt particles of grit find their way under his lids. Hyperventilating, he stumbled out of the shower and felt his way to one of the two sinks cut into a granite slab. He turned the water on full and tried to throw handfuls of water into his eyes.

That only made it feel worse. Finally, he grabbed one of Lisa's new and very expensive white towels and rubbed his eyes until he felt he'd cleared whatever it was off his face.

He carefully opened them.

Then he screamed.

Moments later Lisa came barging into the bathroom and joined him in the scream fest. Because Mike was only able to see a few inches in front of his face, he was missing the true horror of the spectacle.

Black water was pouring out of the shower head, covering the marble and etched glass door with dark muck. The tap Mike had turned on to flush his eyes was also spewing the same viscous liquid. The worst thing, if it was possible to rate any one part of the disaster, was that black water was also overflowing the toilet, bringing with it what appeared to be slivers and chunks of charred wood.

Standing amid the melee was Mike, naked, and covered from head to foot in the stuff. He was still trying to wipe his face with the towel, which by that point looked like an oily mechanic's rag.

Lisa, despite feeling that her sanity was on the very edge of collapse, told Mike to stay still while she dealt with the situation. She first shut off the sink tap, then reached into the shower and turned the four valves off as well. In a truly inspired move, she also shut off the water supply to the toilet then flushed it.

The black water ceased its assault on their bathroom. What was left looked like a black and white remake of Stephen King's *Carrie* (with Mike in the lead role). Their beautiful, brand-new bathroom was covered in black gunk. It was everywhere. Through Mike's attempts at flushing out his eyes by tossing handfuls of what he thought was clear water onto his face, even the ceiling hadn't been spared and was dripping with black mud.

Lisa managed to get Mike into his robe and carefully guided him into the spare bathroom. She helped him into the bath and was about to turn on the shower fixture when she had a thought. She stepped over to the sink and tuned on one of the taps. For a brief instant, she was relieved to see clear water flowing out of the polished chrome fitting. Then, it too began to sputter then turn grey. Moments later, the same black filth began to spew out of the faucet.

"Hurry up," Mike shouted. "The crap is in my eyes."

"We need to go to plan B," she said as she grabbed his arm, helped him out of the bath, then led him downstairs. She walked him to the nearest door leading outside then gently guided him down their new sloping lawn.

The team of landscapers openly stared at the bizarre image of Lisa leading her husband, who looked to have had an accident with a can of black paint, across their lawn to the lake.

"Where are you taking me?" Mike finally asked as he gagged on more of the black liquid that had found a way into his mouth.

"All the water in the house is contaminated. You're about to have a swim in the lake."

"Good idea," he replied, relieved.

Lisa helped him get to the edge of the water, then removed the robe. Mike stepped cautiously into the water, then once he had solid footing, walked to where it was deep enough for him to submerge himself. It took a few dunks, but the black liquid seemed to wash completely away.

"Keep flushing your eyes out until you can't feel anything but water," Lisa commanded.

Daryl, the landscaping foreman, approached her.

"Can we do anything to help?" he asked.

"Did you tap into our plumbing system?" Lisa asked.

"Normally we would have, so we could install the sprinkler system, but we were told that you didn't want one."

"Is there any way that during the digging or excavating the flower beds you could have hit a water line?"

"Not a chance. We checked the plans and made sure to keep away from the main water and utility lines. We also planned everything around not having to break through any more of the concrete slab."

"I thought that the only bit of concrete was next to the house where the fibre needed to go?"

"There's a hell of a lot more of it than just that part. We used ground penetration radar to make sure we didn't dig into anything we shouldn't and found that the slab is roughly a hundred and twenty feet square. Something pretty big must have stood on it at some point."

"So how could all the utilities have been connected to the house?" Lisa asked.

"Someone must have trenched through the concrete and laid in all the necessary whatnots for the utilities and waste disposal. It must have been quite a job."

Lisa felt anger blooming within her.

"I'll tell you what you could do that would be a lifesaver," Lisa said, trying to stay calm. "Could one of your crew nip over to the sales office and get the manager – his name's Walter – to come over here immediately?"

"No problem," Daryl replied. "If he asks why, should I mention that it has something to do with your husband skinny dipping in the lake?"

Lisa glanced over at Mike and saw that he was standing in only thigh-high water, revealing to the world more of him than anyone needed to see.

"For god's sake, Mike, a little modesty would be appreciated," she yelled.

Mike, still dazed by the bathroom trauma, hadn't realised quite how much of himself he was putting on display.

"Sorry," he called back as he lowered the important parts back below the surface of the water.

CHAPTER 21

"Well?" Lisa said with no attempt at keeping the anger from her voice.

Walter looked at the carnage within the bathroom and wanted to make some joke about it looking like a Jackson Pollack painting, but chose to keep that thought to himself.

"I don't know what to say," he said. "I've never seen anything like this. I don't even know how something like this can happen."

"And?" Lisa asked.

"I will see to it that this gets resolved immediately. We will fix whatever is wrong with the plumbing and will have a top-notch cleaning crew in here within a few hours."

"Good. You will also need to get a carpet cleaner for where Mike left a trail."

"No problem," Walter agreed.

"You will also be getting a bill for a new bath robe

for Mike and a new set of towels for me."

"Again, no problem. Is there anything else?" Walter did his damnedest to keep his tone upbeat and humble, even though he was feeling a little peeved about her adding the robe and towels. A couple of times through the Maytag and he was pretty sure they would have been as good as new.

"Yes," Lisa replied. "There is something else. You lied to me again."

Walter blinked rapidly. "I have never lied to you, Mrs Ellis," he proclaimed.

"What about the dead builder?" Lisa shot back.

"That was an error of omission, not a lie."

Lisa gave him her glare of death. It had the desired effect. Walter began to blink even more rapidly, and pink rosacea-like blooms began to form on his face and neck.

"Go on," he said with a sigh.

"When the installers were here from Horizon Cable and their backhoe came up against the concrete, you were asked if you knew anything about it. You claimed that you had no knowledge about there being anything except dirt on this site before you started construction."

"And that's the truth," Walter insisted.

"That's funny, because I just learned that the concrete slab is twice the size of the house and that utility trenches had to have been cut through to get from the street to the house. Was that another error of omission?"

"Actually, it was not," he replied. "Darcey Development did not create this subdivision. The original developer went bankrupt early on during the lockdown. They had already put in the streets, levelled the lots, laid a number of foundations, and installed all the utilities, as well as waste and water drainage."

"That's fascinating, Walter, but what does it have to do with you not knowing that this house was built on a vintage slab of concrete?"

"Yours was one of the lots where they had already laid the slab and done the utility trenching."

"Wouldn't they have left you documents showing everything they'd so far completed?" Lisa asked. "Wouldn't they have shown that there was an original foundation under the slab that they put down?"

"In a perfect world, yes. The problem was, and is, that Motwask Construction did not exactly leave the development graciously. They shredded every document they could find, presumably so that whoever benefitted by their misery, would have no help from them. I'm afraid that all we could confirm was that your house was plumbed and piped into the city utilities. How it got that way was always a little grey."

"Well," Lisa began. "Now it's a little black. It looks to

me as if they did a piss poor job of doing the install and we are the ones who are left to suffer."

"That's not actually the case. Because of the lack of documentation, Darcey brought in a survey crew to inspect all the infrastructure work that Motwask had carried out. Fibreoptic cameras went through every pipe and piece of conduit. Say what you will about them; they may have left themselves a bit thin financially, but they did a first-rate job on any of the work they carried out."

"Then what caused this mess?" Lisa asked, gesturing into the bathroom.

"I don't know. May I…? he asked, pointing to the nearest sink.

"Be my guest, but watch where you step," Lisa suggested.

Walter leaned into the room and managed to turn on the cold tap. A trickle of clean water came out of the faucet. He turned it the rest of the way. There was good water pressure and it looked exactly the way water should.

"How odd," he said as he put his hand under the stream. He smelled the liquid, then much to Lisa's disgust, tasted it.

"Perfect," Walter said as he offered his hand for her to sniff.

"Really?" she said, shaking her head.

"What's going on?" Mike said as he walked into the bedroom.

"The water looks fine now," Lisa announced.

"It tastes good as well," Walter added, causing Mike to flinch.

"I'd best get back to the office so I can get a cleaning crew out here. Is there any time when you won't be home?" he asked.

"One of us will be here all day," Lisa advised. "If at all possible, could this be cleaned up before Kevin gets home from school? He might find all this upsetting."

"I can vouch for that," Mike said, smiling.

*

The rest of the day was organised chaos. Walter had found that another Darcy development only a few miles away had a cleaning crew onsite for a week to give their four model homes a full deep clean. He was able to get them to spare a few hours. By the time Mike had finished breakfast and was starting to feel vaguely normal again, they were at the front door. The crew consisted of three East Asian women who seemed way too happy, considering they were having to clean other people's toilets.

When Lisa walked them upstairs, she had expected some degree of shock from the women. After all, it wasn't every day that a bathroom ended up in that condition; at least she hoped that was the case.

The cleaners weren't remotely fazed. In fact, once they'd examined the room, Lieha, the older sister, looked to Lisa with a cheerful smile.

"Mr Hill said this was going to be very difficult," she said. "This is not difficult at all. We see much worse every day."

Lisa tried not to imagine what 'much worse' could look like. She was about to let them get to it when Lieha asked, "You want us to clean the dirt off the carpet as well? We have a steam cleaner in the van."

"Yes, please, if you think you can."

"This is easy," Lieha said after quickly conferring with her sisters.

Ninety minutes later, the three trouped downstairs, lugging all the tools of their trade. Lieha found Mike and Lisa camped out in the dining room, trying not to get in their way.

"Are you finished?" Lisa asked, surprised.

"Go up and have a look," Lieha suggested. "We'll wait down here."

Lisa and Mike shot each other a doubting glance, then headed up to see what the women had achieved. Lisa had fully expected to be disappointed. Even if they could get the muck off the marble and glass, she couldn't see how they would be able to clean the grout between the floor tiles, or the paint on the ceiling.

The first clue that the sisters were miracle workers was when they reached the stairs and couldn't find a trace of the black ooze that Mike had trailed through the house. The carpet on the landing, which had seen some of the worst of it, looked pristine.

"I thought Walter was going to have to replace the carpet," Lisa said as she tried to find any sign of the soiling.

When the two reached the bathroom door, they stared into it with complete shock. It was cleaner than when they'd been given the keys a few weeks earlier. Not only was the grout clean, but it was a shade lighter and brought out the colours of the tiles.

The real mystery was the ceiling. They stared upwards and did their darnedest to find even a single speck of the black gunk.

They found none.

When they returned downstairs, they saw that the women had cleaned the last remnants off the hardwood floors – something that Lisa had planned to do herself.

"We can't thank you enough," Lisa gushed.

"Really, thank you," Mike added. "You're amazing."

"If you really want to thank us..." Lieha began.

Both Lisa and Mike thought they were about to get pressured into giving a big tip.

"Please take our card and tell your friends." Lieha placed a couple of business cards on the hall table, then left.

"I can see why they're raking it in. What a unique business model," Mike said. "Work hard, be the best at what you do, and be courteous to your customers. I doubt that'll catch on."

"Don't be such a cynic."

*

Moses appeared just before midday as his landscapers were finishing. He walked Mike and Lisa around their property, pointing out what they had done and what the couple needed to do to keep everything looking its best.

"I hear you had an exciting morning," Moses said as he raised his eyebrows at Mike.

"Please apologise to your crew. I don't usually put on quite such a performance."

"None of them were offended in the least."

"That's a whole other concern," Lisa quipped.

"I spoke to a friend of mine who's lived in the area for over seventy years. He used to play on the other side of the lake long before there were any developments here. I asked him about your piece of land and whether there used to be a building where your house now stands."

"And?" Mike said a little too quickly.

"He said he couldn't be sure, but that he seemed to remember there was a shell of a big hotel or something located around this part of the lake."

"What did he mean by a shell?" Lisa asked.

"He's in his nineties now and has a lot of trouble remembering things. All he could say was that he was pretty sure that there was a big place, right on the lake, and that from what he could recall, it looked to be little more than a burned-out ruin."

"Did he ever come over to this side to check it out? I know I would've."

"With all due respect, Mr Ellis, I think that if you'd been a young black boy living in Northern Virginia back then, you'd have been pretty unlikely to go wandering too far from your own property."

CHAPTER 22

For lunch, Lisa whipped up her version of a salad niçoise (no anchovy or raw onion). They were about to tuck into their meal when the doorbell rang.

It was a utilities surveyor who Walter had booked to inspect all the water and waste lines going in and out of the house. The man looked to be around the same age as Mike, but with a full head of bushy hair that was so black it almost looked fake. He was also thin. Really thin. For a brief second, Mike wondered if that was a prerequisite because of the need to crawl into narrow piping.

"Mr and Mrs Ellis?" the man said, his voice a full octave lower that either of them expected. "My name's Hunter Chase. I'm from Marlin Surveyors. I'm supposed to check on your water and waste systems."

"We were about to eat lunch. Do you need us to do anything?" Mike asked.

"I'll start in the front of the house. That will probably

take around forty-five minutes to an hour. I may need you to flush a toilet and run some water in the shower, but that's about it. After that, if I don't find the issue, I will want to check the upstairs bathroom where the blockage was first noticed, but that can be last on the list."

With that, he walked back to his truck, which had the Marlin Surveyor logo emblazoned on the door panel. It showed a smiling caricature of a marlin in mid-leap from a bathtub to a toilet bowl. Lisa could almost see the humour of the promotional image, but there was something about a thousand-pound fish heading for your toilet that didn't seem quite right.

"I love their logo," Mike said as he headed back to the dining room.

Fifty minutes later, Hunter was back at the door.

"That was quick," Lisa said. "Did you solve the problem?"

"No. I ran a camera through every intake and outtake, and they look as they should; brand spanking new. I can show you the video on my iPad if you like?"

"No, thanks," Mike shot back. "We're good."

"If you don't mind," Hunter asked. "I'd like to check out the bathrooms upstairs?"

"I'll show you," Lisa said.

As she led him upstairs, Mike heard her say, "I wouldn't mind having a look at the video."

Lisa came back downstairs with an iPad mini in her hand.

"You're going to watch this with me," she announced as she took Mike's hand and led him to the den.

She entered their wi-fi password, then after turning on their 60-inch Samsung, she activated the AirPlay option. She patted the sofa next to her and Mike reluctantly sat down. She gave his knee a brief squeeze then pressed play.

The image of the inside of a three-inch PVC pipe filled the screen. It looked new, just as Hunter had said. The camera was moving slowly, getting deeper and deeper into the tubular cavern. The only light was from the fibreoptic camera, which managed to illuminate a few inches ahead. The pipe was clean except for a thin trail of clear water running along the very bottom of the curve.

It took about two minutes before the camera ran up against the join to the house system, then the picture went black.

Moments later a new image appeared. It looked almost exactly like the other one except the water run off was slightly discoloured.

"Yuck," Mike said.

"This must be the sewage pipe," Lisa offered.

"Why am I watching this?" Mike asked.

"Because it's our house and we should know every inch of it."

Mike gave her a sarcastic smirk. Lisa suddenly got up and headed for the kitchen.

"Where are you going? You can't leave me watching this crap... literally!"

"I'm just getting some water," she called back.

Mike cringed as the camera moved slowly along the interior of the pipe. The dim light gave the whole shot an eerie feel. Even though everything was brand new, the claustrophobic image was starting to get to him.

Suddenly, the camera shuddered. Ahead in the darkness, Mike thought that he could see something beyond the illumination range of the light. He knew that it was impossible, but he was certain that he could just make out the outline of something that was blacker than the already black interior of the pipe.

Mike leaned forward to get a better view of whatever was in the darkness and saw that it was definitely getting closer. Whether that was because the thing itself was moving or the motion of the camera, he couldn't tell.

Suddenly, the light shone on what appeared to be a piece of lace-like cloth. It seemed to be partially covering an obstacle that filled the pipe.

"Lisa," Mike shouted. "You'd better get in here."

"Just a second," she shouted back.

As the camera reached the object, it brushed against the material, causing it to fall to the side.

A partially decomposed face was only inches from the camera lens. It filled the pipe on all sides. The flesh was lacerated and blackened. Strips of rotted flesh were still attached to the facial bones; the other ends seemed to be moving on some unseen current, as if they were trying to free themselves from the carnage.

Grey-coloured teeth were clenched in some sort of death rigor as the remains of what had once been lips were now only thin strands of leathery fibre.

Mike could clearly see burned bone under the remains of the muscle tissue. The only part of the face that was remotely intact was the area around the eyes. Though charred, he could make out the eyelids that somehow had so far survived the putrefaction. Something made him move still closer. There was something about the eyelids. He wasn't sure why, but he felt that they belonged to a woman.

Then they opened.

Mike screamed for the second time that day. He crawled over the back of the couch and was about to run out of the room when Lisa appeared with two glasses of water.

"What's wrong?" she asked.

Mike pointed back towards the TV screen.

"Look at it," he managed in a croaky voice.

"I am. It's still just the inside of a pipe," Lisa replied.

Reluctantly, Mike turned around. The screen was filled with the shot of the empty PVC pipe.

"I'll show you," Mike stuttered as he got back to the couch and, trembling, picked up the iPad. He wiped the video back, waiting for the face to appear. It never did.

"What did you think you saw?" she asked with feigned calm.

"I thought I saw a…" Mike stopped. He knew that what he had been about to say would sound insane, probably because it was.

"It sounds to me as if you're having another mental blip like when you saw that ash in the basement. I think it's time we make an appointment for you to see Dr Manette in DC. Between the job stress and the exploding bathroom, anyone would start to go a little loopy. Here, hold this." She handed him one of the glasses. "I'm going to get you one of my panic pills."

"I don't like taking those things."

"And I don't like to see my husband cracking up. I'm just going to give you half of one. It'll calm you down."

Mike let out a long sigh and nodded his head, already starting to doubt what he thought he'd seen.

Just then, Hunter came trotting down the stairs.

"Was that the plumbing or did I hear someone scream?"

CHAPTER 23

Mike had Hunter airdrop the recording to his iPhone, then once he had left, he AirPlayed the video to the TV and re-watched the entire seven minutes of footage, showing the innards of every pipe that fed the house, eight times in a row.

There were no heads stuck in a PVC pipe.

He was about to watch it again when Lisa called out, "Alexa, TV off."

The screen went dark.

"Just one more time," Mike insisted.

"You've always had a few OCD tendencies," Lisa said. "But this has all the making of a full-on problem."

She sat next to him on the sofa and took his hand.

"Have you made the appointment with Dr Manette? That'd be something that might actually help."

"I'll call him tomorrow," Mike said. I'll get an appointment for next week. I don't want to go all the way to DC while I'm on vacation."

"You're not exactly on vacation," she reminded him.

"I'm off work and still being paid. What would you call it?"

"I can think of a dozen terms for what they have you doing, and none of them contain the word vacation. I'll make you a deal: call the doctor's office and have a phone consultation with Dr Manette, then have a follow-up in-person appointment next week."

Mike let out a frustrated sigh.

"If you don't call him, I will," she said. "You've had two hallucinations in the last few weeks. That's not normal. Face it, you are under incredible stress at the moment."

"I've been under stress before," Mike volleyed back.

"Babe... think about it. You had to go through the whole interview process. We then had to pack everything and move twenty-five hundred miles to DC. You started what is doubtless the most demanding job you've ever had. Then, we bought a house, did another full move from DC to here, and you are now living under the threat of being fired because of an insane woman who doesn't know what the hell she is doing. Add that to your little adventure in the shower this morning and well... that my love is enough to send anyone over the edge."

Mike studied her face for a moment.

"I'll call Manette right now," he conceded, realising

that she had a point.

Lisa handed him his phone.

"I'll be in the kitchen," she advised. "Tell him everything. He's not going to judge you, so don't hold anything back."

Mike made the call and spoke to the doctor's assistant. She put him on hold, then after a few minutes asked if the doctor could call back at six.

Once he'd made the call, Mike felt a sense of relief. Lisa was right. He was stressed. When the simple act of walking through the security entrance of the bank caused a sense of dread to descend out of nowhere, there was something wrong. After the first instance in the basement, he should have talked to somebody, especially when he knew what he'd seen hadn't been real. It wasn't until Nigel pronounced the house clear of ghosts and ghoulies that Mike fully accepted the fact that what he'd imagined was stress induced and was only in his mind.

By the time Lisa went to collect Kevin from school, she was confident that all traces of the bathroom disaster were gone. The water and sewer system had been pronounced fully functional, and as a surprise bonus, an Amazon delivery arrived from Darcy Development. In it was a full set of white Egyptian cotton towels and a bathmat, as well as a man's bathrobe.

Lisa felt guilty as she and Mike unpacked the box. All the soiled items had gone through an extra hot wash with a generous slurp of bleach and had emerged sparkling white.

"Should we give these back to Walter?" she asked.

"No way! They owe us at least this much just for the inconvenience."

Once Kevin was home and had eaten a snack, he asked if he could go outside to play. As the fencing wasn't due for installation until the following week, Mike and Lisa decided to try out their new faux ratan backyard furniture set so they could keep an eye on him.

It was hot for early fall and at that time of the day, their patio got the full wallop of the sun. Mike offered to move everything onto the lawn, but the day had left him feeling wrung out and just plain lazy. Lisa said to leave them where they were. All she wanted to do was to sit still for a while and hopefully not have to deal with any more calamities or meltdowns.

Mike made a jug of Minute Maid frozen lemonade then set up the portable tetherball set he'd bought for Kevin. It was designed for five to ten-year-olds and was half the height of an adult version. Kevin loved it. Mike tried to play with him but exhaustion took over within a few minutes. Mike wondered what was sapping his strength then remembered that he'd taken one of

Lisa's happy pills earlier in the day.

Leaving his son happily batting the tethered foam ball by himself, Mike joined Lisa on their bricked patio.

"Jesus," he commented. "How come it's so cold here? We're still getting direct sun, but it's got to be twenty degrees colder than on the grass."

"Must be something to do with the bricks," Lisa suggested.

Mike downed two thirds of his glass of lemonade in one gulp as he watched Kevin, hard at play.

"It's beautiful here, isn't it," he said, sounding relaxed.

"It is."

The two watched their son as he swatted the ball time and time again. Despite the repetitious nature of the toy, he seemed content to keep whacking it for hours on end. Beyond Kevin, the gentle waves on the lake were reflecting the sun's light as it traversed further into the western sky. For whatever reason, all avian air traffic appeared grounded, and the waterfowl seemed content to simply float around. The image of the child at play with a backdrop of natural beauty was calmingly serene.

"Shit!" Lisa screamed. "Mike, wake up."

Mike hadn't even realised that he'd dozed off.

"Kevin?" Lisa shouted as she ran to the water's edge. "Kevin, where are you?"

As Mike scrambled to his feet, he noticed that the sun was much lower than it had been last time he'd looked. He joined Lisa at the shoreline. The two of them kept shouting as they studied the surface of the lake, dreading what they might see. It was hard to focus on water because the sun's lower angle seemed to make the surface dance and shimmer with refracted light.

Suddenly, Mike spotted something on the surface. It appeared to be a piece of white material. Before he could say anything, Lisa cried out.

"Kev was wearing a white t-shirt."

Without any forethought, Mike dove into the lake. Despite the hot day, the water was so cold it felt like a million needles stabbing at his skin. The object was about a hundred yards offshore and seemed to be drifting away from their side of the lake.

"Hurry, Mike," Lisa screamed as tears flowed down her face. "Oh god, oh god."

She began rocking backwards and forwards, clutching herself.

Mike hadn't been swimming in a few years and was finding the going much harder than he would have expected. It didn't help that the white object seemed to be drifting away almost as fast as he was swimming.

Finally, exhausted, he lunged forward in the water and grabbed the material. He tried to see what it was, but between him having trouble staying afloat and the glare from the dropping sun, he couldn't be certain what he was holding. It took every iota of his fading strength just to get back to their strip of shoreline.

Lisa helped him crawl out of the water as his legs were trembling too hard for him to stand. She grabbed the material and looked down at it with complete confusion.

"Is it his?" Mike managed to ask between gasping for breath.

"What're you guys doing?" Kevin asked from the open patio door.

Lisa burst into tears of relief at seeing him. Mike managed to get to his feet and together with Lisa, rushed over to hug him, making sure that he was real.

Kevin explained that he got bored with tetherball, and as both Mommy and Daddy were asleep, he went inside to watch TV.

As Lisa continued hugging him and brushing his hair aside with her shaking fingers, Mike walked back to the shore. He picked up the white material to work out what he'd retrieved from the water.

He felt the blood rush from his head as his stomach turned to ice.

In his hands was a white veil made from what looked to be very old, handmade lace. It appeared to be almost new and in good condition except for one end, which looked as if it had been charred in a fire. Michael raised it to his nose.

Even wet, it smelled of burned cloth. It suddenly brought back the memory of his dad, who, while showing off how he could light the barbeque with gasoline, managed to set fire to the sleeve of his shirt. His mother had ripped it right off his chest and doused it with hose water. The smell of the burning shirt obviously still took up space somewhere in his memory bank.

CHAPTER 24

The sound of Mike's ringtone, a snippet of *Spirit of the Radio* by Rush, filtered out of the house. Mike made for the patio door.

"It's Dr Manette," Lisa said as she stepped out of the house. "I'll leave the phone out here so you can have some privacy."

She placed his phone on one of the faux cane chairs, then stepped inside and closed the patio door.

"Dr Manette," Mike said as he tried to focus his thoughts away from the piece of lace. A piece that looked too much like what he'd seen wrapped around the face that had somehow been compressed into the narrow sewer line. "Thank you for calling back."

They spoke for almost fifteen minutes. Once the doctor heard what Mike had to say, he began asking him a series of very direct and very pointed questions, intending to build some sort of prognosis as to what Mike could be suffering from.

"What I'm going to say is very likely the accurate prognosis, but until I can give you an in-person check-up and have run some tests for any underlying physical issues, I could be wrong."

"I understand," Mike replied.

"It seems to me that you have been through a number of emotional upheavals over the course of the last six to eight months. Your mind has found a way to cope with each one of those, but as they began to add up, especially the ones involving your work situation, it didn't have enough ram to store away all the stress, the fear, the anger and I would also assume, sadness."

The doctor's last words acted on Mike as if someone had thrown a switch. He felt his eyes well up. He wanted to say something to Dr Manette but couldn't get the words out.

"From your reaction, I'd have to say that my phone diagnosis appears to have been accurate," he said in a gentle and calming voice. "Mike, you are having a mental breakdown. I don't believe that it's at the point where I need to suggest in-patient care, but you are going to need medication and treatment. I'm going to send a prescription for Effexor to your Gainesville pharmacy. There will be two packs. The first one is a start-up pack that, over the course of the next three weeks, will increase the dosage from 37.5 milligrams to 150 milligrams. It takes between four and six weeks to take full effect so don't expect any instant miracles. I am also prescribing a low dose of clonazepam. I want you take one, twice a day for the next two weeks. There are mixed opinions about prescribing benzodiazepines, but I believe that a low dose at the onset of symptoms can do far more good than harm. I don't believe you to have an addictive personality, so please don't prove me wrong. In addition, I'm going to email you a list of three psychiatrists here in DC. I know all three of them and feel that any one of them will be able to offer you some help getting through this period. In addition, and I know that you are not going to want to hear this, but I suggest you stay away from work for at least the next two weeks. I will send you a note that you can forward to your HR department."

"As I mentioned before," Mike said. "That might be a moot point."

"I understand. But I still want to see you next week on Tuesday at eleven. Try to take care of yourself and keep your mind off the problems. Find something else to occupy your mind."

"I have been wanting to do some work on the basement," Mike said.

"That sounds perfect," the doctor agreed. "If things get any worse, call me. If it's after hours or over the weekend, leave a message with my service. I will get back to you."

"Thank you, doctor."

Mike disconnected the call and turned back to the house. Lisa was standing on the other side of the glass door. Concern was written all over her face.

Mike suddenly jumped as something tried to wrap itself around his calf. He looked down and saw Samantha, their indoor cat, rubbing against him as she coiled her tail around his leg. He picked her up and looked over at Lisa. She seemed as perplexed as he was. Samantha was a rescue cat and therefore came with all the emotional baggage that her earlier life had packed for her.

She was never supposed to go outside. That had been the specific instruction from the animal rescue group that had arranged the adoption. As far as Mike and Lisa knew, she'd never shown any interest whatsoever in stepping into the outside world. Yet here she was, acting like it was no big deal.

Mike carried her into the house and placed her on her favourite spot on the sofa.

"How the hell did she get out?" Mike asked.

"I have no idea; however, we have had a lot of people roaming in and out of the house all day," Lisa replied.

"The surveyor must have accidently let her out," Mike suggested.

"That makes sense," Lisa replied. "God, look at the

time. It's almost seven. It'll be a late dinner tonight, folks."

"What about calling for a pizza?" Mike suggested. "Be easier on everyone."

Lisa rolled her eyes at his feeble attempt at justifying a reason for getting a pizza.

"Pizza!" Kevin shouted from the other room. "We're getting pizza. Pizza pie, pizza pie, it tastes so good, it makes you cry," he recited, running into the room. "I want the one with pineapple on it."

*

After devouring an extra-large, thin crust Hawaiian while watching yet another animated movie involving some kid training a dragon, they put Kevin to bed. Without any preamble of wanting to be read to or have the room inspected for things that go bump in the night, he fell asleep. Mike was envious of his child's ability to just close his eyes and drift off. The only way he was able to do that recently was either by drinking too much or taking one of Lisa's emergency calming pills.

After a brief debate concerning what to watch, Lisa won with The Handmaid's Tale. They watched two episodes before Lisa called for Alexa to turn off the lights and the television. After sluggishly climbing the stairs, they were both fast asleep within seconds of their heads hitting their pillows.

*

The shaking began just after two a.m. It lasted for less than twenty seconds but was violent enough to send both of them charging out of bed and into Kevin's room to make sure that he was okay. Not only was he unscathed, but he was still sound asleep. Samantha, however, who always spent the night at the end of his bed, was wide awake and was staring at the ceiling. The hair on her back was raised and her tail was three times its normal size.

Being from California, they'd both experienced earthquakes. Lisa's memory of 'the big one' in 1994 gave her a different and much darker perspective than Mike, but he was still able to discern a bad one from one of the more common tremblers.

They returned to the bedroom and crawled back under the covers.

"You all right?" Mike asked, holding her hand in his.

"Yeah. It's just that momentary fear – what if this is gonna be a big one?"

"I would imagine that by Virginia standards, that was a big one. What are the odds of getting as far away from California earthquakes as we could, yet still getting one all the way on the other coast?"

"That scared me," she admitted.

"I'm sure it did. What can I do to help?"

Lisa rolled onto her side and kissed him while removing her hand from his grasp and sliding it down the waist of his pyjama bottoms.

Mike almost made a dumb comment about making the earth move twice but decided to just shut up and go with the flow.

CHAPTER 25

"Mike, wake up," Lisa said in a loud whisper.

Mike could sense daylight even through his closed eyelids.

"I don't have to go to work," he mumbled. "Just let me sleep a little bit more."

"Open your eyes," she insisted.

Mike opened them. He was lying on his back and tried to focus his vision. It took a few beats for the ocular data to reach his tired brain, and then a few more until what he was seeing was fully tabulated.

Running diagonally across their bedroom ceiling was a crack. At either end, it was what would be referred to as hairline, but closer to the middle, it widened. Mike estimated that he could probably fit a dime into the widest part.

"I hope the new-home warranty covers that," Lisa commented.

Mike stood unsteadily up on the bed so he could get

a closer look.

"It doesn't look that bad," he said as he rubbed his finger across it. "I don't think it's structural. After breakfast I'll... shit."

"What's the matter?" Lisa asked.

"I knew that there was something we didn't buy for the house."

"What's that?"

"A ladder."

"Why don't you just borrow one from a neighbour," Lisa suggested.

"We should have one of our own."

"We never have."

"That's because every place we've rented had one," Mike reminded her. "The time has come for us to own one of our own."

"You make that sound like some sort of life milestone," Lisa said, smiling.

"It is. First car, wife, baby, then ladder," Mike said, finally noticing how bright it was outside. "Don't you have to make Kevin his breakfast and take him to school?"

"Done and done. I was up hours ago, then snuck back to bed to play hooky, like you."

"No time for that," he said in an exaggeratedly macho voice. "I have to do manly things today."

"What, like pick up your stress medication so you

don't get sad?" she said, teasing.

"That was mean," he replied. "I may just cry."

"There's the man I love. Have a quick shower and I'll get breakfast ready," she said. "Then you can go buy your big boy ladder... and your medication."

"I'll have you know that not only am I going to buy a ladder, but plan to pick up some supplies so I can turn that basement into a game room."

"Can we get a ping pong table?" Lisa asked.

"Might as well. It'll give me something to do while I'm unemployed."

"What? Play with yourself?"

"You really are on form today, aren't you," he said.

"Hey, I had me some sugar last night. Of course, I'm a happy girl."

*

Mike liked to think of himself as some sort of a do-it-yourself expert when it came to home improvements. As he'd always been a renter, he had never been in a position to really hone his untested talents. The repairs he had made in their various homes were more creative than they were durable (or within code). Mike was very proud of the fact that he could fix (or at least conceal) just about anything with spackle, paint, zip ties, or duct tape. The basement would be his first real challenge. It would be his Sistine Chapel, his chance to show Lisa what he was capable of doing.

Mike roamed the aisles of the mega Home Depot looking for the odd collection of items that he planned to use to fix up the space. He knew in his heart that he should frame the wall with wood first, then anchor the drywall screws into that, but like most of his DIY work, he had a better, quicker idea of how to do things.

When it was Mike's turn at the check-out line, he was sure that Makisha (if he was reading her name tag correctly) knew what he was up to and was secretly judging him.

"That was quite a shaker last night," Mike said, hoping to throw her off.

"Whas zat?" she asked.

"The earthquake. You must have felt it."

"Not me." She said as she turned and shouted to the next checker. "Frieda girl, you feel an earthquake last night?"

"Last one I felt was that one back in 2011, and that was plenty enough for me."

Mike filled the SUV with his purchases, then after swinging by the pharmacy and picking up his meds, he headed home as he listened intently to the local news channel. He couldn't understand why there were no reports about the earthquake.

Once Mike started unloading the Honda, Lisa looked

at the odd collection of items he'd purchased but didn't dare ask him about his master plan. She knew that he liked to keep his projects to himself until the 'big reveal'.

Mike wanted to get started on the basement, but Lisa reminded him that a visit to the attic to check on damage above their bedroom was by far the most important task.

The access hatch to the attic was in the middle of the ceiling within the master bedroom walk-in closet.

Wearing his brand-new tool belt, Mike managed to position the new ladder under the hatch, then extended it so it was at a safe angle for him to climb. In all his life, Mike had never had the need or opportunity to go into an attic. His only experience of them was in movies and books and most of those involved something nasty waiting in the shadows.

Mike pushed the hatch insert aside and used his mini Maglite to find the light switch that had been mounted on a support beam. He flipped it on, but nothing happened. He shone his flashlight up at an LED fitting that ran almost the entire length of the space. It looked to have been professionally installed; however, someone had forgotten to put in any bulbs. Mike hoisted himself up onto the plywood walkway that ran between a sea of mineral wool insulation.

Mike took three paces and was pretty sure that he

was directly above their bedroom. With his Maglite held in his mouth to free up his hands, he got on his knees and tried to lift off some of the brown material, with little success. It wasn't until it dawned on him to try rolling back a section from a join that he was able to reveal what was below. He had expected to see the top side of the ceiling drywall. Instead, between each floor joist was a second barrier of thin insulation tiles that appeared to be covered in metal foil.

He managed to remove one without ripping the covering and could finally see the damage, or at least part of it. The drywall was cracked all the way through but was attached to the joists at so many points that it didn't look like it was going to go anywhere.

Mike replaced all the insulation and got back on his feet. He shone the light around the rest of the space to see if there had been any other damage.

At the farthest end of the empty attic, Mike could see something leaning against a roof joist. As he approached it, he at first thought it was part of a gate. Mike crossed over to a parallel walkway to get a better look. As he got closer, he could see that it wasn't a gate at all. It was part of an old metal bed frame. It looked to have once been white, but the paint was worn off in places and rust had taken hold. Mike guessed that it was the headboard end of the bed. What he couldn't work out was why there was a heavy leather strap bolted on each side.

"What's that?" Lisa asked from the other side of the attic as she poked her head through the hatch.

Mike literally jumped, hitting his head against one of the rafters.

"Ow!" he gasped as he tried to rub away the pain.

"Sorry," Lisa said. "I should have let you know I was here."

"Ya think?" Mike said, still rubbing.

Lisa found her way over to where Mike was standing and looked down at the bed frame.

"What's that doing here?" she asked.

"How should I know. Someone must have left it."

"Babe… we are the first people to live in this house… ever. Nobody left this behind. Someone had to have intentionally put it here."

"Why would anyone do that?" Mike asked. "Do you think a builder found it and hid it up here until he could take it home?"

Lisa shrugged then noticed the straps.

"I saw those too," Mike offered. "I couldn't work out what they were for."

"I know exactly what they are for. They're restraining straps."

"Like in bondage?" Mike asked.

"You're sick," she said. "No. Not like bondage. Like strapping someone down so they can't move or run away."

"With leather straps. There must be a hundred better things to use than leather."

"Maybe now. But by the look of them and the bed, it must be old. Very old."

"So where would something like that come from?" Mike asked.

"I have no idea. I think the big question is how it ended up in our house?"

Something was bothering Mike. It took a few more synapses to fire before the thought reached maturity. He marched back to the open hatchway and removed a tape measure from his belt.

"Care to include me in what you're doing?" Lisa said as her husband went into one of his DIY trances.

"Give me a second," he replied, distracted.

Mike measured the hatchway opening. It was thirty-four inches square. He retraced his steps and rejoined Lisa by the mystery headboard and measured the height and width of the thing.

"It's not possible," he mumbled to himself.

"What isn't possible?" Lisa asked.

Instead of answering, Mike picked up the headboard and was shocked at how heavy it was. He was forced to put it down and looked hopefully over at Lisa.

"Want a hand?" she offered.

The two of them manhandled it across the attic to the open hatchway.

"This would be a great time to tell me what we're doing," Lisa suggested.

"I want to see if it fits through the hatch," Mike announced.

"Why? I certainly don't want that thing downstairs."

"You prefer it being up here... above our heads?"

Lisa took a better grip on the thing.

Between the two of them, they tried every angle they could to get it through the opening. Finally, exhausted, they gave up and leaned it against a nearby joist, before looking at each other with growing unease. Mike had indeed proved his point.

There was no way for the bed head to have ever been carried into the attic.

CHAPTER 26

Before accepting such a creepy conclusion, they tried to see if there was a way to disassemble it. There wasn't. All joins had been welded together and showed no signs of ever having been tampered with. They had no choice but to leave the mystery object in the attic.

Mike was again ready to head to the basement and start his project, but Lisa had other plans.

As they emerged from the walk-in closet, she took hold of both his hands and looked into his eyes.

"How much do you love me?" she asked.

"Beyond words," Mike replied, waiting for the reason for such a loaded question.

"I don't know if I can sleep with that crack across the ceiling. For some reason, between that and the thing in the attic, I know that I'll just lie there, staring up at it. Could you postpone your other project and fix that first?"

"Of course," he replied, feeling slightly guilty that he

hadn't thought of that without her having to suggest it. "I'll spackle it now, but I'll have to wait till it dries before sanding it and painting it."

"Thank you," she said as she kissed him on the tip of his nose. "While you're doing that, I'm going to give Walter a call and ask him to explain why we have part of an antique bed sitting in our brand-new attic."

Lisa tried his number as Mike went downstairs to grab the tools he would need. The call went straight to voicemail.

"Walter," she said, putting on her sweetest voice. "After that earthquake last night, we ended up with a nasty crack in the bedroom ceiling. Mike went into the attic to check it out and found part of an antique bed frame, just sitting up there. It is too big to fit through the hatch, so I need you to please have it cut down and removed as soon as possible. Thank you."

It took Mike over an hour to spackle the ceiling. To be fair, it took fifteen minutes to do the job, but forty-five minutes to dash back to Hardware Emporium to buy a mid-sized step ladder as his new telescoping ladder was useless for any task that didn't have a nearby wall for it to lean against.

Once the patch job was done, all he had to do was wait until the pink putty turned white, indicating that it was fully dry. The tub said to expect thirty to forty-five minutes' drying time, which gave him the opportunity to cart his purchases to the basement and take an exact measurement of the space. He hadn't told Lisa, but he planned on surprising her by having the whole room carpeted.

Paul's Discount Floorcoverings in Warrenton had a sale going on and Mike had found a generic, beige, polyester carpet that was on special for seventy percent off, including installation and underlay. Even though it was clearly not a great quality carpet, Mike felt that it was a damn sight better than a concrete slab.

The great thing about Paul's, according to their website, was that you did all the ordering online. They didn't send out salespeople or samples. You just picked the colour and the quality and entered the dimensions of the space. It saved the company a lot of money, which they passed on to the customer. The only downside was that if the client mismeasured and the installer found that there was more carpet needed (closets, alcoves, etc.), you were charged double for the extra bits. This penalty was meant to ensure that clients took the time to measure carefully, and the policy was written in bold print and repeated at every stage of the online purchase.

Once Mike had piled all his purchases in the middle of the basement, he used his new laser measure to get the length and width. Wanting to be one hundred percent certain of the dimensions, he then used his old trusty aluminium measuring tape to check his laser reading. They were the same.

Mike went upstairs to the living room (there was no wi-fi reception below ground level) and finished his order to Paul's. The price was just over $1800, which included installation within forty-eight hours. Considering the basement was almost twelve hundred square feet, that was a bargain. He knew that Lisa would have a fit about spending that much while his earning potential was in jeopardy, but Mike considered it an investment. If they did have to sell their home, a finished basement could add tens of thousands to the value.

Mike checked the time on his phone and guesstimated that the spackle should have dried already. As he made his way upstairs, Lisa came storming down. They met in the middle.

"Can you believe that Walter hasn't called me back?" she fumed.

"It's been less than an hour. He may actually be busy," Mike suggested.

"Too busy to call me back?"

Lisa pulled her phone out of her back pocket and began texting.

Mike couldn't see exactly what she was texting, but by her look of frustration, assumed that she was using all capitals.

"What'd you text?"

Lisa held the phone out so that Mike could see the screen.

'WHAT ARE YOU DOING ABOUT THE DAMN BED FRAME?'

"That should certainly get a response," Mike said with a slight grin.

Lisa didn't see any humour in the situation and stormed down the rest of the stairs.

"What do you want for lunch?" she snarled.

"How about some…"

"We're having tuna sandwiches," she announced before Mike could finish his thought.

"Sounds good to me," Mike called after her.

Mike started back up towards the bedroom when he heard Lisa yell.

"Shit!"

Mike turned around and made for the kitchen. He found her staring at a monthly calendar they kept on the fridge door.

"I forgot that we're having Wayne and Barbara over for dinner," she announced in a panicked voice.

"That's not a big deal," Mike replied. "It'll be a nice way to christen the house. When are they coming over?"

Lisa looked at him as if he was insane.

"Tonight! They're coming for dinner tonight."

"That's okay. I know Wayne likes pizza. We'll just order a delivery."

Mike realised too late that he couldn't have said anything worse. He looked at her face transform. It reminded him of *The Picture of Dorian Gray*.

"Have I ever invited friends to dinner then given them a delivery pizza?" she asked incredulously. "You know how much it means to me to make something special when friends come over."

"I do," Mike agreed. "It's only just past noon. Can't you whip something up in six hours?" he said, compounding his earlier mistake.

"Whip something up?" Lisa's voice went up a full octave. "I don't just whip things up."

Mike held up both hands in a show of defeat. "I'll let you work it out. I know that you'll come up with something fantastic. You always do. Tell me what you need from me."

The rest of Mike's day was spent going back and forth to Wegman's supermarket as Lisa kept remembering things she wanted to add or had forgotten. The only break from his shopping runs was when he picked up Kevin. Because it was the first time that Mike had collected him, the school admin person, who was tasked with ensuring that each child only got into a vehicle with someone she either knew or was on the list (and could confirm their ID), wouldn't let Kevin get into his car.

The woman had never met Mike and his name wasn't on the approved collector list. He had to waste almost half an hour in the admin offices proving who he was and having his name formally added to the records. All the while, the pot of crème fraîche that was so vitally urgent to Lisa's creation was sitting on the front seat of the car as the sun heated the interior to a nice even baking temperature.

By the time he got Kevin home, Lisa sent him straight out again for some fresh tarragon and a new, chilled pot of the ridiculously expensive cream.

Lisa hardly left the kitchen and wouldn't let Mike anywhere near. When she was in her culinary zone, she couldn't be disturbed.

Mike gave the downstairs a quick once over with a Swiffer and vacuum, laid the table, put some nuts and Japanese soy snacks in the living room, and felt that he had things pretty much in control.

That's when he heard Kevin cry out from upstairs. Mike found him standing in front of his bedroom closet. One half of the folding louvered doors was open. Inside was a large wicker chest that held most of his smaller toys. It took Mike a moment to recognise what it was that was sitting on top of it.

He felt icy tentacles creep over his body.

"Did you put that there?" Mike asked.

Kevin shook his head, but kept his eyes riveted on the object.

Mike reached in and picked it up. It was heavier than he expected. Then again, he had never had the need to pick up a chamber pot before, so had nothing to compare it to. It appeared to have once been white enamel over metal, but time and wear had turned the outer coating yellow. Large areas had lost the enamel altogether. The visible metal beneath was rusted and pitted. It was obviously old and well used.

Mike looked inside. A thin layer of brown liquid covered the bottom. He wanted desperately to believe that it was simply rusted water, but his nose was telling him the truth.

"What is it, Daddy?" Kevin asked, fear evident in voice.

Mike was doing his best not to retch.

"It's just something people used to use to go potty if they didn't have a toilet like we do."

Kevin considered his father's words carefully.

"Why is it in my room?" he asked as his bottom lip started to tremble. "I don't want to use it. I like using the big toilet."

"You don't have to use this. I promise. Daddy's going to take it away right now."

Mike looked at the thing with a growing sense of revulsion. He couldn't imagine how it got into the house, let alone their child's bedroom. It was becoming obvious that someone was playing some very unfunny tricks on them.

"Don't move," Mike instructed, as he placed the pot back on the wicker box and dashed into the hallway bathroom.

He grabbed a couple of tissues and a hand towel then returned to Kevin's room. He placed the towel gingerly over the opening while turning his head to the side, trying not to inhale any of the cloying nectar. He wadded the tissues together and used them like an oven mitt to grasp the handle of the chamber pot.

"Where are you taking it, Daddy?" Kevin asked.

"Somewhere safe until I can get rid of it tomorrow."

"Why not throw it away now?"

"Because Uncle Wayne and Aunt Barbara are coming over, remember. We don't want to be dealing with dirty things just before they arrive."

Kevin nodded and watched his father hold the pot as far away from him as possible as he exited the room.

"Can I come with you?" Kevin asked.

"You stay up here and play for a while. I don't want you anywhere near this thing anymore, okay?"

"Okay."

Mike made it down the stairs without mishap. As he was about to open the kitchen door to access the garage, he realised that Lisa would not be very pleased at him traipsing across her food prep area with a chamber pot of unknown origins. Instead, he decided to go out the front door and access the side entrance.

He stepped out front and came face to face with Wayne and Barbara, who were about to ring the bell.

Wayne, who was renowned for his wry humour, looked down at the chamber pot then looked up at Mike.

"You should have told us it was gonna be that sort of a party. We would have brought our own."

CHAPTER 27

After getting the couple to promise not to mention the chamber pot to Lisa, everyone seemed to enjoy the evening. Lisa had made Hungarian goulash with braised fennel and wild rice. Mike thought that he'd become used to her cuisine prowess, but even he was gobsmacked.

Dessert was a simple pear tarte with vanilla-bean ice cream. Over the course of the meal, Mike and Lisa double-teamed to tell the story of the mysterious bed frame. Wayne put it down to being a prank by the builders. As far as they knew, Darcy Development might leave some piece of the past in every one of their homes.

"Maybe it was some sort of good luck tradition," Wayne suggested.

"Why not just leave an old coin or tool?" Mike asked. "Something that could actually be removed if needed."

"Something like a bedpan?" Barb said, keeping a

straight face.

"That would be a little disgusting," Lisa commented.

"Yes, it would, wouldn't it," Barb said as she smiled innocently at Mike.

Lisa wasn't remotely aware that Barb was making Mike squirm.

"Why don't you all go into the living room while I put a few things in the dishwasher," Lisa suggested. "Would anyone like coffee or tea?"

"I'll give you a hand," Barb offered.

Mike gave her a panicked look. Barb returned it with a barely perceptible shake of her head. He got the meaning. She wasn't going to spill the beans.

While Wayne and Mike sat in the living room, Lisa and Barb made fast work of the dishes. The one thing that was banned from going into the dishwasher was Lisa's prized serving platter. She washed that by hand then began to wrap it in a large sheet of bubble wrap.

"What's that for?" Barb asked.

"None of the bigger pieces will fit in any of the cabinets, so I have to store it in the garage."

"That's not possible," Barb exclaimed. "Show me."

Lisa removed the dish from the wrapping, then opening the biggest of the wall-mounted cabinets, she placed one end on the bottom shelf and slid it gently inside.

"Keep going," Barb instructed as she peered over

her shoulder.

"It's not going to fit," Lisa insisted as she slid the plate a little further.

The plate kept on going. It passed the point when Lisa knew it would touch the backing. It finally came to a stop, leaving at least an inch of clearance between it and the cabinet door.

"I don't understand," Lisa said feeling a strange unease settle upon her.

"The plate's oval. You just hadn't hit the exact angle so it would fit."

"Let's find out," Lisa said as she headed for the garage. She opened one of the packing boxes that she knew held her biggest circular serving dish. As she was about to step back into the house, she caught a whiff of something unpleasant; something that should only be present in a sewer.

Then it was gone.

She handed the plate to Barb. "Okay, let's see you find a place for this."

"Shall we make this interesting?" Barb asked.

"You want to bet me that you can make it fit?"

"No. That would be crass. How about, you give me the recipe for that goulash you made if I can find a place for this dish?"

"If you can find a place in this kitchen for this dish, I will come to your house and not only give you the recipe but cook it for you as well."

"Deal," Barb said, grinning.

Barb began opening various cabinets. She settled on one that was under the granite countertop next to the oven. It held an assortment of pots and pans on the lowest level but also had two shelves at the top. The highest one was only being used to store a couple of chopping boards.

"May I try this one?" she asked.

"This is your challenge," Lisa replied. "You can try anywhere you want. I sure did."

Barb grinned back at her then removed the two boards from the shelf. She carefully took the plate from Lisa's hands and gently slid it into the opening. Lisa looked on with an all-knowing expression. She and Mike had already been through this a few weeks earlier.

Barb kept pushing as more of the plate disappeared into the dark recess. It kept on going until all of it was within the cabinet. Lisa stepped closer and gingerly closed the door knowing it wouldn't quite make it.

It shut completely.

"I don't know what your schedule looks like, but I'm available almost any night next week," Barb said, gloating.

"How's that coffee coming along?" Mike asked as he poked his head into the kitchen.

Once the Givens were gone, Lisa and Mike sat in the living room and shared the last bit of red wine.

"That was one of your best meals ever," Mike said.

"I have to agree with you," Lisa replied. "Am I allowed to say that?"

"Only between ourselves. In company it just might sound a little like hubris."

"Well, we can't have that," she said, snuggling up against him.

Lisa could feel his deep steady breathing and felt a sense of security. Her unease about the china dishes fitting into places they couldn't had mostly dissipated. She considered telling Mike about it, but decided that, what with whole bed frame thing, she didn't want to add another anomaly to the list.

Mike loved it when Lisa curled up against him. It was comforting. It reminded him of how good their life was together. Even if things went sideways at work, they would always have each other. As he felt her warmth through his shirt, he felt a momentary pang of guilt. He had always been one hundred percent honest with Lisa and shared everything with her. Yet, for some reason, he hadn't told her about the chamber pot. He knew he should, and probably would. It was just that the day had had so many conflicting emotions, especially after finding the bed frame, he thought it best to keep the latest oddity to himself.

The two must have dozed off because neither heard Kevin come down the stairs and walk into the living room.

They jolted awake the second he spoke.

"My room still smells of poo!" his little voice announced.

*

Once Kevin was settled in bed with his window latched open, Mike considered weaving some complex tapestry of untruths to explain Kevin's pronouncement, but decided that coming clean would, at that point, be by far the safest alternative. He told Lisa about finding the chamber pot in his room and about how he had snuck it out of the house, only to get caught red-handed by Wayne and Barb.

"That explains her mentioning a chamber pot at dinner," Lisa said. "I thought that was a little weird."

Lisa hesitated for a moment, then continued.

"There's something I have to tell you as well," she admitted.

"Oh really?" Mike replied, intrigued.

Lisa told him all about Barb's insistence that her big

serving plates should fit in the kitchen and how they'd managed to fit two of the biggest pieces into places that were too small only a few weeks earlier.

"Somehow, your discovery doesn't sound half as creepy as mine. In fact, yours is kind of a plus. You now have more storage room."

"You don't think the fact that our cabinets seem to be getting bigger is creepy?"

"I think that there is a very logical explanation for the cabinets," Mike said. "As for the chamber pot…"

"You got shit?" Lisa suggested, smirking.

"Very funny. Let's have a look at your magical cabinets," Mike said as he headed for the kitchen.

Lisa pointed to the under-counter shelf where Barb had had no trouble storing Lisa's biggest serving plate.

Mike could see that it was indeed safely tucked away while allowing the cabinet door to be closed. He opened a utility drawer and grabbed a flashlight. He then crouched down so that he was at eye level with the space.

"Please take the dish out," Mike requested.

Once Lisa had removed it, he poked his arm all the way to the back of the cabinet and ran his fingers along the sides where the cabinet met with the backing material. There was a wide gap between the end of the shelf and the wall beyond. Also, the fibreboard backing seemed to have disappeared. The serving dish was able to fit in the cabinet because there was nothing between it and the wall.

Mike removed all the pots, pans and other utensils, then removed the shelves. He then lay on his side and pointed the flashlight onto the wall. He expected to see new sheetrock; instead, he saw brick. Old, worn brick.

"What do you see?" Lisa asked.

"Wall," Mike replied.

"That's a good thing, isn't it?" she asked.

"It would be, if it was ours."

CHAPTER 28

Mike and Lisa stayed up talking long into the night. They couldn't get their heads around what was happening in their home.

Lisa postulated that just maybe, part of an original wall from whatever had stood on the lot before had been incorporated into their construction. It made no logical sense but did qualify as a possible explanation. Wayne's idea about the builders leaving the bed behind as a sort of good luck token, though bizarre, also fit the bill pretty well. Both agreed that the plumbing disaster was almost certainly due to their system being brand new and having teething pains.

That left only one unsolved issue. Neither of them could come up with any rational explanation of how a vintage, well-used chamber pot could suddenly appear in Kevin's room.

They tried to work out when it could possibly have been left there, at which point they could extrapolate who had been in the house within that period of time.

"The plumbing surveyor," Mike said, suddenly remembering that he'd had the full run of the house the day before. He was left completely alone while upstairs and could easily have left it there.

"I get that he could," Lisa said. "But why would he?"

"I have no idea. Just because he has a responsible job doesn't mean he's necessarily running on both rails. I mean who in their right mind would choose a profession where you spend your days looking into other people's sewer lines... staring at other people's..."

"I get your point, but why a chamber pot and why us?" Lisa asked.

"How do we know it's just us?" Mike suggested. "Maybe he leaves something like that behind at every house. In fact, it makes perfect sense. The man's job is to check out plumbing, right? So, what does he sneak into our house? A chamber pot – the alternative to indoor plumbing. The poor guy must have snapped. He's seen so much excrement that he's trying to tell people to go back to the old ways."

Lisa looked at her husband with growing concern.

"Did you take the meds you picked up today?" she asked.

"No," he said, unable to look her in the face.

Lisa shook her head and made for the kitchen. She

returned a few moments later with the unopened pharmacy bag and a glass of water.

"Are you telling me that you don't like my hypothesis?"

"I'm just saying that you need to take one of each pill tonight, then we can talk about your idea tomorrow. Does that sound fair?"

"I forgot to tell you about the earthquake," Mike said excitedly. "I asked a bunch of people at the hardware store and at Wegman's and guess what? None of them knew anything about there having been an earthquake. We should have asked Wayne and Barbara when they were here. They live close. They would have felt it. Right?"

Lisa held the bag of meds out in front of her and shook it. Mike looked like he was going to say something else, then instead, reached over and grabbed it.

*

There was no shaking that night, and with Mike's patching job on the ceiling taking away its ominous appearance, Lisa fell asleep immediately. Mike, however, was having a raging case of monkey brain and was trying to isolate and focus on any one of the dozen or so unrelated thoughts that were bouncing around inside his head. As if that wasn't enough, The Beatles' song *I am the Walrus* was also in his head and snippets of different parts kept sneaking into other thought streams. Thankfully, after an hour and a half of tossing and turning, the clonazepam took hold and swept the jagged mental melee into various dark recesses where his mind couldn't quite get at them.

He slept like a baby.

*

In the morning, he felt rested and not quite as anxious about all the weird goings on. Mike checked his phone and saw that it was past nine. The morning sun was desperately trying to find a way to sneak through the slats of the plantation shutters. Somewhere in the house he could hear Lisa. Her voice was raised, but he couldn't tell what she was saying or to whom she was saying it to.

He shuffled down to the kitchen just as she disconnected her call.

"Problem?" he asked.

"Walter still hasn't called me back or texted. I just left him a third message."

"Do you think he might just be avoiding you?" Mike suggested. "That all caps text about the antique bed would have scared the shit out of me."

"Speaking of shit," she grimaced. "When are you going to empty out that chamber pot?"

"Hopefully when no one's looking."

"I said when, not where. Why don't you just dump it down the toilet?"

"I know this is going to sound crazy, but for some reason, I don't want to get rid of what's inside it within the house."

"You're right…" Lisa said. "It is crazy; however, I'd much prefer you dispose of the contents somewhere that the neighbours won't see you. Getting caught emptying out a vintage chamber pot down a storm drain could ruin our rep within the estate."

"How do we know that all the residents haven't been left their own chamber pot at some point?" Mike asked.

"I'm not even going to respond to that."

"It's possible. What if the guy was sneaking one into every house on the estate, but because nobody knows about the others, everyone is too embarrassed to bring it up?"

Lisa tried to keep a straight face but couldn't. "You are one sick puppy."

"It's my calling."

"Speaking of your calling, are you going to finish the ceiling today?"

"I just have to give it a final sanding, then paint it,"

he advised.

"Will it match?"

"I put a dab of paint on yesterday and now can't even find it, so yes. It should match perfectly."

"After that, what are you going to do?" Lisa asked.

"I plan on spending most of the day in the basement," Mike said before seeing the look on her face. "After painting the ceiling, obviously."

She was still giving him 'the look'.

"And emptying the chamber pot," he quickly added. "What do I do with it when it's empty?"

"I would hope that you'd throw it away," she replied. "Or…" she added as an evil grin appeared. "You could gift wrap it and give it to Kerry."

"That is low." Mike smiled. "Can I really?"

"No. Of course not. But it's fun to imagine."

Lisa could tell that Mike really was thinking about it.

"I was joking."

"I know," Mike confirmed. "But what if it got mailed from somewhere far from here? She'd never know."

"I would," Lisa stated bluntly, in effect torpedoing Mike's scheming. "In fact," she added. "We will go to the dump together so that you aren't tempted."

"Yes, dear," Mike said, feigning extreme disappointment.

Mike ate a bowl of Wegman's generic version of Cheerios, then drank a cup of instant French roast coffee that tasted nothing like coffee but saved him the trouble of brewing a fresh pot of the real stuff.

Mike put his bowl and mug in the dishwasher, took his morning dose of clonazepam, then with a deep sigh, headed into the garage.

The chamber pot was where he'd left it (why wouldn't it be, he told himself). He lifted it up and was struck by the fact that it seemed heavier. Quite a bit heavier.

Holding it as if it was the most fragile object on earth, Mike slowly walked to the downstairs powder room. He pulled off the towel and, despite his brain telling him not to, had a quick peek inside. When he'd removed it from Kevin's room, it'd only had less than a quarter inch of brown effluence swilling around the bottom. Now there was at least a couple of inches of the vile stuff.

Mike gagged and turned his head away. The stench was overpowering. It was much worse than before. He leaned out of the room and breathed in as much clean air as he could, then carefully tipped the contents into their brand-new and gleamingly clean toilet. He took extra care not to let any of the brown slime splash back.

It seemed to go on for ever. It had to be something to do with the shape of the pot, but to Mike, it seemed as if he was pouring gallons of the putrid liquid into the toilet.

Finally, one last ghastly drop departed the pot and joined with the rest of the horror in the bowl. Mike flushed and hoped that it wasn't going to stain the sides of the lav. He watched as the runny ooze formed into a cyclonic funnel then began to empty away. Then suddenly, it began to rise. It was still spinning as it should but was climbing higher in the bowl. Mike could see that it was about to flow over the rim of the toilet.

He flushed again and for the first time ever, appreciated the majesty of a water-saving toilet. Even though hardly any time had passed between flushes, the smaller tank had filled sufficiently to dump fresh water into the melee.

For a terrifying moment, he thought that the rising brown tide was going to breach the lip and cascade onto the Italian tile floor. It didn't. Just as Mike felt all was lost, the bowl emptied completely, leaving only a brown ring behind as a memory of the moment.

Mike used an entire jug of toilet cleaner to scrub away every trace of the unspeakable slop. He then took the chamber pot and walked down to the edge of the lake. By that point, he didn't care if the neighbours saw him or not. He wasn't going to risk hosing the thing out. He could imagine all too well the force of the water curving along the rounded sides of the potty and sending it all right back into his face (and mouth).

Mike shuddered as he lowered it into the warm

water and gently, very gently, swilled it around until there was nothing inside but chipped, yellowed enamel.

After a quick shower (without any plumbing catastrophes), Mike was able to complete the ceiling fix in under an hour. That gave him the whole day to work on the basement walls. He needed to have his part completed before the carpet installer arrived the following afternoon.

Lisa knew not to interrupt Mike as he worked at his 'surprise'. The only time they saw each other during the day was when Mike came into the kitchen foraging for lunch. Lisa made him a ham and cheese sandwich as he stood by and watched.

"I could have done that," Mike commented.

"I don't think you should be touching anything in here."

Mike looked down at himself and was shocked to see that he was covered in white plaster. It was on his shoes, his clothes and, as he felt a little higher, on his face and in his hair.

"Did any get on the wall?" Lisa asked, smiling.

"I'm having to do this quickly," he offered. "I need to finish the wall treatment by tomorrow."

"Why the deadline?"

Mike tapped the side of his plaster-covered nose. "That's my little secret."

Lisa rolled her eyes.

*

At six thirty p.m. Mike emerged from the basement. He'd managed to splatter even more wet plaster onto his clothes, shoes, exposed skin, and hair. He didn't care. He'd completed his challenge to make the basement walls look professionally finished.

Lisa was still not allowed to go down to see what he'd done and he in turn wasn't permitted to go anywhere within the house in his current condition. Though most of the plaster was dry, that wouldn't have prevented it from flaking off and coating their home in a haze of white dust and dry globules.

Lisa had placed a chair next to the basement door. On it was a plastic garbage bag as well as his bathrobe and his slippers. A note on the chair instructed him to place everything he was wearing into the bag, then don the robe and footwear before proceeding to the shower.

He knew better than to deviate from Lisa's instructions. As he was about to remove his t-shirt, Kevin appeared from the den and stood gawking at his father.

"Daddy, why do you have cake frosting all over you?" he asked. "Are we having cake?"

"Sorry, little man. No cake tonight," Mike replied.

Kevin immediately lost interest and wandered off to get into mischief somewhere else.

"Did I hear the voice of my hard-working craftsman?" Lisa said as she appeared at the end of the hallway.

She helped him remove his clothes, trying not to send too much of the plaster onto the new floor. Due to the additional layer that had accumulated on his head and arms, Lisa wasn't comfortable with him traipsing through the house yet. She led him onto the patio and using their Dyson vacuum with the furniture attachment in place, sucked off all the loose plaster she could find.

Because both were outside with the vacuum deadening all sound, neither heard the doorbell. They also missed Kevin open the front door and greet the unscheduled visitor.

The first they knew that there was someone else in the house was when the patio door opened and Rick Greenberg started laughing at Mike's appearance.

CHAPTER 29

"What the hell happened to you?" Rick managed to ask, wiping tears from his eyes.

"I've been working on the basement," Mike replied, trying to sound offended by the question. As Lisa still had the Dyson attachment up against his head, his look of disdain fell flat.

"Rick," Lisa said. "What are you doing here?"

Her tone was not lost on him. Rick could tell that she was not happy to see him.

"I know that you both must hate me at the moment," Rick said, hoping for some sort of denial.

Lisa and Mike didn't say a thing.

"Look, I need to talk to you," he said, looking at Mike. "I know I should have called before coming over, but I assumed that you'd have said no."

"How did you get through the gate?" Lisa asked, her voice frosty.

"I followed another car through. You may want to

have them adjust the sensor. I shouldn't have been able to do that."

"No, you shouldn't," Lisa agreed.

"Give me ten minutes, so I can get most of this crap off me, then we'll talk," Mike advised. "However, if you're here to fire me, you might as well do it now. I don't feel I should have to spruce myself up for that."

"Ouch." Rick flinched. "I'm not here to fire you."

Lisa and Mike both gave him a doubting stare.

"I promise you, that's not why I'm here."

"Babe, would you please fix him a drink while I clean off." Mike tried to walk back into the house with some degree of dignity.

Lisa sighed and turned off the vacuum.

"Arsenic and tonic all right?" she asked as she stepped past Rick and walked into the house.

Mike rejoined them fifteen minutes later. He had managed to rid himself of the remaining plaster and was wearing black jeans and a People Force t-shirt. He liked the irony.

Mike got himself a beer from the kitchen before joining Rick in the den.

"Okay," Mike said as he sat across from the company president. "Here I am. What do you want?"

"I owe you an apology," Rick announced without preamble. "I didn't believe what you were telling me about what Kerry was doing at the bank. It all sounded too implausible. I didn't think that there was any conceivable way that she could screw things up that badly in such a short space of time. I know that you tried to tell me otherwise on several occasions... it's just that, as the vendor, we have to believe what we're told by our clients. If they say that service has declined, we have to assume it has. Logic dictates that there would be no reason for them to lie about that."

"But...?" Mike asked.

"Holy shit, man! She's a one-woman wrecking crew. It's not just that she doesn't know what she's doing; she seems hell-bent on getting rid of anybody and anything that was in place before she arrived."

"I know," Mike said.

"But it doesn't make any sense. We made Martin look good, very good, in fact. He was smart enough to see that and worked closely with the team to keep that synergy going. This bitch, excuse my French, seems perfectly happy to destroy everything, then blame it on everyone but herself."

"Still waiting to hear something I don't know," Mike said.

"I have been there for four days and never once seen her do anything even closely resembling managing the AV operation. All she does is direct blame, redistribute our technicians so they're bound to fail, and then bitch to upper management about the failures. I tried more than a dozen times to have a professional conversation with her, and she either didn't show, or on the two occasions when she did, spent the time telling me what was wrong with my company."

Mike just shrugged.

"I've got to tell you, Mike, I've never encountered someone like her," Rick continued. "I can only assume that her actions come from some deep neurosis and insecurity, but that still doesn't explain why she wouldn't want us to make her look good. I mean, if she's successful in getting our contract cancelled, she'll still end up with another group of professionals who she'll undermine and complain about. I just can't see her end game."

Rick lowered his head into his hands and stayed that way. It only lasted a few seconds, but when he raised his head, his red-rimmed eyes told Mike everything.

Kerry had managed to break him as well.

Rick was invited to have dinner with them, and over leftover goulash, the three tried to come up with some sort of plan. Mike agreed to return once his medical leave expired but didn't see what good he could do at the bank. Rick convinced him that, if nothing else, his being there and doing everything he could to protect his team was, in and of itself, a huge plus. Rick also mentioned the fact that he'd heard through the grapevine that several technicians were posting their resumes and that maybe they'd reconsider with Mike back.

At some point during dinner, the subject changed from trying to find a way to work around her to how to get rid of Kerry.

"Isn't there something that Martin can do?" Lisa asked. "He must have some strong allies within the bank who'd back him up if he went head-to-head with the executive director."

"That's not how things work at the Global Initiative Bank," Mike advised. "The staff are known throughout the city as complainers and manipulators, but when it comes to standing up against senior management, their tails droop between their legs and they run off to find somewhere to hide. We won't get anyone internal will stand up for us... except for Martin."

"That seems completely unfair," Lisa commented.

"Welcome to DC," Rick added.

They continued spit-balling for over an hour without coming up with any good ideas. Rick had floated the notion of a professional hit person, but neither Lisa nor Mike thought he was being serious. At least they hoped he wasn't.

"I wasn't going to tell you this," Rick said. "What with your stress and all, but considering what's been discussed here, I think you should know."

"Know what?" Mike asked, unsure if he even wanted to know the answer.

"Martin was given a second written warning today."

"What the hell for?" Mike was furious.

"He moved a meeting from a room Kerry had insisted they use back to the one that was originally set up to handle the client's needs. She went ballistic and stormed right upstairs to her mentor's office. From what Martin told me, she made a case that he was constantly undermining her and even telling clients to ignore her as she didn't know what she was doing."

"All completely true except the last part. I don't see Martin ever saying something like that about anyone," Mike stated.

"In the new order, truth and facts don't seem to matter. The director reported it to HR and had them issue a second warning. One more and he's gone."

Once Rick left, Mike and Lisa sat up a while longer. Lisa had formally declared their home to be a Kerry-free zone, so there was no more discussion about the bitch or the bank.

Instead, they talked about what would happen if logic and karma did not step in and the contract was cancelled. Lisa was surprisingly upbeat about their prospects. Despite her love of their new home, she made it clear that she would feel perfectly comfortable selling it, if it came to that. She kept driving into Mike that he was still one of the best technical operations directors in the business. He could get hired anywhere in the country, maybe even abroad, and despite Kerry's lies, Mike was just as good at his job now as before she started.

It was midnight when they headed up to bed. Mike was feeling comfortably numb on his meds and fell asleep almost immediately. It took Lisa quite a bit longer as she was still fuming inside. She loved Mike and knew what a good person he was. It was impossible for her to understand how one mentally incompetent woman could bring everything crashing down around him.

*

Lisa at first thought that she was dreaming. The sounds of a child screaming meshed with the nightmare she was having. Kevin was standing by the lake then began moving away from her as he walked across the water. His image became translucent as he started to scream.

Lisa sat up and realised that the screams were real and were coming from his bedroom. She shoved Mike then jumped out of bed.

Kevin was standing in the middle of his room staring at his closet doors. They were both closed. He was wearing his *101 Dalmatians* pyjamas and had wet himself. He stopped screaming the moment Lisa ran into the room. He looked terrified and was shivering all over.

Lisa dropped to her knees and looked into his tiny, emotionally wrought face.

"What happened, Kev?" she asked as gently as she could.

Mike came running in just as he started to answer his mother.

"She c... ca... came out of the cl... closet," he said between sobs. "She tried to take me with her."

"You were dreaming, little man," Mike said as he too knelt on the floor. "There's nobody in the house but you, Mommy and Daddy."

"She... w... was real," he insisted. "She c... came through the d... door in the closet."

"Oh, honey bear," Lisa said as she took him into her arms.

Mike got to his feet and opened and closed the louvered doors a couple of times. "Nobody came through this door."

"I know that Daddy," he said, nodding his little head.

"That's good," Lisa said.

"She c... came through the door at the b... back of the closet."

CHAPTER 30

Mike opened both doors so that Kevin could see everything inside. He then parted his son's hanging clothes, revealing the plain white wall at the back of the closet. There was no door. There was, however, a crack than ran horizontally across the middle of the wall.

"You see," Mike said, trying to mask his surprise at seeing the damage. "No door."

"She told me that it was time for my teat mint," Kevin whispered.

"Teat mints?" Lisa questioned. "I'm sorry, Kev, but I don't know what a teat mint is."

"Little man, why don't you go to the bathroom and take off those PJ bottoms. Mommy will be right there with clean ones."

"I'm sorry, Mommy."

"There's nothing to say sorry for," she said as she kissed his forehead.

The two watched Kevin shuffle off down the hall.

"I think he was trying to say treatment," Mike said, lowering his voice.

"Good grief," Lisa exclaimed. "What the hell was he dreaming about, and what happened to that wall?"

"I assume the wall happened at the same time as our ceiling and..."

"During the earthquake that nobody else felt?" Lisa interrupted.

"As for his dream," Mike continued. "I'm going to take a stab at that being a reaction to what occurred at his school, especially the part where the paramedics were treating him."

"Of course." Lisa nodded. "That actually makes sense."

"I'll fix the wall tomorrow, so he doesn't have to see that crack."

"What did shake the house that night?" she asked. "And don't you dare joke about you making the earth move."

"I would never even have thought of saying that," he replied, thankful that she'd cut him off before saying almost exactly that.

Lisa gave him a playful punch on the arm.

"Stopped you just in time, didn't I?"

Mike nodded.

Lisa rolled her eyes then located a fresh pair of pyjama bottoms within the closet and left the room.

Mike was up early working in the basement. He wanted to see if he could get the electrics done before the carpet installer arrived. For some reason, when they built the room, the only power they'd wired in was to the single bulb that hung in the centre of the room.

What Mike planned to do was to take that single source and wire up three circular LED light fittings, which he had spaced evenly along the ceiling.

The thing he hadn't planned for was that once he removed the existing light, the room was plunged into darkness. Mike realised that he should have bought a work light and a long extension to plug in upstairs. Instead, he ended up placing three flashlights on the floor under where he was planning to work.

Though Mike made up most of his own rules when tackling this sort of project, the one thing he always did was to ensure that power was off at the fuse box before touching any electric wiring.

The problem was, he had no idea where the fuses were in their new house. After fifteen minutes of searching, he still hadn't found them. Finally, he asked Lisa if she'd encountered it in her travels.

The fuse box turned out to be in the utility room. It had been the first place Mike looked, only he never thought to look behind the framed photo of The French Laundry restaurant on the west coast. Lisa found it funny to have the picture hanging in the laundry room. Some sort of utility room irony.

Mike opened the off-white panel door and saw to his delight that every breaker was clearly labelled. There were three for lights: GRND FLR – 2ND FLR – KITCH/GAR. There was no mention of the basement. He tried each one then ran to the top of the basement stairs to check if the single bulb had gone out. It hadn't.

He tried one circuit at a time until, in complete frustration, he flipped off the mains.

"I'm trying to fix lunch in here," Lisa shouted from the kitchen.

At almost the exact same second, Kevin cried out from the family room, "The TV's stopped working."

Despite the trouble he'd caused, the little bulb stayed on throughout. Mike decided that he would just have to go against his rules and be extra careful while working with a live wire.

The first thing he did was to take off the single fitting that was screwed into the concrete. Looking at it up close, Mike was surprised at the state of the thing. He'd assumed that it would be brand new, but it wasn't. It looked like something from the silent movie era.

He managed to remove it and access the wire that had been pulled through the concrete ceiling. Mike was speechless. He'd never seen electric wire like it in his life. It was heavy gauge copper covered in what looked like cloth of some kind. Because of the diameter of the copper, it was a nightmare getting it wired into the three-way splitter he'd purchased.

Mike finally got it attached and was able to finish off the rest of the project by lunchtime. Minutes before Lisa called down to tell him that they were going to eat on the patio, Mike was ready for the big test. Nobody was allowed to see the room until after it had been carpeted, so the switching-on ceremony was a solo affair. He'd had to leave a loop of wire hanging down into the room with a simple on/off switch fitted so they could finally turn the light off. It wasn't very professional, but it would do until he could find a better solution.

Mike activated the switch and waited for the room to fill with brilliant light. The problem was that instead of the promised LED brightness from each of the three new fittings, they were only able to manage a weak, insipid, yellow glow. Mike had no idea how to troubleshoot something like that. Besides, he was being called to lunch.

Lisa was determined to get all three of her family to eat al fresco for something other than barbequed hotdogs or hamburgers. She'd made seared shrimp with mushroom and spinach salad for the adults and a toasted peanut butter and jelly sandwich on rye for Kevin.

Days earlier, Lisa had restricted a number of subjects from being discussed at mealtimes. Items that were barred were work issues, house issues, or pretty much anything else that could qualify as putting out negative vibes.

While Kevin was regaling them with a story about how one of his classmates managed to get a pencil stuck in his ear, Lisa noticed something strange about the flower beds that abutted the house.

The flowers looked to be dying.

When they were planted only a few days earlier, they'd been glowing with vibrant, colourful life. Now their hues were muted, and most were starting to wilt, mid-stalk.

"Babe," she said in a cheery voice so as not to alarm Kevin. "Have you seen the owerflays recently?" she said in her best Pig Latin.

It took Mike a beat to understand what she'd just said. Once he'd got it, he casually glanced over at the nearest bed.

"I'm going to walk around the house and check for purple gorillas," he announced, using their code for checking to see if something was wrong.

"Can I come, Daddy?" Kevin asked.

"Sure you can, but if we see any, remember, don't

give them any walnuts no matter how much they beg."

"I don't have any walnuts," Kevin advised.

"Good. We'll be safer that way."

Mike and Kevin did one circuit of the house then returned to the patio.

"It's okay, Mommy," Kevin said proudly. "There are no purple gorillas anywhere."

"That's a relief," Lisa replied, trying to keep a straight face.

"Can I bring some toys outside?" Kevin asked.

"Of course, you may. Just don't play near the lake," Mike answered.

As soon as Kevin was out of earshot, Mike spoke.

"They're all dying. Plus, at the front, I can't be sure, but it looks as if the grass is starting to go yellow as well."

"It can't be from too little water. I've run a hose on the flowers every day and gave the lawn a soaking yesterday and this morning, as instructed."

"Can we be overwatering?" Mike asked.

"I don't know. I've been doing exactly what Moses said to do. I've even used that sprinkler thingy that he left with us."

Before either could say anything else, Mike's phone began vibrating while blasting Rush's anthem.

"This is Mike," he answered. "Great. It's 1-9-4-2. Stay on the main drag and I'll meet you out front."

He disconnected the call.

"Gotta go," he said with a wink, just before heading into the house.

"Enough of the mystery!" Lisa shouted.

A Ford van appeared around the corner and Mike waved it onto their driveway. It was covered with the image of a family smiling down at a roll of golden carpet.

"Right on time," Mike said cheerily as the driver exited the gaudy vehicle.

The installer was a short man with a receding hairline. That, along with his oily complexion and a sour-looking expression, rounded off the 'look' perfectly. Mike could tell from the man's body language that there was not going to be much comradery between the two of them.

"You Mr Ellis?" the man asked with a frustrated sigh.

"That's me. Shall I show you where the room is?"

"If you want me to work in it, then... yeah," the installer replied.

Mike wanted desperately to tell the guy to lighten up, especially as they were paying for his services, but there was something about the guy that screamed, 'Mess with me and I'm gone.'

Mike led him to the basement. The first thing the installer did was to look at the dismal lighting and snort.

"This all the light you got?"

"Yes," Mike answered. "I installed it yesterday," he added for no good reason.

The man made the same snorting sound.

"What's with the walls?" the installer said, approaching one with his arm outstretched. "Weird," he said as he rubbed a hand across the newly completed surface.

Mike didn't say a word. The guy was starting to piss him off and just wanted him to do the install and get the hell out of their home.

The man removed a laser measure from his pocket and held it against the nearest wall. He took a measurement, then moved to one of the side walls. After noting the numbers, he turned and gave Mike a long head shake.

"You people are always trying to pull some sort of scam."

"I have no idea what you're talking about," Mike replied indignantly.

"You ordered carpet for a room that was thirty-two and a half feet wide by thirty-eight feet long."

"I know I did. What's wrong with that?"

"What's wrong is that the room is thirty-four feet by just over forty-one feet," he said, almost sneering. "You guys think that you can measure low and we're gonna just let you off cause it's only a couple of feet?"

"I measured it myself with the same brand of laser

that you're using. Here I'll show you."

Mike grabbed his measure from where he'd left it on the bottom rung of the stairs. He stood against a side wall and pressed the button.

He looked at the led screen and saw it blink: 33.99. He tried it again, not believing the first reading. It said the same thing. He went to the next wall and took that reading.

41.1.

Mike looked at the installer in complete shock.

"I swear to you, the numbers I put down on your website were the numbers I saw yesterday."

"Sorry, mister, but I can only use today's measurement for the job. I've got enough carpet to cover the excess, but you know you have to pay double for the extra feet, right?"

Mike could only nod.

"Come out to the van and I'll ring you up. Once that's done, I can get started."

CHAPTER 31

Mike plopped down next to Lisa, who was watching Kevin play with his toy airplane on the grass.

"Everything all right?" she asked. "You look funky."

"It's nothing. The installer's kind of an asshole."

"What installer?" Lisa asked.

"Whoops," Mike laughed. "I almost gave it away."

"Honey," she said as she patted his hand. "The bright orange van from Paul's Discount Carpet, which by the way is leaking oil on our driveway, kind of blew the lid off the great mystery."

Mike was about to say something when *Spirit of the Radio* exploded from his phone.

It was Wayne, telling him that he was going to be in the area in a couple of hours. He wanted to drop off the Tupperware that Lisa had loaned them when she'd sent them home with enough goulash for another meal.

"Do you still have that drone you were telling me about a few weeks ago?" Mike asked, having a minor brainwave.

After Mike explained what he wanted it for, Wayne sounded excited at the prospect of using it for a real purpose instead of just annoying his neighbours.

Wayne agreed to bring it with him.

"Dare I ask?" Lisa said, doubting that any good could come from the two of them flying a drone around the neighbourhood.

Before Mike could answer, they both felt a cold draft sweep across the patio.

"In another few months, it'll turn into Siberia out here," Mike said.

"That's a bit of an exaggeration, don't you think?"

"Do you remember last January when it was so cold, we couldn't walk home? I distinctly remember your eloquent words when we ended up on Virginia Avenue and the wind was hitting us straight in the face. It was so poetic."

"What did I say?" Lisa asked.

"I think it was something about… oh yeah. You said 'Shit, even my snot's starting to freeze.'"

Lisa guffawed.

Though the sun was beating down and they could see heat shimmers rising above the lake, Lisa suddenly shivered.

"It's actually cold out here," she commented.

"I know. I'm thinking of putting on a sweatshirt."

Just then, Kevin's plane did a spectacular loop, crashing nose first into the grass resulting in one of its wings careening off in the other direction. Kevin just stood there and stared. Both parents were wondering if tears were imminent.

Mike got to his feet and stepped off the patio to collect the plane parts. The wing was about twenty feet from the house and as Mike bent to pick it up, he noticed something very strange.

He felt hot.

It had to be at least twenty degrees hotter than on the patio, yet there was no reason for it. The patio wasn't in the shade. They were sitting under the same sun, yet standing on the grass, he could feel its heat on his skin. He looked back at Lisa and saw that she'd grabbed her woollen throw from the back of the living room sofa and had it draped across her shoulders. She saw Mike watching her.

"I'm freezing," she called out.

Puzzled, Mike collected the main part of the aircraft and carried the two segments over to Kevin, who was still staring at the house.

"You okay, little man?"

Kevin didn't even seem to notice that his father was standing next to him.

"Kevin?" Mike said, his voice a little louder.

There was still no reaction. He reached out and felt Kevin's forehead. It was ice cold.

"What's going on?" Lisa shouted from the patio.

Mike stood directly in front of his son, blocking whatever he was staring at. Kevin still didn't seem to see him. Mike was about to give him a gentle shake when Kevin blinked twice, then looked directly at his father.

"Hi, Daddy," Kevin said in a subdued voice.

"Did you not see me all this time?" Mike asked.

Kevin shook his head.

By that point, Lisa had run over to the pair and was feeling his forehead.

"I just did that," Mike mentioned.

Lisa shot him a mini glare then carried on with what she was doing.

"Do you have a headache?" she asked.

Kevin nodded.

"Is it a bad one?" she asked.

"Not yet," he replied.

"But you think it might become a bad one?"

He nodded again.

Lisa was so focused on her son that she wasn't consciously aware that she'd pulled off the throw and was rolling up the sleeves of her shirt.

As they both looked on, tears began forming in the

corner of Kevin's eyes. One by one they ran down his face, pausing at the chin line as if summoning courage, then dropped to the ground.

"What's the matter?" Lisa said as she knelt in front of him.

He looked into her eyes and for the briefest second, Lisa was convinced she saw a flash of yellowy-orange flit across his eyes.

"They all died," Kevin said in a much lower register than was normal.

"Who died, Kev?" Mike asked.

Kevin looked confused as he looked over at him.

"You said they all died," Mike gently reminded him. "Who were you talking about?"

Kevin suddenly noticed the plane parts his dad was holding.

"Is it broken?" he asked with a slight tremble to his bottom lip.

"No, we can fix it," Mike assured him.

"Can we fix it now?" Kevin asked as he gently took the wing from his father's hand.

"Of course, we can."

As Mike and Kevin walked back to the house, Lisa kept re-seeing the flash of orange and yellow she'd seen reflected in her son's eyes. She knew it was just a trick of the light, yet she couldn't help feeling that it meant something, as if it was a reflection of what Kevin had been seeing.

Though it could have been just about anything, Lisa knew deep inside what she'd seen in his eyes.

She'd seen flames.

CHAPTER 32

The carpet installer finished the installation and asked Mike to sign off on the order. Mike followed him down the basement stairs and walked the length and breadth of the room hoping to find something wrong with the man's work. He had acquired an inexplicable need to get back at the guy over the whole mismeasuring mess. Even though it didn't appear to be the installer's fault, Mike wanted to have something to gripe at him about.

The carpet, however, looked great. Mike couldn't find anything wrong and signed a screen on the man's phone. Without another word said by either of them, the installer then grunted and exited the house.

Mike stood in the middle of the room and admired his completed project. He still had to do something about the dim lights, but apart from that, the space looked great.

"Can I see it now?" Lisa called from the hallway.

"Come on down," he shouted back.

Lisa's first reaction was to say, "Wow!"

Her second was to start laughing as she walked the perimeter of the basement. She kept touching the walls in amazement.

"Don't they look good?" Mike asked.

"How did you do it?"

"I skimmed a thin layer of plaster over every wall but did it roughly, leaving some bumps and swirl marks. Once it dried, I painted it matte white."

"It looks like the walls of an old English cottage," Lisa said. "It looks amazing."

"Sorry about the lighting," Mike shrugged.

"I was going to ask about that but was worried that it was intentional. That maybe you were trying to continue the old English theme."

"Nope," he replied. "I was actually going for bright and cheerful."

She laughed again. "The biggest surprise is how good the carpet looks. At the price you paid, I thought it was going to look cheap and nasty."

"How do you know what I paid?" Mike asked, stunned.

"Next time you buy something you don't want me to know about, don't do it from an account where we have a monitor alert for any unusual charges."

"I'll try and remember that. Next time I'll use one of our offshore accounts," Mike joked.

"Hello?" a voice called from upstairs.

"That sounds like Wayne," Lisa said as she headed for the stairs. "We're down here."

Wayne poked his head around the door frame.

"Nice job, boss," he said nodding his head approvingly.

"Come down and have a look," Mike suggested.

"I can see everything from here. I'm kind of in a rush. Barb wants me to pick up something she needs for dinner so I can't stay long."

"Do you have the drone?" Mike asked.

"I most certainly do."

They used the patio table as the launching site. Wayne's drone was not one of the professional ones that cost thousands. It was a mid-range consumer unit he'd found at Costco for fifty percent off. It was white and had four down-facing rotors.

As Wayne prepped the craft for take-off, he suddenly shivered.

"Why is your patio so cold? It's ninety degrees everywhere else."

"We think it's something to do with the used bricks and the proximity to the lake," Mike lied, making it up on the spot.

"You ready?" Wayne asked, ignoring Mike's lame explanation for the cold.

"Go for it."

Wayne tapped the start button on his iPad screen. The little rotors began to spin. With practiced skill, he moved his index finger across the screen and the drone rose above the table.

"See if you can get it right above the house so we can see all of our property at once," Mike requested.

"No problem," Wayne replied.

Sounding like a swarm of angry hornets, the drone rose quickly into the sky.

"Houston, we have a small problem," Wayne said as he squinted at the screen.

"Looks good to me," Mike commented.

"It's too bright out here for me see the video feed."

Mike joined him and looked down at the iPad. Sure enough, the flight controls were visible, but it was almost impossible to make out anything in the video window.

"What I'll do is fly around at a bunch of different heights and angles, then we can watch the recording later inside."

After about five minutes at higher levels, Wayne brought the craft down to about fifty feet from the roof and let it hover for a few seconds. As he brought it down for an even lower pass, its angry insect-like noise stopped abruptly and a red warning began flashing on the screen. As the two watched, the little craft fell like a stone, bounced off the roof (losing one rotor assembly), and almost got tangled up with the guttering before dropping down into one of the flower beds.

Mike and Wayne ran to the crash site.

"I've seen worse," Wayne said. "They're designed to come apart during a bad landing. We just need to find the missing rotor."

They found it about ten feet away under a dead rhododendron bush. Wayne carefully packed away the two parts of the vehicle while Mike turned on the TV in the living room. Wayne entered their wi-fi password into his iPad and mirrored the video to the big screen TV.

Four minutes into the six-minute video and they still hadn't been able to see anything unusual. One problem was that the day was so bright that all the higher angle shots looked washed out and made the detail appear murky.

It wasn't until the final, fateful pass at the lower level that they captured the footage that Mike had wanted. Though closer to the house, the wide-angle lens still managed to capture not just the house, but their entire piece of property as well.

Wayne paused the image and squinted at the TV screen.

"What the hell is that?"

Surrounding their house was an outline of

something. From the ground it was impossible to make out, but from the air, the yellowing grass and dying flowers revealed the footprint of something else.

"It looks like the outline of another building," Mike said.

"If that's what it is, or was, then it was a big one. It's at least double the size of your house."

"They found a concrete pad when they were installing the fibre," Mike advised. "I wonder if that's what we're seeing."

"I don't know, Mike," Wayne said. "But if I were you, I'd want to find out what was here before they built your house."

"Will that explain why our new landscaping is dying?" Mike asked.

Wayne shrugged.

"Keep playing the video," Mike asked.

They watched as the drone rotated in place and started to drop a little closer to the roof. Suddenly, when it was only about twenty feet from the top of the house, the camera view tipped violently, whirled around once, then went black.

Both men turned and faced each other.

"What was that?" Mike asked nervously.

"If I didn't know better, I'd say the drone hit something."

"But there was nothing there," Mike pointed out.

"I know, but it looks exactly like when I first got it and flew it too close to a tree. I couldn't see it on the video, but the result looked a lot like that." Wayne gestured with his head towards the TV.

"It might look the same, but there's nothing there for it to have run into."

Wayne took a deep breath.

"I gotta go," he said in little more than a whisper. "Barb's waiting."

"I'm not wrong, am I?" Mike asked. "There's definitely nothing there, is there?"

Wayne tried to find the right words to describe the thought that was starting to scramble his reasoning.

"Wayne, talk to me. There's nothing there, right?"

Wayne looked over at his boss and friend.

"There's nothing there," he concurred.

Mike visibly relaxed.

"At least nothing we can see," Wayne said, finishing his thought.

CHAPTER 33

Before leaving, Wayne sent a copy of the video to Mike so that he could show it to Lisa, as she'd missed the viewing.

"Is he still sleeping?" Mike asked as Lisa joined him in the family room.

"Yes, but I can tell from just looking at him that it's going to be a bad one."

"Poor little guy. Did you give him anything?"

"I don't want to start medicating him just because I think he *may* be getting a headache. That sounds like a bad routine to get into. That nose spray is strong stuff. I only want to use it when it's essential."

"If he does get a bad one, it would kind of disprove Nigel's theory about it being his mind's reaction to there being a spirit force nearby. We know that Sebastian is gone, and the house is brand new, so..."

"What if there is still something in the house?" Lisa asked.

"Like what?"

"What if all the little things that we've felt or seen, including the stuff that you experienced, and I put down to stress… What if they were an indication that something is still here?"

"Nigel checked out the whole house and once Sebastian was gone, he said we were spirit-free," Mike replied. "I'll tell you what, if anything else happens, I'll give him a call and ask him to come back out."

"I have a better idea," Lisa said. "I don't want him to think of us as one of those couples who picks up the phone every time they see a shadow, or hear a thump in the night…"

"We did have a thump in the night and it damaged part of the house," Mike reminded her.

"Good point. But I still don't want him to think we're crying wolf. So, what about inviting Nigel and his wife to dinner. We won't even mention our concerns and see if he brings up the subject. I would like to think that if he felt a new presence, he'd say something."

"That sounds like a plan," Mike agreed.

"How did your screening go with Wayne?"

"Want to see it? He gave us our own copy."

"Was there anything to see?"

"I'll let you be the judge," Mike said as he reached for his iPad. "I'm going to fast forward to the last bit of the video. The earlier stuff didn't come out well."

"Why?" she asked.

"It was the footage shot from the higher altitudes. For some reason the sunshine messed with the camera. Everything looked like it was shot through a fog."

Mike started the playback four minutes in. Lisa immediately saw the pattern that the dying vegetation revealed.

"Am I losing it, or does that look like the footprint of a bigger building surrounding our house?"

"You tell me," Mike replied.

"Damn it!" Lisa said. "I bet that's the concrete slab that nobody seems to know about. I even asked whether it could be a problem for the landscaping and was told that it wouldn't have any impact." She pointed at the screen. "I'd say that's quite an impact, wouldn't you?"

"Want to see the rest?"

"Sure."

Mike played through the part where the drone went goofy, and the picture stopped.

"That's the part that freaked Wayne out," Mike advised.

"Why? It's pretty obvious what happened."

Mike looked at her with a questioning stare.

"It must have hit a bird, or a bird hit it," she stated, as if it was blindingly obvious. "Considering the god-awful noise it makes, I'm not in the least bit surprised that something attacked it, are you?"

"I should call Wayne and give him your theory," Mike said.

"Let me have the iPad. I want to see the video from the beginning."

Mike left the room so he could make a call and not disturb Lisa's viewing pleasure. Wayne answered on the second ring. His voice still sounded stressed. Mike gave him Lisa's theory. There was silence on the line, then he heard Wayne sigh.

"That actually makes sense."

"I know, right," Mike said. "Lisa always puts things into a rational context."

"What a nerve," Wayne said, laughing. "I'm glad you called and shared. I have no idea why that footage got under my skin, but it did."

"I'll pass on your thanks to Lisa."

Mike disconnected the call then returned to the family room.

Lisa had frozen the image and was staring up at Mike with a look he'd never seen on her before. She appeared to be well and truly scared.

"What did you see?" Mike asked as he sat beside her.

"Did you look at the earlier part of the video?"

"Not really. As I said, it looked all blown out, so we went right to the part that was clear."

Lisa reversed the video to a shot that was taken at the highest altitude – probably about a hundred feet above the house. The image was blown out and almost looked as if there was a white mist between the drone and the ground.

"It's too messed up," Mike said. "That's why we…"

"Wait," Lisa said, her voice overly intense.

Mike was about to ask what he was supposed to be waiting for when he saw something. Even through the white filter, he could see, beyond the perimeter of the dying lawn, two dark, shadowy objects move into frame. It was impossible to discern what they were, especially when shot from directly overhead, but there was something about the way the two dark blurs were moving that made him feel that he was watching people.

He was about to say something when Lisa held up her index finger. It was her signal for him to shut up and look at the screen.

They both watched as the two objects approached the footprint of the buried concrete slab, then seemed to come to a stop, inches away from the yellow grass. One of them appeared to reach for something then stood aside. The other shadow moved forward and vanished. The other figure followed, then it too disappeared.

"Play that again," Mike said as icy tendrils began

crawling up his spine.

Lisa played the same segment as the two watched in silence.

"If we assume they're people," Lisa said. "It almost looks as if one of them lets the other go first."

"What, like through a door?" Mike asked. "No. That's not possible. Whatever we're looking at disappeared over twenty feet from the patio. Wayne and I were on the patio while this was being shot and we didn't see a thing."

"Did you notice how they disappeared the moment they reach the beginning of where the grass is dying?" Lisa asked. "What the hell is that about?"

A thought sprinted through Mike's head, but he refused to take hold of it.

"You have an idea, don't you?"

Mike decided that she had a right to share in his ludicrous pondering.

"It looks as if..." he hesitated.

"Go on."

"If we take a huge leap of incredulity, it could almost look like two people walking into a building."

Lisa's mouth suddenly went dry.

"I don't understand. There is no building. They just disappear."

"What if that footprint is where a building used to be?" Mike asked.

"Then that would make what we're seeing…" She left the sentence unfinished.

"Exactly!"

"Maybe we should call Nigel sooner rather than later?" Lisa suggested.

Before either of them could say anything else, the house was filled with a loud yowling.

Mike jumped to his feet and tried to work out where it was coming from. He tracked it to the basement. By the insipid glow from the dim overheads, he saw Samantha, her hair on end and her tail three times the size, standing in the centre of the room. On top of the yowling, the cat was spitting and hissing at something that only she could see. As Mike looked on, she got into her sideways attack stance and took a swipe at nothing but air.

Then, as if something pushed her aside, she rolled across the carpet, got back on her feet and streaked up the stairs, passing Mike at full tilt.

"You may want to call him right now," Mike shouted to Lisa.

"Way ahead of you," Lisa replied, having just seen Samantha tear past at breakneck speed.

"Mommy," Kevin cried from upstairs. "My room's cold."

"What fresh hell is this?" Lisa mumbled to herself as she headed upstairs.

Mike caught up with her on the stairs and the two of them entered their son's room together.

It was freezing.

Kevin was under his summer blanket, which was no match for the frigid temperature in the room. The child's breath was forming into small, expelled clouds of condensation.

"I'll get some more blankets," Lisa said. "Find out where the cold air is coming from."

Mike checked the windows, but though open, there was no draft coming through them. He moved under the ceiling vent and was stunned to feel icy air blasting out of the opening. He couldn't fathom how that was possible as the system, even at full fan setting, only pushed gentle wafts of air into the room. What he was feeling was like a car air conditioner turned up full.

As a temporary stopgap until he could work out what was going on with the system, Mike adjusted the angle of the vent blades so the air flow was restricted. Just as he finished forcing the finicky adjustment lever, he heard Lisa gasp from just outside the room.

Mike joined her in the hallway and looked at what she was staring at within the linen closet. The neatly arranged shelves that held their towels and bed linen were all hanging askew, having dumped their sheets, blankets, and towels unceremoniously onto the floor.

Mike used his phone's flashlight to check out why

the shelves had partially collapsed. He found that they all appeared to have been cut too short. Mike couldn't see how they'd ever managed to sit atop the support mounts that protruded from the side walls. The other anomaly was that he couldn't understand why the shelves were so narrow, considering how deep the space was.

After helping Lisa sort out the jumbled pile on the floor then getting Kevin snuggled under a couple of heavy blankets, Mike grabbed his phone so he could call Nigel.

"I take it Walter still hasn't called you back?" Mike asked as he looked up Nigel's contact information on his iPhone.

"No. I've been leaving messages for days. It's as if he's intentionally ignoring me."

"I'll walk over to the office and if he's not there, I'll leave a note."

Lisa was about to make a comment when Mike signalled that Nigel was on the line.

"Nigel," Mike tried to sound upbeat and casual. "It's Mike Ellis."

After some generic pleasantries, Mike got to the point of the call.

"We were wondering if you and Trish would like to

come over for dinner one night?"

Much to Mike's relief, Nigel advised that they had been thinking of asking him and Lisa over to their house.

"Let me ask Lisa," Mike said as he looked over at her.

"Tomorrow?" he mouthed silently.

She nodded.

"I know it's short notice but what about tomorrow?" Mike asked. "I could barbeque some steaks."

A couple of seconds later, Mike gave her a thumbs-up.

Only moments after speaking with Nigel, they both heard Kevin calling from upstairs.

"Mommy... it's too hot in here."

They both headed upstairs and were shocked to find that their son's room was now tropically hot. As Lisa freed Kevin from the layers of blankets, Mike stood under the vent. Sure enough, hot air was blowing into the room. Hard. As if the change in temperature wasn't weird enough, Mike immediately saw that the vent blades were back in the fully open position, presumably, Mike hoped, because of the force of the air flow.

While Lisa tended to Kevin, Mike went downstairs to check the thermostat. He saw that the temperature was set at seventy-two degrees and that the fan was set on automatic.

Mike's next stop was the garage so he could see what the furnace was up to. He was by no means an expert on HVAC within the home, but he knew the basic principles of heating and air conditioning. That said, he couldn't even begin to understand how hot air was pumping into one room only, especially as the furnace was, at that moment, off.

Mike stepped back into the house and as an experiment, set the thermostat to eighty degrees. By the time he returned to the garage, the furnace had been activated and was rumbling away exactly as it should.

"We have to get a hold of Walter," Mike announced as he walked into Kevin's room.

"I just told you that I can't seem to reach him."

"Then let's move Kevin into the guest room until we can get Walter to sort out the HVAC problem."

"I think we need to give him the medication," Lisa said, clearly upset. "The headache's getting worse, and that heat hasn't helped at all."

They moved Kevin, together with a few of his favourite toys, into the guest room just down the hall. Lisa then had him sit up in bed as she broke the seal on a single-use nose spray applicator. Lisa gently placed the tip of the device just inside one of his nostrils then told him to hold the other one with a finger.

"Do I have to have the medicine, Mommy?" he

asked. "It runs down my throat and tastes yucky."

"I know, babe, but it also makes you feel better," she replied. "You ready?"

"Yes."

"Okay, we want a big breath in through your nose in… 3… 2… 1… now."

Lisa pressed the plunger. There was an audible click as the unit ejected its medicinal cargo.

"You all right?" she asked him.

He nodded his head then suddenly cringed.

"Eww! It tastes so bad."

"Want me to get you a juice so the taste goes away?" Mike offered.

Kevin nodded. "Can I have grape?"

"Of course," Mike answered.

Once Kevin was tucked snuggly into the guest bed Mike went back to Kevin's regular bedroom to try and work out where the heat was coming from.

His task was made impossible as the room was back to feeling normal and there was no air being pushed through the vent.

Mike decided that while he was there and Kevin was using the room down the hall, it was the perfect time for him to patch the crack on his closet wall. He lifted out all of Kevin's hanging clothes in one smooth move from the closet to his bed. Once he had clear access to the wall, he was stunned to see the full extent of the damage. The crack looked about the same as when they'd first seen it but now appeared to have minute tributary fissures that spread out in every direction.

Mike decided that the job was beyond the scope of simple spackle. Thankfully, he just happened to have a third of a bucket of premixed plaster left over from the basement makeover. An hour later, Mike was standing back admiring his work when Lisa walked into the room.

"Not bad," she said, nodding. "I take it that the old English cottage look is the only choice?"

"It is if you want me to do it," he replied, giving her a raised eyebrow. "How's he doing?"

"He's sleeping. The headache seems to be getting a little better and he dozed off while I was reading *Lucy* to him."

"*Lucy*? The movie with Scarlett Johansson?"

"No, you goofball. It's a lovely book about a dognapped golden retriever who manages to escape with his other dog friends."

"Sounds good," Mike said.

"It is. You can read it after Kevin and I are finished."

*

After a wonderful dinner of blackened shrimp linguini, Lisa and Mike watched a little TV then decided on an early night. It had been quite a day, and both were mentally exhausted.

"You don't seem particularly freaked out by that drone video we watched earlier," Mike said, before sleep took complete hold on him.

"I'm not. You know how pragmatic I am," Lisa said. "We have no idea what we saw on the screen. We recognised what we thought were people because of our predisposition to find recognisable shapes within anything we look at. It's called pareidolia. It's why we can find faces in almost any complex pattern."

"So, what do you think we did see?" Mike asked.

"I have no idea, and until I do, I have no intention of letting it get into my head. I've got enough worries as it is and just want to get to sleep and forget about everything."

"That's a shame," Mike said.

"Why's that a shame?"

"I was hoping we could both forget everything else together," he said as he nuzzled her neck.

Mike distinctly heard her make a mewling sound.

"Like that, huh?" he asked.

"That wasn't me," Lisa replied, laughing. "Samantha's under the bed. She's been hiding there all afternoon."

"Now I feel self-conscious," he whispered.

"No reason to. If she's comfortable licking her butt

in front of us, we shouldn't feel weird about having sex
in front of her."

CHAPTER 35

As was their Sunday tradition, Mike got up before Lisa so she could get a little extra sleep. He first checked on Kevin who, though seemingly having done serious battle with his bedclothes at some point during the night, was fast asleep in a foetal curl. Mike felt his forehead and was delighted to find it cool to the touch. The miracle nose spray had saved the day, yet again.

Mike made his way downstairs and got coffee started. He microwaved a bowl of oatmeal, added toasted almonds, blueberries, honey, and a dollop of cream (Lisa being asleep was the only way he could get away with not using almond milk). He took the bowl with him to the basement. He wanted to work out what exactly to turn it into now that the room was finished.

Mike heaped a large spoonful of oats into his mouth then switched on the lights. Even by their dim glow, he could tell that something was wrong. It took a few moments for his sleepy brain to recognise what had changed.

There was a visible gap between the carpet and the wall. Not just in one spot; the gap ran the whole way around the room. Mike almost choked on the porridge, such was his shock at seeing the state of the new floor covering.

He couldn't work out what he was seeing. There were no jagged edges or signs of rending where the carpet ended. Mike placed his bowl on the stairs and walked to the nearest wall. He felt the edge of the carpet and it struck him that it was still firmly attached to the grip board that the installer had glued to the concrete.

For some reason, Mike's first thought was that somehow, the installer had done something wrong and caused the carpet to shrink overnight.

Then an alternative option snuck into his head, one that caused goosebumps to sprout on his bare arms. What if the guy had snuck into the house and had cut the carpet while everyone else was sound asleep as revenge for Mike's perceived attitude?

Mike measured the carpet and found that it was exactly the size that the installer had told him the previous day. As an icy chill bloomed from within his guts, Mike then measured the exact distance from the wall to the edge of the carpet.

It was just over two inches wide. Mike grabbed his porridge bowl, climbed up the stairs then locked the basement door from the outside.

He knew he should tell Lisa but decided not to mention the shrinking carpet (or expanding walls) until Mike had seen Nigel's reaction to the house.

As he returned to the kitchen, Mike smiled at the weird irony of the situation. People spend thousands of dollars just so they can enlarge their home. Yet here they were in a house where it was happening for free. The problem was that they had no control over the remodel, and it was starting to scare the shit out of him.

Once Lisa was awake, and after she had Kevin up and fed, she went into full dinner party mode. Even with Mike assigned to be the primary chef, she still insisted on making enough side dishes to feed the whole estate.

By the time Nigel and Trish arrived, the Ellis family were showered, dressed in their casual barbeque best, and were looking forward to some fine food and interesting conversation. As it was a barbeque versus a formal sit-down dinner, Kevin got to eat with the adults. Any talk of spirits, except for the fermented kind, would have to wait until the little man had retired for the night.

When Mike and Lisa had visited Nigel's home, they'd had almost no opportunity to talk with Trish. They were surprised to find that she had a PhD in abnormal psychology. Despite that serious grounding, she had a sharp and cynical sense of humour.

Though any mention of strange goings on with the house were stalled until later, the adults got a creepy little 'amuse bouche' before the meal was even served.

Mike didn't believe in propane barbeques and swore by his trusty Weber kettle that had been with them for years. He was also dead against using charcoal lighting fluids or bricks. He felt they left an aftertaste of something resembling jet fuel. Instead, Mike used an electric charcoal starter.

While the others sat watching him prep from the patio, Mike waited until the briquettes had a layer of white ash on them before he removed the electric starter. Once the coals had lost most of their furnace-like heat, he placed four steaks on the grill with the intention of adding a couple of hot dogs for Kevin a few minutes later.

For a moment the air was filled with the sound of sizzling meat and the smell of his 'secret' dry rub. Then, as he was about to brag about his barbequing prowess, a look of shock found its way onto the others' faces.

Mike turned back to the Weber and saw what he later could only describe as a funeral pyre rising into the evening sky. There was a yellow flame that looked like it should have been coming from the underside of one of Elon Musk's rockets as it jetted straight up out of the kettle barbeque.

Trish made some comment about wanting the name of the charcoal he used before humour was overtaken by the seriousness of the situation. The flames were so intense that it began melting the underside of the Weber. Lisa screamed for him to put the top on the barbeque to smother the fire.

Mike looked at her as if she was insane.

"Does that look like it can be smothered?" he snapped back.

Things got more frantic as they noticed that the top of the fire seemed to be curving towards the house. The area Mike had deemed safe for outdoor cooking was a good ten feet from the building, however the flames seemed to be trying to reach out for it anyway.

While the men fired possible solutions at each other, Lisa walked over to the barbeque and kicked it over, sending flaming coals streaming out onto the new lawn. Before anyone could even compute what she'd done, Lisa turned on the garden hose and pointed it at the flaming debris.

The group watched, riveted as one by one, the coals lost their fiery mantle and turned white. The last thing to stop burning was the nearest steak. For some reason, a small flame managed to persist at one charred end of the piece of meat, then, with a final sizzle and a whistle of white-hot steam, the blackened sirloin gave up the fight.

"That one's mine," Trish said, with feigned calm.

"While I make some mac and cheese for Kevin," Lisa said to Mike. "Why don't you go online and get Uber Eats to pick us up some chicken."

As soon as Lisa had steered Kevin into the house with her, Nigel looked over at Mike.

"Something tells me that our being here is not solely a social thing."

"What gave it away?" Mike replied.

*

Mike booked the food delivery, then, while Kevin was still inside, explained what had been going on within their home. He started with his original supposed hallucination of a basement fire and finished with the expanding basement and obviously the spectacular barbeque fire show.

"We weren't going to say anything, hoping that you would sense something out of the ordinary," Mike explained.

"I sensed something as soon as we stepped out of the car, but I have to tell you, I don't know what it is," Nigel said. "I feel a force, almost like a vibration as if the whole place is humming. I've never encountered anything like it in my life. The weirdest thing is that I'm not sensing any particular spirit presence. I'm also not feeling any of the emotions that I would have expected around a displaced entity. Trish, what do you think?"

Neither had been looking at Trish and were stunned to see tears rolling down her cheeks.

"What's the matter, honey?" Nigel said as he sat next to her and took her arm.

"I don't know what I'm feeling," Trish replied. "I can't explain it. I suddenly feel... loss. Great, unresolved loss."

Trish excused herself to use the powder room.

"While Lisa's in the kitchen with Kevin, may I show you the basement? I can't help feeling that whatever is happening here has something to do with that room."

Nigel followed Mike to the basement door. He unlocked it then swung it open.

Nobody spoke until they reached the bottom of the stairs and Mike reached for the wire-loop switch.

"I thought you said there was about a two-inch clearance from the edge of the carpet to the wall?" Nigel questioned.

Mike wasn't sure how to answer. Since being in the room earlier that day, it had grown even bigger. The gap between carpet and wall looked closer to three or four inches. The already dim light hardly even reached the new position of the walls.

"What's this?" Nigel asked from the centre of the room. He was pointing down at a dark smudge on the new carpeting.

Mike kneeled and touched it. "It's warm," he said as he withdrew his fingers.

Nigel grabbed Mike's hand and studied it. It was covered in a black powdery substance. Nigel rubbed his index finger on the floor, then smelled it.

"It's ash. It's as if there'd been a fire here. Is this where you found the remains of the fire the first time?" Nigel asked.

Mike could only nod.

"Food's here," Lisa called from upstairs, interrupting the myriad of thoughts that were bouncing around inside their heads.

*

Mike discovered an important food fact that night. If you add Lisa's incredibly prepared side dishes to a bucket of extra crispy Colonel Sanders, you get a meal that's as close to perfection as most folks were ever going to get.

Somehow, his eleven herbs and spices made the Colonel's chicken meld perfectly with Lisa's sweetcorn salsa, red potato and spring onion salad; her version of a Greek salad (adding avocado), and fresh sourdough garlic bread.

Just as Lisa was serving her special ginger and pecan pie, the ground beneath them shook. It was brief, but it was enough to cause one of the roof gutters to come loose, emptying its contents onto the far end of the patio.

At first it was just a bunch of leaves and dried twigs, but then after bouncing along the plastic guttering, a dead crow fell out with a sickening plop.

Mike assumed that it must have died recently. It looked almost normal if it weren't for the fact that its head was turned almost completely around the wrong way.

Trish held up her wine glass in a toast. "To Lisa, Mike, and Kevin. I like eating here. Your house is fun."

She then downed her almost full glass of Merlot in one long gulp.

After dinner was cleared away and the dead bird was given a quick burial in one of the flower beds, Kevin was tucked into bed for the night. All semblance of normal conversation filtered away with the last vestiges of the dusk light.

"Before we start to discuss our situation," Mike began. "I think there's something else you should see."

Mike led them inside and powered up the big TV screen in the living room, then played the drone video.

"The image at the beginning is blown out by what we had initially thought was the sun, but Lisa persevered and found something a little unusual."

Mike started the video and both he and Lisa kept silent while the footage rolled through. They both wanted to get their guests' impression of what was happening at ground level.

"Stop it there," Trish said, just as the dark forms first appeared on screen.

"What are those?" she asked.

"We were hoping that you could tell us," Lisa said.

Nigel and Trish both kneeled close to the screen and stared at the image.

"Okay," Trish said. "Keep playing it."

They all watched the two dark shapes approach the start of the yellow lawn, then disappear.

"Before you say anything," Mike advised. "I want to show you the other footage that gives a much clearer idea as to the shape of whatever it is that we seem to be living on top of."

Mike advanced the video.

"Freeze that, please," Nigel requested.

With the image paused, they could easily make out the exact shape of the subterranean object by the death of the flora and lawn above it.

"That looks like the footprint of a much bigger house," Nigel observed.

"It looks to me that they built your home right on top of another foundation," Trish observed.

"So, what does that tell us?" Lisa jumped in. "Does that explain what's been happening to our house?"

"I wish I could say yes," Nigel replied. "But the fact is that we have no idea what that building was and why it should be having any effect on anything."

Nigel paused to get his thoughts in order.

"I know that this is going to be a really stupid

question, but are we sure that the changes to your house aren't simply the result of slippage or the building settling?"

"I'll accept that could be possible in the bedroom and closet, but the expanding basement doesn't fit that scenario at all. It's not settling; it's expanding. Plus, what about that burn mark?"

"I was wondering about that," Nigel said. "The point where that seems to have happened is directly under the antique wiring that you split to get power to the other two fittings. It's obvious by the low wattage that's coming out of those lights that the wiring is funky. What if there was sparking at the join that caused something hot to land on the carpet and char a section of it?"

"But what about the ash I found before I even worked on the basement?" Mike asked.

"Wasn't it the same wiring that's above that same spot?" Nigel asked.

Mike simply shrugged.

"I think you may have a wiring problem, not a spirit issue. From what you told me, it was very old. What amperage is the breaker it's fed from?"

"I couldn't find any breaker that feeds that room," Mike admitted. "In fact, I switched off all the mains, yet the light in the basement stayed on."

"Not wanting to make light of your situation..." Nigel

paused momentarily to see if anyone got his pun. "But you seem to have rooms that are getting bigger and free electricity. I'm not exactly sure that you should be questioning it."

"What about the figures that seemed to walk into the perimeter of the original building?" Lisa asked.

"I'm not sure that's what we saw at all," Nigel stated. "If you'd told me that you were being plagued by visible, malevolent spirits roaming the house, then those images could have been an indication of some sort of presence. However, I think that what we all saw on that video was what is referred to as a plasmatic echo. When we were sitting outside, I took the liberty of taking a few readings with my EMF flow meter. For some reason, the electromagnetic energy around the exterior of your house is quite a bit higher than normal. Usually, such readings are the result of charged magnetic material in the ground.

"I think that the heightened energy reading, plus the high-end drone camera, which I suspect uses ultraviolet filtration, was able to pick up what is basically an electro-plasmatic echo from people who lived here at some time in the past."

Mike gave him a doubting look.

"We are all made up of energy, and though we are completely unaware of it, we leave traces of it behind wherever we go. I think that whatever is generating the electromagnetic field is acting like an invisible energy recorder. Nobody would ever have seen the playback from that energy loop had it not been for the filtration matrix of the camera."

"Is anything you just said even possible?" Lisa asked.

"Completely," Nigel replied. "The research isn't even relegated to the supernatural study units anymore. This is becoming a whole new science that will, over the next ten years or so, change our perception of ghosts and spirits."

"Are you saying it proves that there are, in fact, ghosts?" Mike asked, amazed.

"Exactly the opposite. What they're now able to prove is the existence of electromagnetic images that, under the right circumstances, can be captured on video."

"So, they are ghosts!" Lisa insisted.

"No, they're not," Nigel patiently explained. "These are images of living people whose electrical field was somehow captured and stored while they were very much alive. What we are seeing is not a haunting by spirits of the dead. We are looking at an electronic playback of living people just going about their business."

"So those figures walking into that building...?" Lisa asked.

"They were living people that, unbeknown to them,

had their electrical energy recorded within the electromagnetic field."

"Jesus," Lisa said, shaking her head. "So, does that mean we are haunted or not?"

"It most likely means that the video has nothing to do with anything else that's going on here."

"What about the hot and cold temperature in Kevin's room?" Lisa asked.

"And the linen closet that seems to have gotten bigger?" Mike added.

"I believe that all of those things can be explained, though I would like to come out here tomorrow and take some readings just to be certain," Nigel said. "I think that the foundation of a previous building is still in place and is doubtless what is responsible for the dying plants and lawn. I also believe that the basement was part of the original structure, hence the electrical problems.

"As far as the phantom earthquake, I put that down to settling. It is a brand-new house and settling happens. Even though it appears to have been built on top of an older, existing foundation, who's to say how well that was laid. The settling would almost certainly have caused the ceiling crack, the one in Kevin's wardrobe, and the collapsed shelving in the linen closet. The hot and cold air sounds to me like teething problems within the HVAC system, especially as it's brand new."

"Okay, say I buy all that," Mike said. "How do you explain the walls moving in the basement and the cremation that occurred in the barbeque earlier?"

"When did you last clean the Weber?" Nigel asked.

"About a week ago."

"Did you deep clean the kettle or just the grill?"

"What does cleaning the barbeque have to do with...?" Mike interrupted.

"Humour me... please."

"I just cleaned the grill," Mike admitted.

"When did you last deep clean the bottom of the kettle?" Nigel asked.

Mike shrugged.

"Oh, babe," Lisa said, a little shocked that her husband had been remiss at keeping his barbeque clean.

"I gave it a good hosing!" he declared.

"How did you dry it?"

"I left it out in the sun," Mike said, just a tad defensively.

"Where did you leave it to dry?" Nigel kept on pushing.

"Over there." Mike pointed out the window to a flat spot in the middle of the lawn. "The grass wasn't there when I did it."

"It's a little hard to tell as it's getting dark, but it

looks as if there's a substantial pine tree that overhangs that part of your property."

"There is," Lisa said, intrigued to know where Nigel was heading.

"I don't mean to sound too much like the science guy, but I think that your barbeque probably had a decent layer of burnt-on drippings within the kettle. That's perfectly normal and bound to happen. The fact that you don't clean that part regularly means that the layers just kept compounding and formed a second skin within the base. This time of year, pine trees literally ooze sap. It's nasty stuff, it's sticky, and unfortunately, highly flammable. I think that when you left the kettle under the pine tree, sap dropped into it and coated the burnt-on fat that was already there. When you got the coals nice and hot, the heat eventually ignited the sap, which in turn acted as an accelerant for the fatty coating. We all saw the results."

Mike could sense Lisa glaring at him.

"You almost burned down the house because you couldn't be bothered to clean the barbeque?" she said in disbelief.

"No!" Mike replied.

"What does 'no' mean?" Lisa asked, shaking her head.

"I watched a podcast back in LA about Southern barbeque. The host, who's considered to make the best ribs and brisket in the country, said that one of his tricks was to never clean the bottom of the cooking drum. The smoke from the old dripping apparently adds a depth of flavour to the meat."

"Oh, my sweet lord," Lisa said, looking up to the ceiling. "I've done married me a simpleton!"

"That still leaves the basement," Mike reminded him. "I can't think of any rational reason for the room to be expanding. Can you?"

"No, I can't," Nigel answered. "I was thinking about the burned carpet in the middle of the room. When synthetics are heated, they contract. I wonder if the charred spot in the middle could have pulled the edges inwards. That's one possibility. Another is that your bad-tempered installer skimped on carpet and overstretched it so that it reached the wall without cutting to fit the new measurements. Over the course of a day, the tension became too much for the nail strip and you got your gap. The fact that it seems to be getting bigger makes perfect sense as the carpet slowly goes back to its true, smaller size."

"But, what about the…?" Mike tried to ask.

"Another possibility is that your basement walls are slightly bowed inwards. If you measured the wall halfway up it showed as being a few inches smaller than at the base."

"I measured the floor," Mike stated emphatically.

"And it is definitely getting wider."

"I believe you," Nigel replied. "We're just theorising here. Unfortunately, over ninety-five percent of my time is spent having to find a rational reason for what customers believe is a haunting. You'd be amazed at how many things can go bump in the night that have nothing to do with spirits."

"And the other five percent?" Lisa asked.

"They're either real, or I can't find a reason for what's occurred."

"How do you tell which is which?"

"That's easy," Nigel said, beaming. "If they're real, they'll tell me."

"The client tells you?" Mike asked.

"No. The spirits do."

CHAPTER 37

The next day, Lisa was out doing a quick shop at Wegman's on the way back from dropping Kevin off at school. Mike was at the back of the house picking up what was left of his Weber and the other detritus that was strewn across their lawn. What was especially frustrating to Mike was that most of the fire damage was to the part of the lawn that wasn't already dying.

"Barbequing is a dangerous job," Nigel said as he walked around from the front of the house. "I rang the doorbell then heard you out here."

Mike checked his watch.

"Am I early?" Nigel asked, concerned.

"Actually no," Mike answered. "I seem to be running late."

"No harm."

"Did you bring all your ghost-busting gadgets?"

Nigel tilted his head to one side in a show of disappointment.

"I hope that's not what you really think I do?"

"Of course not," Mike said. "That was a dumb thing to say, especially to someone who's here to help us. Can I make up for it with a cup of coffee?"

"It was a big insult, so it better be a damn good cup." Nigel grinned.

After coffee, Nigel grabbed an aluminium-framed road case from the trunk of his car and began assembling various meters and sensing probes.

"All this stuff is for confirming the presence of spirits?" Mike asked, amazed. "I would never have guessed that there was enough money in that to warrant what it must have cost to develop all this equipment."

"Most of this is pre-existing scientific test equipment that was originally designed for something other than what I use it for."

Nigel pointed to a squat black box with an orange dial and numerous knobs and switches.

"The technology in this little baby came from SETI," Nigel advised. "It was designed to sweep space for any variations in radio frequencies."

Nigel could almost see Mike's eyes glaze over.

"If we send out radio waves that are set at a particular frequency, then light years later hear that same transmission come back but with a change in frequency, we know that something out there has caused it to shift."

"Wow," Mike responded. "That's cool, but how does that help you find something local. Surely spirits don't sit around changing radio frequencies?"

"You're absolutely right. They don't. This device has been modified from the SETI technology and sends out a multi-frequency sweep of white noise. It's believed that some entities are able to garner energy from the signal and use it to communicate."

"They talk through your radio?" Mike asked.

"No." Nigel smiled. "If they do interact, I would see an interruption in one particular frequency, but that's about it. All this equipment lets us know is that something is there. We're a long way from being able to record voices and even further from capturing a clear image on a camera."

"It seems to me that you are able to sense and communicate with a spirit without any of this stuff," Mike replied.

"Usually, yes, but in cases like yours, where neither Trish nor I can get a good sense of who or what is sharing your house, a little science can sometimes make all the difference. Besides, everything I have brought today can work remotely. If you don't mind sharing your wi-fi password, I can monitor everything from my home."

"No problem, remind me and I'll give it to you when

you're ready to leave."

"Before I give the whole place a sweep, I have to ask you the same thing I ask all my clients," Nigel said, his voice unusually serious. "If I were to find something here, something that was more than a simple haunting…"

"Like Sebastian?" Mike asked.

"Like Sebastian," Nigel agreed. "If it's something darker and less simple to relocate, how would that impact you and your family's willingness to continue living in the house?"

"That's a question I never thought I'd be asked… or would have to answer. I'd have to talk with Lisa to find out…"

"Talk with me about what?" Lisa said as she appeared from the kitchen. "What have you done now?"

"Nigel, would you mind asking Lisa the same question."

"I am about to take measurements, and if needed, use myself as a conduit with whatever may be in your home. I asked Mike whether my findings could change your perception of the house and whether you'd even be willing to remain here."

"That's a big question for this early in the morning," she replied. "Mike, what did you answer?"

"I waited for you. I felt that this was too big a

question for the answer not to come from both of us."

"I have a question for you, Nigel," Lisa said. "Why are you asking that now? When we first spoke to you about the dead builder, you didn't ask it then."

"Good point," Nigel said. "Sebastian was a newly deceased entity and most likely felt no animosity towards you or any member of your family. In fact, from what you'd initially told me, he'd already spoken to Kevin and from what I could tell, was simply confused and needed a gentle push in the right direction."

"So, why don't you think that whatever is here now just needs the same little push?" she asked.

"First of all, I have no idea if there even is an entity within your property. There is certainly a sensation that vibrates throughout your home, but that tells me nothing. It could be part of a vortex of some sort."

"Like in Sedona?" Mike asked.

"Exactly," Nigel replied. "It's possible that's what I'm sensing, but until I dig a little deeper, I won't know. I just want to make it clear that if I do a full-on evaluation and do find a presence, you must be prepared for it to be something far more entrenched than poor Sebastian. If there is an entity here, I doubt that it's the result of a recent passing. It could relate to whatever building used to sit on this spot or even to occurrences going back tens, hundreds, or even thousands of years."

"Occurrences?" Lisa said, raising her eyebrows.

"People seem to think that hauntings are based on relatively recent passings. That doesn't have to be the case at all. All the land around this part of Virginia has borne witness to unspeakable atrocities over time. This was Civil War country and before that it was Indian land. A great deal of blood has been spilled over time. It's not beyond the realms of possibility that, leftover from some horrific battle, one lone soul is still trying to find its way into the light."

Mike and Lisa were both staring wide-eyed back at him.

"That said," Nigel added. "I might find nothing at all, in which case my earlier question is moot. I just want the two of you to be prepared just in case."

"I would like to think that we would be able to see past whatever you find, so long as you're able to send it on its way," Lisa said. "At no time have I felt any strange sensations or negative vibrations, within the house. It's brand new and it's what we've dreamed of for as long as I can remember. The house couldn't have a dark history, only the land itself. If you can fix that, we're good to stay here."

Lisa turned to Mike to make sure he agreed with her statement.

He did.

"Good," Nigel said. "I'll get started. Is it all right if I walk through the house? I want to check everywhere. When I've done that, if I haven't stumbled across the source of the problem, we can talk about the best locations for me to leave my equipment. The sensors will have to be high enough to be out of Kevin's reach and ideally somewhere where the cat can't get at them."

"I take it we're going to have some new equipment around the house?" Lisa asked.

"Sorry, babe," Mike gave her hand a squeeze. "I forgot to tell you that Nigel is going to be able to remotely monitor everything that goes on in the house."

"With video cameras?" Lisa asked, shocked. "Like in *Paranormal Activity*?"

"You can relax," Nigel assured her. "There won't be any video cameras. I will be putting up thermal imaging devices, but I won't need to put those anywhere inappropriate. Besides, most of the data will come from electromagnetic sensors, temperature gradient monitors, and white noise frequency disruption sensors. It's only for twenty-four hours, but I think being able to see data covering a full day within your home should tell us whether there is something here or not."

"What about when we wander around the house?" Lisa asked. "Especially Samantha. She spends her nights creeping around, keeping us safe."

"I've got used to filtering out family members and even their pets. The equipment is so sensitive, I can set it to tell the difference between your cat and even something else on four legs."

"Something else on four legs?" Lisa said, concerned.

"Last year I set up my equipment in a home just the other side of Culpeper," Nigel explained. "They were convinced they had a poltergeist. Every night their living room and kitchen were ransacked. They were certain it had to be a poltergeist because it even managed to get into their kitchen cabinets and throw all the food onto the floor. The couple both used earplugs at night so never heard a thing. Turned out they had a family of racoons living in their attic. Once the house was quiet, the little rascals found a way down an unused chimney and had a field day."

"Do you think our problem is racoons?" Lisa asked, smiling.

"I do not," Nigel replied. "Do you?"

"That reminds me," Mike said, ignoring their banter. "What about the iron bed head in our attic and the potty in Kevin's closet?"

"You both already gave me possible options for both of those, but why don't we leave any more deducing until after I've done a full house check and have monitored the place for a day. I always feel that it's better to juggle with facts than battle with imagination."

"I like that," Lisa said.

After airdropping the wi-fi password from Mike's notes app, he and Lisa retired to the kitchen to stay out of Nigel's way.

"I stopped at the sales office to see if Walter was there," Lisa said. "I still can't believe that he refuses to call or text me back."

"Was he there?" Mike asked.

"Nope. There was some young guy who was filling in, but he didn't have a clue where Walter was. I even asked if he could help, and he said we'd have to wait for Walter to get back."

"But he didn't know when that would be?" Mike asked, surprised.

"He said he didn't."

"I don't want to spoil your quest to get him to call you back, but have you considered exactly what you plan to say to him at this point? A lot has happened since you left that first message. Complaining about an antique bed head in our attic has lost some of its urgency."

"There's plenty left to shout about," she reminded him. "We've still got the leftover foundation that's killed our landscaping, then there's the settling, which he can now pay for."

"And the basement," Mike threw in. "Don't forget the basement."

CHAPTER 38

Lisa lay awake for most of the night. Despite her statement that they could put up with almost anything and still remain in their home, she couldn't help questioning that premise. The house was a big deal, there was no doubt about that, but if Mike's job really did go down the crapper, was there any real point to living on the wrong side of the Rockies (as her dad referred to the entire east coast)?

After all, life in LA hadn't been that bad. Sure, they'd moved way too much, but that was their own fault. They could have stayed in the same rental for decades if they'd wanted. Even if home ownership was never likely to happen due to the ludicrous cost of buying property in LA, they could still have created a stable home.

As she lay there with a million thoughts all fighting for cerebral dominance, she looked over to see if by any chance Mike was even partially awake. Lisa suddenly felt the need to feel his arms around her. For some reason, she was experiencing a wave of loneliness that made no sense whatsoever.

In sleep, Mike's features had softened and even in the low light of the room, she could clearly make out the younger face she recalled from a time before life's stresses had added age lines and muscle tension. She thought of rousing him but realised that her need was purely selfish and that he deserved what sleep he was getting, even if it was the result of the little yellow benzodiazepine pill he'd ingested right after dinner.

Until just over forty-two hours ago, she would have taken one of her own happy pills, as she liked to call them, but after peeing on three test strips a few days earlier, she'd known then that anything beyond a baby aspirin and a cup of camomile tea would be out of the question for quite a while.

Lisa had been waiting for the right moment to tell her husband, but between his suspension from work, his mini breakdown, and the never-ending issues with the house, she'd been putting it off until she felt it was the right moment. It was starting to dawn on her that sometimes there was no such thing as a right moment. She desperately wanted to wake Mike and tell him their news but decided that even something as momentous as her being pregnant could wait until morning.

*

At some point, Lisa did sleep. The smell of coffee and bacon, plus the bright sunshine that was managing to illuminate the edges of the shutters, gently pulled her awake.

She threw on a robe and started downstairs, careful not to wake up Kevin.

A panicked thought took away all remnants of her sleepiness bringing her fully awake.

Lisa charged into the kitchen and was about to go all nuclear on Mike when he managed to speak first. "I took Kevin to school hours ago," he blurted out. "You looked so peaceful, I decided that I might as well do the morning school run and let you sleep."

Lisa, her adrenaline at peak level, didn't know quite how to react.

"Go sit down and I'll bring you breakfast," Mike said, smiling proudly at his accomplishment.

The eggs were a little dry and the bacon was too crispy, but still, it was one of the best breakfasts she'd had in years. Ever since Kevin had joined the family, mornings had become a brutal routine of trying to get him fed, battling to get him dressed, and then driving him to day care (or more recently, school). To have Mike step in without even having to ask was perhaps not a miracle, but the effect on Lisa's mood was still miraculous.

"I have something I want to tell you," Mike announced while he finished his last bite of bacon.

"I have something to tell you as well," Lisa replied.

"I just wanted to say that what you said last night about our being willing to get through whatever it is that's effecting this house, meant a lot to me. I know that I'm not the one who's been pushing for us to have a real home, but now that we're here, I'm glad you did."

"Thanks, babe," Lisa replied. "Want to hear my news?"

"Absolutely… unless it's that you're going to tell me that you're pregnant. That's old news. I've known that since I saw your test kits in the bathroom waste basket."

"Why didn't you say something?" Lisa asked, stunned.

"Excuse me, but why didn't you?" he shot back, grinning. "And if you think that I didn't see you pour two glasses of perfectly good wine down the sink the other night, then you really are the worst sneaky person ever."

"Why didn't you say something?" she insisted.

"I'm not sure that I can imagine a more important and intimate thing that a wife can tell her husband. For you to have waited meant that you must have had a good reason. I felt I should honour that."

"There are moments when I'm sincerely glad that I married you," Lisa said as she leaned across the table and kissed him.

"What about the other moments?" Mike asked.

"We don't talk about those," she replied with a straight face.

"By the way, I did some online checking about our lot," Mike said. "Apparently, the entire Lake View development was owned by some sort of retreat."

"That sounds very cheerful and zen," Lisa commented. "What exactly did they do there?"

"That I couldn't find out, but there was only one habitable building on the land, and it was situated next to the lake."

"What's left of it must be our mystery foundation."

"Probably. I couldn't find any plat maps, just a description that mentions Manassas Lake and an old pine tree," Mike added.

"Did you find out what happened to the building?" Lisa asked.

"Nope. The other bit of information was that the owner of the land, a Mr Edward Wainsborough, purchased the property in 1919. That was it."

"I think we need to find out more about the retreat and Mr Wainsborough, don't you?" Lisa suggested.

"I was thinking that we could drive into DC today and see if Abe Goldstein knows anything about Wainsborough or Sunny Meadows. He's always said that when he was still a paid cultural historian for DC and Northern Virginia, he knew every secret there was."

"And you believed him?" Lisa asked.

"Enough to give him a shot at proving himself," Mike replied.

CHAPTER 39

Driving into the city between the morning and evening rush hours was a breeze. They made it door-to-door in just over an hour. Abe buzzed them straight up and met them at the front door. He seemed happy to have some company. Abe was in his early seventies, still had a full head of hair, albeit grey, and stood over six and a half feet tall. At some point, probably early on in his career, he developed the habit of bending at the waist when talking to people of lesser height, which was just about everyone.

After being seated, Mike and Lisa gave Abe a highly abridged overview of the new house and what it was like to live so far out in the 'boondocks'.

"As I mentioned on the phone," Mike said, getting to the point. "I was hoping to pick your brain about the house that was originally on the property where we now live."

"After you called, I went downstairs to our storage

unit and fished out my notes from when I researched all persons of wealth who either lived or had business enterprises in your part of Northern Virginia from the 1950s back to 1900."

"Did you find your notes?" Lisa asked.

Abe leaned over and patted a sizeable leatherbound notebook on the table.

"Now, as for your question about Edward Wainsborough. I knew I'd researched that name before and was able to find mention of him within a matter of minutes. Edward was quite well known in DC back in the early 1900s. He was a congressman representing the fifth district of Virginia. The young man had quite a reputation from day one. It appears that he preferred the company of young women far more than that of his peers within the House. He was cited on several occasions for failure to appear for his committee duties, and for public behaviour that was deemed wholly unsuitable back then."

"What did he do?" Lisa asked.

"Suffice it to say that alcohol, opium, a short temper, and spending time with countless prostitutes ended up with his being considered a ne'er-do-well and he was ultimately ostracized by most of DC society."

"Wow," Mike said. "Nowadays those traits would either get you a TV special or into the White House."

"Different times, Mr Ellis," Abe said, trying to hide a

growing smile. "Different times."

"What finally happened to him?" Lisa asked.

"The House expelled him for moral turpitude in 1917. He then proceeded to use the contacts he'd made while in congress to set up several businesses, all of which ultimately failed due to questionable legality and poor management. In 1919, he bought the property we discussed earlier and registered his new endeavour as Sunny Meadows."

"What exactly was this endeavour?" Mike asked.

"There are two answers to that question," Abe said as he sat up straight and stretched his back muscles. "The formal name of the business was The Sunny Meadows Retreat. It was promoted as being a centre of mind and body well-being for the elite of Washington DC and Northern Virginia."

"I sense a 'but' coming," Lisa commented.

"What Mr Wainsborough really created was a residential hospital for the supposed care of those with complex emotional issues."

"Are you saying that Sunny Meadows was an insane asylum?" Mike asked, shocked.

"That, again, is another difficult question," Abe continued. "You see, The Meadows, as it was referred to within DC society, was a most unusual facility. It was the first of many such places where, for the right amount of money, a relative or spouse could be interred indefinitely without any formal diagnoses of mental illness or instability."

"I'm not sure I understand what you're saying," Lisa said, as an icy sensation crawled up her back.

"Say you were married to a woman you no longer loved, and for social, moral, religious or financial reasons, could not divorce. For the right amount of money, you could have her committed to a facility such as Sunny Meadows. The onsite psychiatrists would deem her to be mentally unfit and a danger to herself as well as others. She would be kept sedated and given what, to the untrained eye, would appear to be professional and customised treatment. All of that was a complete charade.

Other than the drugs to ensure that she was kept docile and completely submissive, there were no other treatments. Sunny Meadows, like many others that chose to emulate their business model, was no more than a storage facility for the unwanted kin of the extremely wealthy."

"That's horrible," Lisa said, shaking her head. "Why didn't the government do something about it?"

"First of all, there was nothing new about sending family members to insane asylums. The Victorians had been doing it for years. What Wainsborough offered was a boutique level facility for the super-rich. To any layman, the place looked to be what they said it was:

luxurious and filled with kind and caring staff and highly skilled practitioners. Each patient had a private room, the meals were restaurant quality, and discretion was at the highest level. Even if someone did begin to see through the veneer of authenticity, senior government officials were themselves in complete favour of such a facility.

They considered it almost a public service. A successful man could send his poor troubled wife to a beautiful place like Sunny Meadows while at the same gaining sympathetic understanding from the voting public. With his wife safely and securely out of the way, she could no longer threaten him with divorce and public ruination. He would suddenly be free to meet up with his mistress and should any member of the public see such interaction, they would most likely understand his need for companionship, considering the dreadful hardship he was being forced to bear because of his wife's unfortunate condition."

Lisa was having trouble holding back the disgust and anger she was feeling.

"So, he was a monster," she declared.

"I don't know if monster is quite the right word. They were different times and as abhorrent as his actions appear today, The Meadows was providing a service that was clearly desirable back then."

Lisa was about to erupt into a full-scale diatribe

when Mike took her hand in his.

"What became of Mr Wainsborough and Sunny Meadows?" Mike asked.

"That's one of the most interesting parts of the story," Abe replied. "In the early 1930s, an investigation began into The Meadows. Apparently, an inmate, the wife of a shipping magnate from Norfolk, managed to escape and found a kind ear at the Warrenton police station. A young and highly ambitious assistant district attorney listened to every word she had to say. The young DA, one Peter Kessler, must have had to overcome numerous obstacles, most likely from powerful people with ties to the facility, but finally in 1932, he was granted a warrant to have Sunny Meadows searched, its inmates interviewed, and all documents examined by both a medical and a criminal auditor."

"That's wonderful," Lisa said.

"Let's not get ahead of ourselves," Abe said as he gave his glasses a quick clean with the end of his tie. "A judge in Charlottesville issued a stay order only days before a team of investigators was scheduled to serve the search warrant. From that point on, there is almost no information about Sunny Meadows or Edward Wainsborough. It appears that not only was the warrant never served, but no other documentation concerning the man, or the facility, ever surfaced. My belief is that the judge somehow buried the case by sealing the documents and imposing a gag order."

"So that's it?" Mike asked.

"Not quite. Though no other formal documentation could be found, there was a small news item in the June 26th, 1941 edition of the *Manassas Tribune* that a researcher found many years later. It simply said that after sufficient passage of time, county vehicles were finally going to be permitted to enter the abandoned property situated on the eastern-most point of Lake Manassas. Though the only building on the property, which had been abandoned almost a decade earlier, was deemed uninhabitable, the grounds were to be opened to the public."

Abe took a deep breath and placed the notebook back on the table. "That, I'm afraid, really is all the information I have. I've put out some feelers to a few local historians out in Fauquier County who may have some other sources, but as things stand, that's about it."

"So, we have no idea what happened to Wainsborough or to the property?" Lisa said, frustrated.

"How can there not be records about what physically happened to the facility?" Mike asked.

"Back then," Abe explained. "Sunny Meadows was literally in the middle of nowhere. The property was over five hundred acres. Their nearest neighbour was miles away. A small bomb could have gone off and nobody would have been the wiser."

"Do you have any theories?" Lisa asked.

"I would suspect that a man like Edward Wainsborough would have found a way to move to another state, change his name, and start over. If he had the funds, which he almost certainly did, maybe even leave the country altogether as soon as he heard about the case that was being built against him and Sunny Meadows."

"I hate cliff-hangers," Lisa stated. "I hoped that with you being able to come up with all that information, there would be a satisfying, or at least enlightening, ending."

"This is real life, not a Hollywood movie, I'm afraid," Abe said with a sigh. "We're talking about actual events from almost a hundred years ago."

Mike got to his feet. "Thank you, Abe, it was nice seeing you."

"It was my pleasure. By the way, it would be good to be able to get Kevin and Patrick together again. My grandson doesn't have that many friends and he always seemed to enjoy his time with your son."

"Let us get out from under this little mystery we're having with our house," Lisa said. "Then maybe Patrick can come over and have a sleepover."

"He'd really like that," Abe replied, as he stood and walked Lisa and Mike to the door.

"Please say hi to Gilda," Lisa said as she gave Abe a hug. "I'm sorry she wasn't here today."

"Her annual girls' pilgrimage to Atlantic City is probably the highlight of her entire year, though she will be devastated to know that she missed seeing you both."

*

"What'd you think?" Mike asked as he drove the Honda onto the feeder on-ramp for the bridge back across the Potomac.

"I'm not crazy about there having been an insane asylum on the spot where we now live."

"To be fair, it wasn't a real asylum. From what Abe just told us, the inmates were most likely as sane as we are. They weren't locked up because of their mental issues, it was just a place to hide people you wanted out of the way."

"Like they still do with the elderly?" Lisa said.

"Sadly, yeah. Exactly like that," Mike agreed.

"So, after all that, we still don't know what happened to the building that used to stand on our lot."

Lisa suddenly pulled her phone out of her bag and

began typing something. "Now that we have a name…" she mumbled.

"What are you doing?" Mike asked.

Lisa was scrolling through page after page of thumbnails before she stopped the screen.

"Pull over," she said, emphatically.

Mike took the next exit and pulled up a few blocks from the town of Falls Church.

"What have you found?" he asked.

Lisa held the phone out so they both could see the image. It was a black and white photo of a place called Sunny Meadows Retreat taken in 1922.

Neither said another word for the rest of the trip back to Lakeview Estates.

The moment they got home, Lisa made them a quick sandwich while Mike transferred the image onto the flatscreen TV. The photo was old and grainy, which, considering its age, wasn't that big a surprise. The shot had been taken on the opening day of the Sunny Meadows Retreat. A huge 'GRAND OPENING' banner was draped above the building's entry portico.

The thing that struck Mike and Lisa the most was the size of the place. They had an idea of the footprint because of the dead vegetation, but they'd had no clue how tall it was. It had five floors as well as what looked to be generous space under a steeply pitched, wood-shingled roof, out of which jutted a row of dormer windows.

Despite a few attempts at architectural softening, the building was clearly utilitarian and could only have been a hospital or something closely related.

Disregarding the fact that the photo was black and white which therefore added its own contrasts, the building and property looked featureless and drab. Even with a glimpse of the lake in the background, there was something depressing about the image.

"Jesus!" Lisa was the first to break the silence. "Is it me or is that the most depressing-looking place you've ever seen?"

"It's certainly up there on my top ten list," Mike replied.

"I wonder what it was like on the inside?"

"Something tells me that we don't want to know," Mike said.

"Turn it off," Lisa implored. "It's making me sad just to look at it."

"Thankfully," Mike said as he switched off the flatscreen. "We don't have to look at it anymore. Whatever it was is long gone and has been replaced by our very attractive and beautifully designed home."

"And your haunted basement," Lisa added, smiling.

"Let's not use the 'H' word until we hear from Nigel. Speaking of which, aren't we supposed to call him soon?"

"It's only two thirty," Lisa said. "We told him we'd call after I pick up Kevin. Why don't we go to the school together? He'll get a kick out of that."

"If we leave now, I could stop by the Hardware Emporium. I want to see if they sell carpet stretchers. I'm hoping I can fix the gap myself."

"Uh, oh," Lisa said, laughing.

They decided to collect Kevin first then all go to the hardware store. Kevin loved to roam the aisles and look in wonder at the miles of fittings and gadgets that were a complete mystery to him.

Mike's quest was successful. He found an electric carpet stretcher that could be used from a standing position instead of one of those ones he'd have to bash with his knee.

Kevin was so tired after his time in the hardware store that he fell asleep the moment they headed back home.

As they rounded the last corner before reaching the house, Mike and Lisa both noticed the same thing at the same time.

There was smoke pouring out of their chimney.

CHAPTER 40

Panic didn't set in until Mike activated the automatic garage door opener. A plume of grey smoke seemed to almost unfold from within the garage before billowing up into the sky.

"You stay here," Mike shouted as he was about to step out of the car.

"What the hell's the matter with you?" Lisa shouted at him. "You are going to stay right here with Kevin and me until the fire department gets here."

She kept her eyes locked on his as she hit the 911 'hot' button on her phone.

Once she'd disconnected the call, she suggested that Mike move the car sufficiently away from the house so as not to impede the firefighters.

As they waited for help to arrive, numerous neighbours began gathering on their respective front lawns to check out where all the smoke was coming from. As they'd only recently moved into the house, they were yet to introduce themselves to any of them beyond an initial wave or smile.

Lisa suddenly gasped. "Samantha's in there," she said, her words catching as she tried to calm her breathing.

"Let me check," Mike said, again opening the car door.

Lisa was about to shout at him for the second time when he assured her that he was only going to check the garden.

"We left her in the house," Lisa insisted.

"She sure as hell found a way to get out the other day," Mike said. Maybe she did that again."

Mike ran to the back of the house, certain that he wasn't going to see their beloved cat ever again. He scanned the lawn and the bushes close to the house. He called her name countless times despite knowing full well that she'd never once responded to that. The only thing she ever reluctantly acknowledged was the sound of a spoon tapping the side of a tuna can.

Mike tried to see into the house through the patio doors but all he could see was dark grey smoke.

His heart felt like a useless lead weight suspended within his chest as he turned to head back to the car, dreading having to tell Lisa that he'd had no success. He'd only walked a few steps when an extra couple of dormant brain cells came to life and he realised that his eyes had seen something that his brain had been slow to acknowledge.

Mike spun around and saw the tip of a tawny coloured tail that was just visible under the patio dining table. His eyes teared as he approached one of the six chairs and gently slid it out from the table. Curled up and seemingly unaware of there being any current issues requiring her attention was Samantha. She looked up at Mike with sleep-filled eyes. Then, as a show of complete trust, rolled on her back, offering up her tummy.

Lisa was getting worried. There was no way that it should have taken Mike that long to have a quick look around the exterior of the house. Her fingers curled around the car door handle just as Mike stepped into view with Samantha snuggled into the crook of his arms.

Just as Mike sat next to her, the first fire engine arrived. They looked on as oxygen tanks were donned and a two-man team got ready to enter the house, axes at the ready. Mike managed to get their attention and handed over his keys, hopefully averting the need for the axes. Both Lisa and Mike assumed at that point their dream of home ownership was about to end.

Instead, within than five minutes, windows began opening from inside their home. Moments later, the two firemen stepped out of the front door and removed their face masks. Mike could see that they seemed far more relaxed than when they'd entered the house. He got out of the car and approached them.

"How bad is it?" Mike asked.

"Not sure what to tell you, Mr…?"

"Ellis, Mike Ellis," he responded.

"There's no sign of a fire now or… ever," the fireman advised. "We checked every room and couldn't find any source point for the smoke. We used thermal imaging and found no hotspot either."

"So, the house is okay?" Mike asked, stunned.

"It's fine. I'm not sure why, considering the amount of smoke that was there when we arrived, but once we aired the rooms out, there was no residual smell. That much smoke normally would have left a heavy odour that should have permeated everything. That didn't happen. You and your family can go back inside."

"Do you have any idea where the smoke came from?" Mike asked.

"Absolutely no idea. The only thing I can say for certain is that when we first walked into your house, the heaviest layer seemed to be coming up from your basement, but as I said, there's no sign of an ignition point, a recent fire, or even any smoke residue. You're a lucky man, Mr Ellis."

After thanking the crew, Mike returned to the car and started the engine.

"Where are we going?" Kevin asked while yawning from the back seat.

"We're going home," Mike said as he drove past the fire engines and up their driveway.

*

The fireman had been right. They walked through every room in the house and couldn't smell any trace of smoke. What was even stranger was that the home still smelled as they'd left it. The kitchen still had a lingering scent of morning coffee, their bathroom still smelled of Mike's tea tree oil shampoo, and the basement still had the slight odour of the carpet glue that the installer had used days earlier.

While Mike was in the basement, he noticed that on the left side of the room, one section of carpet had come loose from the floor. Mike got on his knees to see what would have caused it to become detached. He saw that the underfelt in that one spot no longer matched the green colour of the rest of it. It had turned black. He rubbed his fingers across it and felt some sort of greasy residue. Though it looked like oil, there was no smell.

He gently lifted one end of it and was shocked to see what was beneath. The concrete floor looked to have been charred in a very distinctive way. Mike tried to carefully lift more of the carpet and underlay while battling against nail strips and glue. He finally managed to fold back a ten-foot section and saw the same burning of the concrete. Mike ran up the stairs so that he could get a better view from a higher vantage point.

Against the left wall, midway along the room, was an eight-foot square section of concrete that had obviously been badly burned. Mike descended back down and took a closer look at the anomaly. The scorched area was not random. The line between the burned and the unburned area was precise. It almost looked like a stencil.

As Mike was trying to work out what could have made that mark and whether it had been responsible for the smoke, he noticed the wall directly above the black square. Though not nearly as burned as the floor, his brand-new wall treatment had a definite discolouration that was the exact width as the mark on the floor but reached all the way to the ceiling. Because of the dim lighting, the firemen had obviously missed seeing it.

"Babe?" Lisa called from upstairs.

Mike didn't want her to see the floor just yet. He was determined to try and work out the cause of the problem before adding another stress to the growing list. He did as good a job as he could of putting the carpet back in place, then climbed out of the basement and locked the door.

"Did you call me?" he asked.

"Nigel just called. He wanted to make sure we were here before he came over. Apparently, he has something he wants to show us."

"Did he say what?" Mike asked.

"Nope, but he said he'd be here in about half an hour," Lisa replied. "I didn't tell him about the smoke."

Once Nigel arrived, Mike could tell the moment he opened the front door that something was wrong. His face looked ashen and there were dark circles under his eyes.

"This can't be good," Mike said as he stood aside to let Nigel enter the house.

"I'm not certain what it is exactly that I have to show you, so let's not discuss anything until you've seen what my equipment captured. We should probably watch this without Kevin seeing it.

"How about Lisa's office?" Mike suggested.

"If that's okay with her."

Nigel followed Mike to the far end of the house. Lisa was on her knees, surrounded by hundreds of tightly typed proofing pages, trying to sort out the ones she needed to mail to an author who flatly refused to do anything online.

"Hi, Nigel. Let me just put this lot back in order."

Despite offers of help, Mike and Nigel were

relegated to sitting on the tiny sofa while Lisa collated all the pages back into one orderly pile.

"Did Mike tell you about our fire scare a few hours ago?"

While Lisa remained on her knees, Mike gave him the highly abridged version of events.

"And there was no sign of anything having been burned?" Nigel asked.

Mike shrugged, hoping that response would be answer enough. He didn't want to tell them about his find in the basement until he'd heard what Nigel had to say.

"Done," Lisa announced proudly as she deposited the tome on her desk. She then sat in her ergonomic chair that looked like an early version of HR Giger's alien from the movie of the same name.

"Did your equipment pick up something interesting?" she asked as she swung her chair so she could face the others.

"Actually, they did, but I have to say right up front that I am not entirely clear what it is that they recorded."

Nigel produced an iPad from his well-travelled backpack.

"There were no unusual readings within the house until just after three a.m. The first alert was from a wireless EMF sensor I placed in the upstairs hallway. It began fluctuating gradually at first then the reading went off the scale. Moments later, the same thing happened in all the bedrooms. The unit over the stairs was next. Moments later, every sensor reacted the same way on the ground floor."

"What does that mean?" Lisa asked.

"It means that there was a drastic change in the electromagnetic field within the house."

"What can cause that?" Mike asked.

"Various things," Mike explained. "Severe solar activity, a surge in overhead powerlines, x-rays…"

"Maybe I should have asked, what can cause it in our house?" Mike replied.

"That's the problem. I don't know. That amount of radioactive energy should have left residual hotspots, but less than a minute after the readings went wild, the sensors all went back to showing completely normal levels."

"Yet you don't know what any of that means?" Lisa asked.

"Could it have anything to do with the smoke in the house?" Mike asked.

"I don't see how," Nigel said. "But there's more. As you know, I mounted thermal imaging cameras as well as the EMF readers."

"Did they go nuts as well?" Mike asked.

"That's what I want to show you," Nigel said as he

held the iPad screen so they could both have a clear line-of-sight.

"All I see is a purple screen," Mike observed.

"Just wait," Nigel advised. "The software is able to sync the image from various cameras when a heat source is in motion. We are currently looking at the output of the one mounted in the upstairs hallway."

"That's great," Mike said. "But all I see is…"

His words stopped in mid flow as a tiny flicker of yellow light appeared at the top right of the screen. It looked almost like a firefly. As they watched, more of the tiny specks appeared. They were an intense yellow that was surrounded by a softer, bluish aura.

"What the fuck?" Mike blurted out.

"Nigel, what are we looking at?" Lisa asked, her voice tense and raspy.

"Keep watching," he instructed.

Dozens of tiny dots of light stretched the length of the hallway. Suddenly, the ones at the farther end began moving towards the stairway. As the hall emptied, the stairway camera took over as the armada of light descended into the ground floor vestibule. A different camera followed the lights to the back hallway, where they hesitated at a closed door.

A chill ran the length of Mike's spine. Even in the purple murk that surrounded the light dots, he knew where they were waiting.

It was the door to the basement.

"Can't they simply pass through the wood?" Lisa asked.

Nigel didn't respond. He knew what was coming. The two kept their eyes glued on the screen, then both jerked backwards at once.

The basement door opened.

The hallway camera captured the yellow flickering dots as they passed through and began their descent into the basement. Because of the lack of any power sockets, Nigel hadn't left any cameras or sensors beyond the entrance to the lower level. Thankfully, the wall-mounted unit in the hallway was at the right angle for them to see all the way down into the space.

The lights all gathered against the left side wall and for a few moments, floated in place without doing much of anything. A few dots then began to circle in the air. Soon the others joined them. Their light intensified as they rotated and formed into what appeared to be a glowing tornado.

As they watched, the luminous body suddenly grew exponentially larger. The room appeared to be filled with the cyclonic light until, suddenly, it seemed to expand up the stairs. The basement door slammed shut as the iPad screen was filled with a white-hot flare.

Though invisible to the conscious mind, both Lisa and Mike sensed that they'd seen something within the burst of illumination. It was like the after-burn on a TV when white lettering from credits seem to remain on the screen even after the TV has been switched off.

Lisa and Mike, however, had not seen letters.

They had seen, or at least believed they had seen, dozens of faces caught up in the final burst of light.

The detail was too fragmented to see any details other that the fact that they all appeared to have been screaming.

The office was deathly quiet. No one knew what to say. Finally, Nigel spoke.

"Did you see the faces?" he asked in little more than a whisper.

Lisa and Mike both nodded.

"Suffice it to say," Nigel said. "You do seem to have some sort of spirit entity within your house."

"No shit," Mike whispered.

"Who are they?" Lisa asked, moving closer to her husband.

"I have no idea," Nigel replied.

"Can you do anything about it… or them… or whatever they are?" Mike asked.

"Now that we at least know that the entities appear to have once held human form, I believe I can, yes."

"Want to run that 'once held human form' part again?" Lisa glared at him.

"There have been instances of hauntings where it's

never been confirmed that the entity was, in fact, human.”

“If a ghost wasn’t once human,” Mike said in a monotone. “Then what the hell could it have once been?”

“Nobody knows, but you have to remember that this planet of ours has been here for a great deal longer than mankind…”

He was interrupted by Lisa clearing her throat.

“Sorry,” Nigel realised his faux pas. “Longer than humankind is what I meant to say. We pretend to know what roamed the planet throughout its history, but scientists are, in many cases, just creating data-less guestimates to fill in the gaps of knowledge or quantifiable proof. It’s long been believed that spirit entities can only evolve from sentient beings and that we are the only species that fit that bill.”

“You’re saying we’re not?” Lisa asked.

“All I’m saying is that there is no definitive proof that some other sentient creature didn’t once roam the earth and that their lifeforce, in some rare instances, could still be trapped in our plane of existence. Then there’s another school of thought that believes we are often visited by sentient beings from alternate dimensions. If that’s true, who’s to say that a few such creatures weren’t able to return to their place in space-time and perished here with us. Perhaps the reason for those hauntings that didn't fit any human mould was that the entities had never been human."

"Please tell me that our haunting is one of the boring human ones," Mike said.

"I can. I can also say that there does appear to be more than one. Why they are trapped here, however, is another issue altogether."

"But you think you can communicate with them?" Lisa asked anxiously.

"I'll be honest with you," Nigel replied. "I've only ever had to communicate with solitary entities before now. That's probably why I couldn't detect one lifeforce that I could focus on. I have heard of spiritualists communicating with multiple spirits at once, but I've never done so myself."

"Can you try it?" Mike asked. "I mean, isn't that the quickest way to find out if you can?"

"That may be the quickest way to find out, but not the best method if I'm to actually have a discourse with them. I'm going to need to go home and confer with some colleagues about how best to approach this. I should be able to be back here mid-afternoon tomorrow if that's okay?"

"What the hell do we do in the meantime?" Mike asked.

"Nothing has changed," Nigel answered. "You are as safe now as you've ever been in this house. Just because my instruments have shown you a different view of your reality, doesn't mean you shouldn't carry on as before."

"In your experience, do you think we are completely safe here?" Lisa asked, her voice mirroring her concern. "I mean, I know that nothing's changed… but it has, hasn't it? We have to consider Kevin. I'm not sure that it would be a responsible thing for parents to put their six-year-old boy in a situation where there's even the slightest chance of his being injured or…?"

Mike put his arm around her.

"Lisa's right," Mike looked to Nigel. "Would you leave your son, if you had one, in a house like this?"

Nigel thought hard about how to answer their questions.

"I don't know. Being used to dealing with spirit entities has taught me that despite all the books and the movies, they usually don't mean to cause any harm."

"Sounds like you're saying that they still can, even if it's unintentional," Lisa said.

"On occasion, when a lifeforce becomes sufficiently agitated, it can accidently cause some physical damage."

"What about when it's more than one, like in our situation? Can multiple lifeforces exponentially cause more harm?" Lisa asked.

"I don't know," Nigel admitted. "I've never heard of such an instance, but that doesn't mean that it's out of the question. Perhaps you should all leave the house until I've come back and attempted communication."

Lisa and Mike glanced at one another and seemed to silently ask and answer the prevailing question.

"We'll have Kevin spend the night with friends," Lisa said. "But we want to stay and see whatever this is through to its natural, or even unnatural, conclusion. Then, depending on how successful you are at convincing the entities to leave, we'll either all move back in together or be on the next plane back to Los Angeles."

"I'm curious," Nigel asked. "Most people I deal with would have already moved out after seeing those thermal images, yet you are planning on staying at least one more night. My question is, why?"

"I know this sounds ridiculous," Mike said. "But it feels like we already have a lot of skin in the game. This is our home and knowing what we now know, we feel we should stay and be a part of helping whatever's here to move on."

Nigel nodded. "That's a very empathetic reaction."

"Are you going to leave the equipment here?" Lisa enquired.

"If you don't mind. You never know what else we'll capture."

Mike swallowed hard as he took Lisa's hand.

*

Once Nigel was gone, Lisa called Abe Goldstein in DC and asked whether they'd like to have Kevin sleep over. Abe was delighted but asked if he could quickly call his son and confirm that they were onboard.

Abe called back less than ten minutes later. They could drop Kevin off at any time.

Lisa had planned to stay in the house while Mike drove their son to the city, but at the last minute decided that she wanted to go along for the ride. Being alone in the house just didn't seem that temping after the video and the conversation they'd had with Nigel.

By the time they dropped Kevin off for his sleepover, it was right in the middle of the evening rush hour. They decided to wait until the worst of it was over before heading home. They walked from their old apartment building to Pennsylvania and 25th. As they approached the Thai restaurant they'd discovered their first week in the city, they both had a momentary wave of nostalgia for being able to just walk out of their unit and find everything on the doorstep.

When they walked into the restaurant, the owner greeted them as if they'd been gone for years.

"This feels good, doesn't it?" Lisa said as they tucked

into their favourite extra-hot, green curry and jasmine rice.

"Better than living in a safe, quiet suburb?" Mike asked.

"Not better. Just different."

"We could always sell up and move back?" he offered, half joking.

"We haven't even given our place a chance," Lisa replied.

"To be fair, that hasn't been entirely our fault," Mike responded. "We've got spooks, remember?"

"We haven't even been living there for a month," Lisa pointed out. "Remember your rule: always give a place six months before deciding if it's a keeper or if it's time to up-stakes and move on."

"Hopefully, we'll have a better idea about our future after Nigel has had a little chat with our house guests," Mike said.

"Not wishing to sound overly pedantic, but they were there first. I think we need to remember that in their eyes…"

"If they have eyes," Mike said, interrupting.

Lisa carried on as if she hadn't heard him. "In their eyes, we are the interlopers, not the other way around."

"That's not how the courts would see it."

"I'm not sure property disputes between owners

and ghosts end up in court," Lisa said, smiling.

Mike shrugged then aimed his chopsticks at a prime piece of chicken protruding from the green curry.

They left DC at seven thirty and were home almost exactly one hour later. As they approached their house, the automatic exterior lights were on, and it looked as they'd always hoped it would. Inviting and safe.

It took them a while to get back into their relaxed routine and stop worrying about what may or may not be lurking in the shadows. Mike poured them both a drink (Amstel Light for him, peach iced tea for Lisa).

They settled in front of the TV and started watching *Bridesmaids* for the third time. Usually, when alone, they'd watch a well-reviewed creepy movie but decided that as they were living in their own low-budget horror, a comedy would be a better bet if they wanted to have any chance of sleeping.

The movie turned out to be a good choice. By the time Kristen Wiig gets them all thrown off the plane to Vegas, they were having trouble keeping their eyes open and decided to watch the rest the next day.

They were both asleep the moment their heads touched their hypoallergenic pillows.

*

Lisa woke up shivering. The bedroom was freezing. Still

half asleep, she stumbled her way to the linen closet to grab an extra blanket.

She opened the door and screamed.

Mike found her standing, facing the open cupboard. She was backed against the wall and was frighteningly pale. He looked to see what she was looking at.

Mike had had to jury-rig the shelves a few days earlier when they'd collapsed onto the floor.

Things had changed since then.

The shelves were again lying on the floor entangled with sheets and towels. The space had grown. It was almost as if they'd gained a small room, though not one that anybody would ever want to step into.

The inside was dark and dank and smelled of age and cheap disinfectant. Lisa recoiled from the odour.

Strangely, the added square footage wasn't the thing that was scaring them both the most. What was within the newfound room was what made the discovery all the more impossibly wrong.

Sitting off to one side was a cheap, metal bedside table. It looked to have been in a fire. Its cream-coloured enamel paint was partially burned away. On it was a lone water glass. It was half-filled with yellow-brown liquid. Just visible within the murk, resting on the bottom of the glass, was a pair of ancient, discoloured dentures... and they were moving.

Lisa knew it to be impossible, but they were

gnashing together, causing a hollow, wood-on-wood sound.

Tok, tok, tok.

Lisa slammed the door shut.

The sound was muted but was still there.

Tok, tok, tok.

CHAPTER 42

Lisa woke up screaming.

It took a few moments of Mike's reassurances that she had only been dreaming to calm her rapid heartbeat and raspy breathing.

"Do you want to tell me about it?" Mike asked, concerned.

"In a minute," she replied as she swung her legs out of bed.

Lisa walked straight to the linen closet and opened the door. Her breath momentarily caught in her throat when she saw that the shelves and linen were again on the floor. Thankfully, that was the only similarity to her nightmare. The cupboard ended in a solid wall. There was no extra room and most importantly, there was no water glass with false teeth chattering within it.

Mike appeared by her side.

"Shit," he said as he saw the collapsed shelving.

"Don't worry about it," Lisa said, relieved. "Things

could be much worse."

Mike gave her a questioning look.

"I'll tell you over breakfast," she replied. "First I want to call and see how Kevin's night went."

"It's five a.m.," he advised.

"In that case, I may wait," Lisa said. "I was thinking that instead of rushing to DC then dropping Kev at school halfway through the morning, I wonder if he should stay in DC until after Nigel's finished with what he needs to do. That way, we won't have to be concerned about him if things go to shit."

"Are you suggesting that things could actually get worse?" Mike asked.

"I'm suggesting that we don't have a clue what's going to happen. The part that really scares me is that Nigel's never faced anything like this. I just pray that his contacts can give him some insight about what to do."

"I hope you're right."

Lisa patted him on both cheeks.

"I usually am." She forced a weak smile.

*

While Lisa shut herself off in her office to finalise the manuscript before mailing it to the author, Mike spent the morning checking out every square inch of the house prior to Nigel's arrival.

He started in the attic and from the hatchway, it looked the same as when he'd last been up there. The metal headboard was where they'd left it and the rest of the space was devoid of anything new and unexpected. Mike sighed with relief as he started to back down the ladder.

He suddenly stopped.

He had been so intent at checking out the floor area that his conscious mind hadn't immediately noticed the rather substantial change a little higher up.

A dormer window now jutted out where previously there had only been the underside of the roof. Mike climbed up into the attic and walked over to the recent addition to their home. Sitting amidst the brand-new construction, the vintage window looked utterly out of place.

Unlike the triple glazed windows throughout the rest of the house, this one was single pane and couldn't be opened. Its only purpose had to have been to provide natural light to the attic. It wasn't providing much light anymore. The glass was coated in a grey/black film.

Mike swiped a finger across the surface and saw that it was a thick layer of soot. He wiped a little more away and stood there looking out of the window. He could see the lake and the shoreline on the far side. The film on the glass made the view appear to be in black and white as if it was a photo taken a hundred years ago.

Only a few days earlier, Mike would have dragged Lisa up to see what had appeared, but that was then. A lot had transpired in the last forty-eight hours and Mike decided not to spring their new house addition on Lisa. Trying to shut the image of the charred window from his mind, Mike continued his inventory to see if there were any other unexpected alterations to their home.

His next stop was the master bedroom. He glanced up at his ceiling repair and noticed that his patch job seemed to have been undermined. A new crack, though subtle, had formed right down the middle of his repair.

The next stop was the linen cupboard. Though Lisa had seemed relieved at what she saw (or didn't see) within it, Mike had been quietly unnerved at the shelves having again fallen free of their supports. He had gone to a lot of trouble to mount extra-long drywall screws to the side walls so the shelves would be secure on top of them. When Mike tried to place one of shelves back on the screws, it didn't come close to reaching them.

Upon closer examination, Mike saw that, though the door frame appeared untouched, the walls on either side, which had originally butted up to the frame, were now set back a good few inches on either side.

Oddly, Mike simply accepted this extra issue and

considered it to be another chore he'd have to deal with later. He was starting to become almost blasé about the fact that their home was not behaving as bricks and mortar usually do.

Mike finished his examination in the one room that always seemed to have been off-kilter.

The basement.

It had been where the first anomaly took place and since then seemed to be the area with the most inexplicable activity. He unlocked the door and saw that the lights were on, despite specifically remembering turning them off with his improvised switch.

As he looked down at what he'd hoped would one day be their family game room, he felt a heavy weight settle in his stomach.

Things had changed overnight.

It was hard to quantify which changes were the most unsettling.

The space was now easily double the size it had been. There was no sign of the carpet as the room was filled to a depth of three or four inches with what looked like black oil. His brand-new wall treatment now had what appeared to be a black tide mark just above the oily layer. To make matters worse, the plaster seemed to be absorbing the oil, causing web-like tributaries to rise from the undulating liquid.

On the left side of the room, a massive boiler sat against the wall surrounded by the sea of black ooze. Mike's innovative approach to adding light fittings to the ceiling had somehow reverted to the single low-wattage bulb at the end of a cloth-covered cord.

The light was slowly swinging from side to side, as its ghostly reflection undulated on the surface of the oil.

Mike stepped back and shut the door. For the first time since the troubles began, he started to doubt whether they would be able to continue living in their new house.

As he leaned against the wall and tried to get a mental handle on what was happening around them, he heard Lisa's phone ringing within her office.

Mike could hear her raised voice, though the words themselves were garbled. Suddenly, her door swung open and she stepped out.

"Mike?" she shouted.

"In the back hallway," he replied.

"Walter is on the line," she said as she approached him.

"We're both here," she said as she put the call on speaker. "Do you realise how long I've been trying to get hold of you?"

"As I said, I only just got all your messages." Walter sounded distant. "I'm in Mexico on vacation. I've been on a fishing boat the whole time. There was no signal."

"You could have told us you were going on vacation," Lisa snapped at him.

There was a long silence.

"Mrs Ellis, I am not at your disposal every moment of every day. I am sorry that you've had a few issues, but I too am allowed my own time and don't believe that I have to report what I do to you outside of work. The office was manned, and you could easily have told whoever was on duty that you had an issue."

"I wanted to talk to you," Lisa insisted. "The issues have been a little beyond the scope of the temp in the sales office."

"I saw your text about the headboard in the attic, but I honestly don't know what I can do about it. You'd be best to just remove it yourself."

"We can't," Mike stated. "That is the whole problem. It doesn't fit through the hatch."

"Can't you disassemble it?" Walter asked.

"No. It's made of metal, it weighs a ton, and is welded together," Lisa said. "Where are you? It would be much easier if we could just show you what has been happening."

"We're in Cabo St Lucas. I won't be back until Monday. Can it wait until then? I'm sure we can find a way to get the bed frame out when I'm back."

"That's just the tip of the iceberg," Lisa continued.

"The HVAC is out of control, the landscaping has died, we've got cracks in the ceiling and walls, and the basement seems to be enlarging."

There was another lengthy silence.

"Did you hear me?" Lisa asked.

"I thought I did, but what was the last part you said?" Walter asked, his voice sounding confused.

"The part about the basement?" Mike said, enouncing his words with exaggerated clarity. "Yeah, it's been getting bigger, but that's old news. Now it's full of oil."

Lisa looked at her husband in shock.

"I'm very sorry, Mr and Mrs Ellis, but I keep hearing you say basement."

"That's because we keep saying it," Lisa replied bluntly.

Another silence filled the hallway.

"Walter?" Mike said.

"I'm sorry," Walter finally responded. "I find myself at a loss for what to say that could possibly help you."

"Why is that?" Lisa asked. "When we bought this house, you promised that you would always be available to help us with any problems we might have with the property."

"I did say that," Walter agreed.

"Then what's the problem?" Mike asked.

Another silence descended on the pair.

Finally, Walter's voice came back through the phone. He sounded concerned and maybe even a little frightened.

"While I still plan on living up to that promise, I can't fix something that's out of my control."

"Such as?" Lisa said, coldly.

"Such as the fact that your house is a two-storey, Cape Cod design, 2600-square-foot home. That is what you purchased."

"So?" Mike said, frustrated.

"Mr Ellis, your home doesn't have a basement."

CHAPTER 43

The phone call ended soon after Walter's bombshell. It had to. There was nothing else to be said. How do you respond to someone who has just told you that one entire floor of your brand-new home doesn't actually exist?

When Walter told them that there was no basement, Mike asked, "If there's no basement, what's the door for in the middle of the downstairs hallway?"

"There's only one doorway off that part of the hallway and it opens to your coat closet," Walter had replied.

"We don't have a coat closet," Lisa shot back.

"You most definitely do. I saw it when I did my walk through a week before you took possession."

"Did you look inside?" Mike had asked.

"Of course. I even made certain there were some hangers there for you to use."

After they disconnected the call, it dawned on Mike

that he had indisputable proof that the basement had existed. He had the bill from the carpet installers.

"You could always just take a photo of it as it looks now," Lisa suggested.

"There's no way I'm opening that door again."

"Even to show me?" she asked.

"Especially to show you."

They made their way to the living room but before Lisa could say anything else, Mike's phone erupted with a croaking frog, notifying him that he'd received a text.

"Nigel's on the way."

"I want a drink," Lisa announced.

"What do you want? Lemonade, iced tea…?"

"No, I'm craving a real drink," she stated. "I'm talking tequila or vodka shots."

"You know you can't have either," Mike said.

"Of course, I do, but that doesn't stop me craving them. I feel I need to numb myself. Either that or pack a few things and get on the next plane heading west."

"Can I come with you?" Mike asked.

"Of course, but you know I don't mean it don't you?"

"The part about the plane or the tequila?"

"The plane," she replied. "I'm deadly serious about the tequila."

"You haven't drunk tequila for years."

"I haven't been in a situation before where the home I've always dreamed of is being systematically destroyed by a bunch of ghosts."

"To be fair, the worst of the destruction is happening in a basement that we don't actually have, so things really aren't all that bad," Mike joked. "Oh... that reminds me, we gained something else overnight. We have a nice dormer window in the attic now."

Lisa looked at him as if he was talking gibberish.

Mike got to his feet and held out his arm. She took his hand and let him lead her out onto the patio and onto the yellow lawn. She looked up at the roof and saw the new window.

"Are we sure that wasn't already there?" she asked.

"Positive."

As he looked at his wife's face, he could see her resolve crumble right in front of him. She turned into him and lay her head on his shoulder as she began to cry. Mike held her tightly as her tears became sobs.

Something made him look up to the window. Whether it was a trick of the light or just his ever-increasing stress level, he thought he saw a face looking down at him. It was only for a microsecond, but he felt he'd seen the features of a young woman, her face pressed against the glass.

"I'm sorry," Lisa said, sniffling. "I'm trying to hold it together, but this dream is falling apart faster than I ever would have believed possible."

"Don't give up yet." Mike tried to soothe her. "Nigel

was able to get rid of Sebastian in a matter of minutes. Maybe he can sort this…"

Mike looked at her without speaking.

"What are you thinking?" Lisa asked.

"When he spoke to Sebastian, do you remember what Nigel told us the ghost kept saying?"

Lisa thought for a moment.

"Yes, I do. He said he needed to stay here so he could protect Kevin."

"We never asked what it was that Kevin needed to be protected from," Mike said.

"Are you saying that Sabastian knew that the house had other occupants?"

"It makes sense, doesn't it?"

"Now it does," Lisa agreed. "But back then…"

"I know. Back then we didn't care so long as *his* ghost was gone."

"Whoops," Lisa said, trying to make light of his comment.

Mike closed his eyes as Lisa held him even tighter. He had to will himself not to look up at the soot-streaked window.

Lisa suddenly released him and headed back into the house.

"You okay?" Mike asked, knowing full well that she wasn't. Hell, neither of them were okay.

"I've got to fix my face before Nigel gets here," she

said, as she vanished from sight.

Mike, in a rare display of domesticity, tidied the downstairs area in anticipation of their visitor's arrival.

Lisa splashed water in her face, then after an overly vigorous soaping and rinsing, she kept her eyes shut as she felt for the face towel on the granite counter. Instead of finding the towel, her hand encountered the sides of something curved and hard. She opened her eyes and saw the same water glass from her dream. She was about to scream for Mike when her blurry vision cleared, and she saw that it was only her coffee mug she had forgotten to take downstairs.

"What the hell!" she said as she stared at her reflection in the mirror.

For a moment, she felt the same wave of hopelessness that she'd experienced during and after the earthquake that killed her father. Her heart was beating way too fast, and she could feel perspiration forming under the layer of water that was still clinging to her forehead. In 1994, she'd had her one and only panic attack. It had left her feeling out of control and vulnerable. She'd never told Mike about it and certainly didn't need a recurrence at this point in her life, especially as he was himself battling stress and anxiety. Lisa knew that she had to be the strong one while they got through this mess. Falling apart now was an unacceptable option.

By the time she'd dried her face and applied the minimum amount of make-up, she heard the doorbell.

"Nigel's here," Mike called from downstairs.

CHAPTER 44

Nigel looked as if he'd been up all night, which in fact, he had. They sat in the dining room as he updated Lisa and Mike on the latest advice he'd received from his peers, as well as what data had been captured by the sensors and cameras.

"I don't think we should waste time watching the thermal images," he advised. "We should focus on…"

"What is it you don't want us to see?" Lisa interrupted.

Nigel managed to force a smile.

"You are a very perceptive person," Nigel replied. "You're right. I don't want you seeing last night's recording. It's very similar to one we looked at yesterday, but it ends…"

Nigel tried to find the right words.

"With fire?" Mike volunteered.

"Yes. Every camera showed a massive spike in temperature then went bright white and stopped recording."

"When you say a spike?" Lisa asked.

"I mean the temperature went off the scale," Nigel said.

"How high does the scale go?" Mike asked.

"A hundred and eighty degrees," Nigel stated.

"That's hot but not that high," Mike started to say.

"A hundred and eighty degrees Celsius," Nigel clarified.

Mike had no response to that.

"So, what are you going to do?" Lisa asked.

"I thought I'd start in the basement and..."

"I should mention that we spoke to the builder's agent earlier today," Lisa interrupted. "He advised that we don't actually have a basement. The door we've been using is supposed to lead to our coat closet."

Nigel took a moment to let her words sink in.

"That's different," he said with a sigh.

"The basement we don't have is now filled with what looks to be heating oil and there appears to be an antique boiler down there as well," Mike added.

"That's not good," Nigel said. "I spoke to my friend and spiritual mentor who lives in England. I told him about the situation here and he was most concerned."

"About the entities?" Lisa asked.

"Actually no. He was more concerned about the changes within your home."

"Speaking of which," Mike butted in. "Did you notice our new window poking out of the roof?"

Nigel looked at Mike with growing concern.

"Actually, you wouldn't have," Mike added. "It faces the lake so you couldn't have been able to see it from our driveway."

"When did it appear?" Nigel asked.

"Overnight, I guess. I only found it this morning."

Nigel slowly shook his head.

"My friend in England told me of an incident just outside Inverness in Scotland. The situation there wasn't that dissimilar to yours. A new home had been built on the site of an old manor house. The buyers moved in and almost immediately began noticing odd things occurring around their new property. At first, they were insignificant – a cupboard seemed a little larger, an object that they didn't own mysteriously appeared in a bedroom."

"That's exactly what happened here," Lisa said, almost sounding relieved that theirs was not a unique happening.

"I know. But I need to warn you that the history of that property differs greatly from this one."

"Does that matter if the effects are the same?" Lisa asked.

"Maybe… I don't know," Nigel answered. "After a few weeks of small occurrences, which the buyers put down to it being a new home, things kicked up a notch. Cracks began forming in walls and ceilings. There were tremors and all three members of the family began feeling uncomfortable as well as sensing that they weren't alone in the house. The builder inspected the property with a surveyor and determined that the entire house was over one hundred and twenty centimetres wider than when they'd completed construction. They also found that the roofing joists were no longer in the same position in relation to the supporting walls. Exterior brickwork was damaged and, in a few places, had separated to a dangerous degree.

"The family was moved out and were rehoused in a different home. The builder, wanting to understand the cause of the damage, investigated the history of the estate and more specifically, the house that had once stood on the same spot. He found that the manor house had been torn down almost a hundred years earlier after repeated reports of hauntings and strange occurrences within the building. As he delved a little further into its history, he found that the property had a very dark history. The original owner had been a successful local shipping magnate who'd helped set up regular supply runs to the Scottish Isles within a couple of hundred kilometres radius of Inverness.

"After a decade of dominance over the local waters, other shipping companies began offering the same services but at far lower prices. Within three years, the owner had lost all his local trade routes as well as most of his fortune. His ships were older and had been worn down by the high seas and harsh weather. Their value wasn't even enough to pay off the man's debts. He began drinking heavily, and according to reports from the local constabulary, started taking out his anger on his wife and their six children.

"One evening, one of their children was found on the road into Inverness. She was bruised, near frozen to death, and was close to being catatonic. While she was admitted to the local hospital, a constable rode up to the manor house."

"I don't think I'm going to want to hear this, am I?" Lisa asked.

"I'll make it brief and sufficiently redacted," Nigel said. "Basically, it's believed that the owner went insane and murdered his own family before taking his own life. How the young girl managed to escape was a complete miracle."

"I get how the manor could end up being haunted after that, but I don't see the connection to the new property and why it started falling apart," Mike said.

"Neither did I until my friend explained a little-known phenomenon called a regressive temporal haunting, or RTH."

"What the hell is that?" Mike asked.

"It's when a new and supposedly untainted property is built on the site of a much older site where the lifeforce of displaced spirits are still attached."

"But surely homes are built all the time on land where old homes have stood. If spirits can remain, why is this RTH so rare?" Lisa asked.

"Very good question and one that I myself asked just last night," Nigel replied. "The force can only remain within the original structure, not vacant land. The reason for such few cases is that most developers, when faced with having to demolish a property, especially one with a history of hauntings, would remove the entire building, including the foundation. It would be pure laziness to basically anchor a brand-new building on top of a hundred-year-old slab."

"How can spirits survive in only a foundation?" Mike asked.

"They can survive in a single brick or even a teacup if it was linked to the original structure. You mustn't think of a lifeforce as a solid or even a consciously sentient being. In fact, from what I learned last night, it seems most likely that these displaced souls can remain dormant for centuries. The only thing that can revive them is when they come into direct contact with new, living energy. The spirits of the old property, in this case, Sunny Meadows, were somehow trapped within the building until it was demolished.

"And then what, they just scurried down into the foundation?" Mike asked.

"Mike, you're not grasping what I'm telling you about spirits. They don't just stay in a room. They're part of the energy of a structure. If a house is haunted, unless the spirit has the energy and the will to focus itself into one place at one time, its energy is intermingled with the atoms and molecules of the building itself."

Lisa shook her head. "I don't understand how a spirit gets stuck with a property in the first place. Forget the RTH thing – any spirit."

"Very simply," Nigel explained. "It happens when a person dies without any knowledge or understanding that they have passed away. When a natural death occurs, the lifeforce is drawn to the next plane and understands that its mortal time is complete. When someone dies unnaturally, through an accident or even intentionally..."

"You mean murder?" Mike said.

"Especially murder," Nigel continued. "The lifeforce has no understanding of what has occurred or where it's supposed to go. Some believe that when you die naturally, a chemical trigger somehow activates telling the lifeforce that it's all right to pass over. In the other instances, no such trigger is activated, and the spirit becomes untethered to the energy that's trying to lead it into the light. It remains exactly where it was when the living body passed away."

"So, every time an RTH happens, the ghost can somehow tear the new building apart?" Mike was trying to follow what Nigel was saying but finding it hard to match the story to his basement full of oil.

"No, not at all. The usual ramification would be that the entity that was still present in the old building would simply become part of the new one once it was bonded together with the existing foundation. In the case of the property in Scotland, six entities were trapped in the new house. Confused and suddenly amidst a new, vibrant, living energy that was being emitted by the young buyers, their lifeforce began trying to change the modern home back into what they were used to. This occurred because their imprinted memory had no knowledge of the new structure, only of the original manor house. Because of their numbers and the way that they had died, their lifeforce was six times as strong when coupled together. Add that to the new energy, especially that of a young child, and you have a formidable though disorganised power."

"You believe that whatever is haunting our home is trying to turn it back into Sunny Meadows?" Lisa asked, wide-eyed.

"Yes."

"And they've been feeding off our energy?"

"Especially Kevin's," Nigel said.

"That means that a number of people within Sunny Meadows did not die naturally, doesn't it?" she asked, dreading the answer.

"It means that they most likely died suddenly and without warning or understanding."

"Jesus!" Mike said, trying to get his breathing under control. "We need to find out exactly what happened to Sunny Meadows."

"Shit," Lisa exclaimed. "Shit, shit, shit."

She jumped to her feet and ran to her office. Both men heard her printer make its strange rooster-like call as it spewed out a couple of pages.

Lisa walked back into the room as she read what was written.

"What are those?" Mike asked.

"I got an email from Abe Goldstein yesterday evening then completely forgot about it and never opened it."

"Was it important?"

"Kind of," Lisa said as she continued reading. "He found out what happened to Sunny Meadows."

"Why it closed?" Mike asked.

"No," Lisa replied in barely more than a whisper. "Abe found out that it was burned to the ground."

CHAPTER 45

Lisa placed a piece of paper on the table between Nigel and Mike. It was a scanned copy of an old document. Text was legible at the very top; the rest had been blacked out.

Mike read, "Pump officer Lewis Granger of Warrenton, Virginia reported arriving at the premises of the facility known as the Sunny Meadows Retreat, but the building was already fully engulfed in flames. His pump crew had to wait almost four hours before they were able to get close enough to douse the remainder of the blaze, and before they were able to inspect what was left of the property, they were notified that the building had been vacant and that the firemen were to leave the property immediately as the owner did not want the premises to be disturbed. The officer stated that he suspected arson but could not verify it before having to leave."

"What about the patients and staff?" Nigel asked.

"That's all I can read. The rest of the page appears to have been redacted," Mike replied. "What's on the other sheet?"

Lisa placed the other page on the table. It was a very grainy photo of Sunny Meadows after the fire. It had been shot from almost the same position as the opening day photo that Lisa had found online. Most of the building was gone. The ground floor walls were still standing, though severely damaged. Nothing else appeared to have survived.

"But the place had to have been occupied," Lisa insisted.

"My guess," Nigel said as he studied the redacted report. "Is that all records concerning what happened to the occupants were either destroyed, or as in the case of this one, made illegible."

"Why would anyone do that?" Mike said as studied the fire damaged shell of Sunny Meadows.

"Isn't that obvious?" Nigel looked from one to the other. "For there to be no eyewitness accounts, one has to assume that everybody within the building perished."

"That seems a bit of a stretch," Lisa said. "If every record has been destroyed or doctored, how do we know that witness reports weren't included in that purge? They may have been able to eradicate witness records created immediately after the fire, but I greatly doubt that whoever was guarding the details of that night could have kept a lid on what surviving staff and patients may have said at some later date."

Nigel nodded his agreement. "I think that no other subsequent reference to the event or to the survivors is a clear indication that nobody was left alive to pass along the story."

"But what about their remains?" Mike asked. "At some point someone must have searched the property."

"Not necessarily," Nigel replied. "The firemen were ordered to leave, weren't they? I think that whatever evidence of what occurred that night was destroyed."

"How is that possible?" Mike asked. "There would have had to be remains if people had died. Even in a fire there's always something left, isn't there?"

"I'm sure there was," Nigel agreed. "However, knowing what we do about the owner of Sunny Meadows and the highly questionable practices that went on there, I'm sure that the ability to dispose of any remains would have hardly been that difficult. Let's not forget that the patients had been placed in the facility, not just by the wealthy, but by government officials who, back then, had almost unlimited power."

"Even so," Lisa continued. "Why would they even want to cover up the results of the fire? Wouldn't everyone perishing in the blaze be a godsend? In one fell swoop, all the people that were being hidden within Sunny Meadows were eliminated. I would have thought that the people responsible for locking their spouses or relatives away would have been only too happy to make public the fact that their beloved wife or whomever had sadly died in a tragic accident."

Nigel smiled back at her. "Unless they were the ones who arranged the fire."

"Why would anyone want to risk doing such a thing?" Mike asked.

"You yourself told me that your friend found evidence that a search warrant had been issued," Nigel reminded him.

"But a judge stopped it being served," Lisa said.

"That may have slowed down the process, but if the district attorney was serious about following through on what he believed was happening at Sunny Meadows, it was only a matter of time before he could have that ruling overturned. I think that some very powerful people became concerned that they were about to be tied to a scandal that would undoubtedly not only destroy their political future but could also land them in jail. I believe that the timing was way too convenient to be coincidental. They obviously arranged for the staff and patients to die before they could have the chance to tell anyone what really went on within the facility."

"Why would they kill the staff?" Lisa asked. "Surely some of them had to be in on the whole scheme?"

"You're right. I don't believe they did kill everyone. There's no way they could have carried out a mass murder of that scale without inside help. To pull off the malpractice that had been going on for years, there had to be people within Sunny Meadows that were very much part of the overall scheme. I'm certain that they were the ones who somehow arranged for the innocent staff and falsely imprisoned patients to die on that night."

"My god," Lisa replied, shocked.

"If we are to accept all of this as fact," Mike said. "There's still one thing that's bothering me. Not everybody who died could have been unaware that they were about to perish. If that's true, how could what's happening here be one of those RTH things that you were telling us about? If people were burned to death they must have known, even if only for a few seconds, what was happening to them and that they were going to die. So why weren't they able to pass on to… what did you call it… the next plane?"

Nigel looked as if he'd been hit in the face. His head flinched at Mike's words.

"I don't know," he said, stunned by Mike's revelatory question.

"Are there any other reasons that would stop an

entity from passing on?" Lisa asked. "Is there something that could hold them back?"

"Oh my god," Nigel said as his hand rose to his mouth. "I never even considered that."

"Considered what?" Mike and Lisa asked at the same time.

Nigel's eyes darted nervously to each of them in turn.

"Considered what?" Lisa asked again. This time her voice was icy calm.

Nigel took a moment to find the right words. "I don't think that their remains were ever removed from the property."

"Then where the hell are they? They can't just…" Lisa started to ask.

"Oh, shit," Mike said, his voice shaky.

"What?" Lisa asked.

"The basement!" Mike stated. "It's always been about the basement. That's where all of this began."

Before the others could say a thing, Mike was on his feet heading for the hallway. They caught up with him at the basement door. Mike was standing staring at it, trying to get up enough nerve to open it.

"We've come this far," Lisa prompted him. "Go ahead."

After glancing over at her and Nigel, he grasped the handle and turned it. After a brief hesitation, he pulled the door open.

The others couldn't see inside, but instead saw Mike fall to his knees and bury his head in his hands as he sobbed unrestrainedly. Lisa walked up next to him and with a hand on his shoulder, looked through the door.

"Oh my god!" she managed to say before lowering herself next to her husband.

Nigel stepped over and looked over the top of them. He felt momentarily lightheaded as a wave of disbelief washed over him.

Beyond the door was an empty coat closet. Hanging on a brand-new chrome plated rail were six cheap plastic hangers. While the closet was unsettling enough considering what had been there only moments earlier, what unnerved Nigel the most was what was on the back wall of the small space.

Written in what appeared to be black charcoal were the words:

HELP US

CHAPTER 46

Less than three hours later, Daryl, the same landscaping foreman who had supervised their yard, arrived in one of Moses's trucks. He was initially shocked by the condition of the grounds. He wanted to first find out what had happened to the pristine landscaping, but something about the fixed stares from Mike and Lisa told him to just get on with what he was there for.

He wheeled the ground penetrating radar unit off his truck as the others watched. It looked like a bright yellow lawnmower with an iPad screen mounted on the handle.

"Looks heavy," Mike commented.

"It is heavy," Daryl replied. "Do you have any towels or cardboard you can put on the floor, so I don't scuff it?"

Mike nodded. "The garage is full of the flat-packed wardrobe boxes that we used during the move."

It took only a few minutes to lay down a protective pathway from the front door to the centre of the living room. Because of all the measuring Mike had done in the basement and his knowledge of which way the space had been oriented, he was able to pace out where the basement would have been in relation to the rest of the house.

"Shall I start here?" Daryl asked, pointing to the area just in front of the unit.

"That's as good a place as any," Mike replied. "Will the cardboard affect the imaging?"

"This thing can penetrate a military grade slab of reinforced concrete. I don't think that some compressed paper will make much difference."

Daryl activated the screen, selected the grid search mode, then pressed start.

The room remained quiet.

"I thought it would make more noise," Nigel commented.

"Nope," Daryl replied. "It's quiet but powerful."

Having helped him move some of the bigger pieces of furniture off to the side, they watched as Daryl slowly wheeled the GPR up and down the living room floor. It only took a few minutes before a shape began to appear within the screen's normal grey background.

"I've got something here," he announced, slightly surprised.

The others all gathered around him.

"See this light area with a black base?" he asked.

They acknowledged that they did.

"That's a void about five feet under us," Dylan explained.

"How big is it?" Mike asked.

"Big," Daryl replied. "Very big. I won't know the exact dimensions until I run a full grid, but from what I'm seeing, I may have to scan some adjoining rooms."

"Can you get an idea of how tall the void might be?" Mike asked.

"That I can do," Daryl said as he pressed the menu button on the touchscreen. "It looks to be about seven feet high."

"I don't think you need to measure any further. You found what we were looking for."

*

Mike contacted the police. They were initially reluctant to pay any heed to a homeowner who kept insisting that there was a secret basement under their house and that he was convinced that there were human remains within it.

Finally, Mike ended up calling Abe Goldstein to ask if he knew anyone of authority in Northern Virginia who would listen to him. It was no surprise that Abe had a high-ranking contact within the governor's office.

Ninety minutes after Abe called and ultimately spoke to the governor himself, a van from the medical examiner's office arrived, followed a few minutes later by a white truck with 'INTERIOR EXCAVATIONS INC' emblazoned on the side.

Mike, Nigel, and Lisa hunkered down as a team covered everything in the living room with plastic sheeting before attacking the floor itself.

As the men were prepping the space, Mike and Nigel watched as the beautiful dark wood flooring was ripped from the centre of the room. Lisa had to leave the room. Mike wasn't sure if it was because of what they were digging for, or that she couldn't handle seeing her home be systematically destroyed.

Once the pneumatic digger began breaking up the concrete, the noise was impossibly loud and the three gathered outside on the patio. Even Samantha couldn't stand the din and found a way to exit the house so she could curl up on one of the patio cushions.

From their position outside the patio doors, they had a ringside seat to see what was going on in the living room.

Finally, after almost two hours, they heard one of the men shout, "We're through."

A fibreoptic camera with a built-in LED light was snaked into the opening they'd made. The three could see the group gathered around a dark tablet screen. Suddenly, they saw the men visibly tense up. There was some urgent sounding murmuring then one of them opened the patio door.

"Mr Ellis, you may want to see this."

Mike was surprised that he was being afforded such a courtesy, but then remembered that these men were there at the behest of the governor, so the manners and consideration suddenly made more sense.

"Can they come as well?" Mike asked, gesturing to Nigel and Lisa.

"It's your home," the technician said as he stood aside to let them back inside.

The three gathered around the flatscreen monitor and tried to work out what exactly they were seeing. The quality of the image seemed razor sharp, but it was hard for them to comprehend the chaos on the screen. Though the camera and monitor were producing a hi-def picture, everything was dark. It wasn't until the medical examiner enlarged the image and was able to point out a few recognisable objects that they were able to understand the horror of what was being captured on camera.

Almost everything was black. The result of what the ME suspected had been a very hot fire that must have started in the basement space then spread up and consumed the above-ground facility. Dotted among the charred floor and walls were small clusters of black debris that were only able to be distinguished from the blackness by patches of grey and occasionally, a speck of something off-white. As the camera zoomed in on a dome-shaped object, they could see that its carbonised outer layer had fallen away, enabling the ME to recognise an eye socket.

They were ultimately able to locate thirty-nine separate clusters, each one being the burned remains of a human being.

"Dear god," Lisa said, as the last one was found nestled against the side of a blackened hulk that one of the technicians suggested may have been the boiler.

"We are going to have to open up the floor so it's wide enough to get some people down there. This is obviously a crime scene, but what with the ferocity of the fire and the fact that the crime was committed almost ninety years ago, the likelihood of finding anything evidentiary is almost zero."

Mike and Lisa could only nod. They had no clue as to what else they could possibly say.

"I don't know what your long-term plans are, but for the next few days, I would suggest that you find alternate accommodation. The removal process of the remains will not be quick, nor will it be pleasant."

Mike and Lisa looked at each other hoping the other had a plan.

"Why don't you all come and stay on the farm until they've finished here?" Nigel offered.

"That's very generous," Lisa replied. "But, and please don't take this the wrong way, I kind of feel that I want to try and forget all about hauntings for at least a few days."

Nigel nodded his understanding.

"Why don't I call Wayne and see if he wants a chance to really suck up to his boss?"

Lisa tried to smile, but it was obvious that her heart just wasn't in it.

Mike reached Wayne just as he was leaving work. After Mike explained their situation, Wayne pointed out that it was Friday so not only were they welcome, but they could even try to make the weekend fun and distracting for the weary adults and for Kevin.

"Maybe we could barbeque some ribs?" Wayne suggested.

Mike unconsciously glanced over at the crowd gathered at the monitor looking down at the mass cremation site.

"No barbeque."

CHAPTER 47

It took a crew from the medical examiner's office two days to remove the remains, at which point a county contractor filled in the entire basement void with cement. Though the state picked up the cost for creating the hole and then plugging it, they regretfully advised Mike and Lisa that they would not be able to replace the missing wood flooring.

When the Ellis family returned home Sunday night, they were astonished at how clean the technicians had left the place. Other than some furniture still being out of place, the missing wood flooring and the raw concrete (that was covered by a tarp that they were forbidden to walk on for at least two weeks), the place looked normal.

Lisa made a simple pasta dish and the three ate at the dining table. The parents kept the conversation light to try and keep Kevin's questions to a minimum. The one item he wouldn't drop was his pleading for them to let him leave his initials in the new cement.

Lisa promised him that if it was still wet enough when he got home from school the next day, he could leave an imprint in it.

Once he was in bed, Lisa and Mike settled into the family room to watch the part of *Bridesmaids* they'd missed when exhaustion and subsequent events overtook them a few nights earlier.

"How are you feeling?" Mike asked.

"Actually, pretty good. I thought I'd feel kind of creeped out, but somehow knowing that the remains have been removed and their spirits have gone wherever they're supposed go, seems to have taken away the taint."

"That's good to hear," Mike replied. "I was worried that you'd be done with this house."

"I didn't say that I've come to terms with what happened here. Whether we stay or go is going to be contingent on my being able to compartmentalise what was buried under this house. The only reason I'm going to give it a try is that I have to believe that the worst is over, at least as far as the hauntings go. Obviously, there's still the matter of your work situation. If you lose your job, it's going to be your call as to whether we stay here and you look for something else, or whether we take all of this as some sort of an omen that the east coast just wasn't right for us."

"I've got another week before I go back, so who knows what could happen. Maybe the bank will realise that Kerry is a vindictive flake and get rid of her."

"I love it when you say such positive things," Lisa joked.

"Okay, let me try something else," Mike said. "Did you notice the lawn when we drove up?"

"No. Why?"

"Maybe I'm going crazy, but the yellow parts looked a little bit greener."

Lisa glanced out into the dark night. "I'll check that out tomorrow."

They snuggled under Lisa's penguin quilt and managed to watch the rest of the movie without dozing off.

*

Lisa was the first to wake up. She looked about the dark bedroom wondering what had disturbed her sleep, then she heard it. The sound was like the sizzling noise a firework sparkler makes when lit.

"What the hell is that?" Mike asked as he sat up next to her.

"I've no idea, but it sounds as if it's right here in the room with us."

Mike was reaching for his bedside lamp switch when

Lisa grabbed his arm. Just beyond the end of the bed, about four feet off the floor was a pinprick of light. As they watched, it grew until it was the size and shape of a pencil. A golden, shimmering pencil. Mike was about to reach out to it when a second dot of light appeared.

"What are they?" Mike whispered out of the side of his mouth.

Lisa could only shake her head as a third one appeared. The first one no longer looked like a flickering pencil. It now looked almost like a child's stick figure drawing of a human but made up entirely of quivering light.

The head, if that's what it was, seemed to turn as if checking out the room. Suddenly, dozens of other dots of golden light appeared, encircling their bed. They all quickly morphed into the same form as the original one.

The sparkler sound filled the room as their luminance changed from gold to a gentle shade of violet. Without warning, they all joined arms, or at least what Mike and Lisa assumed were arms, then raised them up and spread them above the Ellis's bed.

Lisa grabbed Mike's hand.

The sizzling sound suddenly stopped and in a chorus that was only just audible, they heard a single musical note. It filled the room and caused both Mike and Lisa's eyes to well up, though neither knew why.

The figures began to brighten as their hue changed to a pale blue, then, as if on command, they rose into the air then vanished through the ceiling.

Lisa felt a release of pressure a little like when ears pop as a plane loses altitude. She turned to Mike and saw that he was trembling.

"What was that?" Mike asked in little more than a whisper.

Before Lisa could answer, a rich, Mexican-accented voice wafted over them both.

"*Ellas te dan las gracias,*" the voice said.

A shape began to emerge from the darkness. It was clearly that of a man but had no real detail. It was as if a shadow had somehow been backlit.

"Sebastian?" Lisa asked.

It took a while before he could generate enough energy to respond.

"*Si, señora.*"

"Why are you still here?" Mike asked.

"*Para tu hijo,*" the image replied.

Mike held up both hands, hoping that Sebastian would understand the 'wait' gesture. He grabbed his iPhone, found Nigel's details then face-timed him.

"What the hell's happening now?" Nigel asked, obviously just awakened.

"There's someone here who needs your translating skills," Mike replied, as he changed the camera orientation so that it was pointed at the outline of Sebastian.

"What am I looking at?" Nigel asked, now fully awake and intrigued. "Sebastian?"

"*Si,*" the spectre replied.

"*Pensé que te habías marchada?*" Nigel said.

As Mike and Lisa looked on, Nigel and Sebastian carried out a brief conversation in Spanish.

"Basically," Nigel explained. "Sebastian remained here to protect the boy. He was afraid that the other spirits would be attracted to him because of his youthful energy."

"Were they?" Lisa asked.

"I asked him the same thing. He said that only one ever communicated directly with him but that there was no doubt that they were very interested in Kevin."

"Does he know if they are really gone?" Mike asked.

"Yes, he does," Nigel answered. "He says they thanked Mike and his family for what they did then they all passed through. There is nothing left here but him."

"Is he leaving soon?" Lisa asked.

"Sabastian said that now they have all gone and the boy is safe, he is also ready to go as well."

"Ask him to wait a minute... please," Mike suddenly jumped in. "Nigel, you said before that spirits could exist even within a small object that was tied to the property?"

"Yes, that's right. Why?"

"I wonder if you could ask Sebastian if he could do us one last favour before passing on?"

*

It felt strange walking into the bank. It was very early in the morning and though it never formally closed, the building seemed deserted except for a small security contingent. Mike scanned his ID as a night guard waved him through without a second glance. He'd been worried that they might have wanted to check out the Whole Foods shopping bag he was carrying, but they didn't seem the least bit interested.

Mike made his way to the second basement level and the AV suite. He didn't even stop at the People Force enclave and made directly for the narrow hallway where Kerry's office was located. He carefully removed the gift-wrapped box from the bag and left it outside her door, then calmly walked back up to the ground floor.

As he stepped through the security turnstiles, the same guard that had watched him enter the building said, "That was quick?"

"Just needed to check on something," Mike replied as he stepped back out into the chilled morning air.

CHAPTER 48

Mike was sitting on the patio drinking an Amstel Light when his phone rang just after midday that same morning. He looked at the screen and saw that it was Rick Greenberg.

Smiling, he accepted the call. "What's up?"

"I wish you'd been here this morning," Rick said, his voice excited and breathless.

"What happened?" Mike asked with feigned innocence.

"Kerry! Kerry's what happened," Rick said, his words coming through the phone a mile a minute. "She went berserk. I'm not talking about the regular lunacy. This time she was totally out of it. She came into our area just before the morning meeting holding a chamber pot..."

"A what?" Mike asked.

"You heard me. An actual chamber pot... and not a nice clean new one. This looked like it had recently been used."

"Yuck."

"I know, right?" Rick continued. "She wanted to know who'd given it to her."

"How weird," Mike said, trying to keep his voice calm.

"She finally went back to her office, then about twenty minutes later we hear her screaming her head off."

"Who was she screaming at?"

"Not who… what! Security found her on the floor wedged between her bookcase and the wall screaming at the chamber pot."

"What was she screaming?" Mike asked.

"Mostly it was complete gibberish. She almost seemed to be trying to exorcise some evil spirit…"

"Why do you think that?"

"'Cause at one point she actually screamed, 'Get back in there you evil demon.'"

"Get back in where?" Mike tried to keep his voice serious.

"The chamber pot!" Rick shrieked. "She was trying to command something back into the chamber pot."

"Wow. Where is she now?"

"They took her away in an ambulance."

"Do they think she'll be okay?" Mike asked.

"I don't know, but here's the best part. When Kerry

was flipping out and ranting on about demons and voodoo and all sorts of wild shit, Madame Ambode was standing in the hallway. She tried to reason with her, but Kerry totally flipped out and told Ambode to mind her own fucking business.

"Needless to say, Kerry's outburst really freaked her out. Once the paramedics had taken her away, Ambode said that she was clearly infected with bad joojoo and that she wasn't going to permit such a person anywhere near her or the main bank building."

"Can she do that?" Mike asked.

"She's the vice president of the African sector. She can pretty much do anything she wants. Besides, I have this sneaky suspicion that Madame Ambode didn't like her much anyway. Apparently, Kerry made a habit of talking down to her."

"So, Kerry's gone?" Mike tried to keep the excitement out of his voice. "Really and truly gone?"

"Sure, looks like it."

*

When Mike returned to the bank one week later, Wayne was already in his office.

"Welcome back," he said as he peered around the doorway.

"Thanks. It feels good to be here."

"Did you hear what happened on Friday?"

"No," Mike replied.

"HR met with Kerry, who's still completely batshit by the way, and told her that she could no longer work within the GIB headquarters. They offered her some lesser position in the M Street building, but she went berserk and told HR that nobody was going push her aside. And that she hadn't been screwing the executive director for all these years so that some low-class dimwit from human resources could tell her where she could and couldn't work."

"Wow! What happened after that?"

"The first thing was that the dimwit from human resources was in fact the director of human resources. She fired Kerry on the spot. Then turned around and immediately started an internal investigation into Gary Schneider!"

"The executive director?" Mike asked, stunned.

"But wait... there's more," Wayne said. "Schneider's now on indefinite paid leave and guess who's acting ED?"

"Not a clue," Mike announced.

"Crap," Martin said as he slid by Wayne and stepped into the office. "I wanted to tell you myself."

"Tell me what?"

"Shouldn't there be a 'sir' in there somewhere? I mean you are, after all, talking to a senior executive."

"You?" Mike's jaw dropped.

Martin grinned.

"I hope you'll do a better job of picking the person to take your old job. The last ED really screwed things up."

"I have someone in mind," Martin said.

"Do I know this person?"

"Intimately," Martin said as he gently nudged Wayne back out into the hall. He then closed Mike's office door so that he could formally discuss the offer with the only person he'd ever felt was qualified to take over the position.

*

Later that day, as Mike pulled into his driveway, he could see Lisa and Kevin through the kitchen window. They both appeared to be licking icing from a couple of wooden spoons. Lisa, sensing his arrival before she even heard or saw his car, looked up and smiled as she gestured to the last glob of icing clinging to the wooden utensil. Mike nodded.

He was glad they'd decided to stay. Somehow when the spirits left them in such an indescribably moving way, he'd known then that Lisa wouldn't want to give up the house. It was what she'd always dreamed of.

It was home.

EPILOGUE

The house was quiet.

Mike was at work, Kevin was at school, and Lisa was running errands in Gainesville.

Samantha was curled up on the family room sofa, twitching and jerking as a dream interacted with her motor neurons. Her eyes suddenly snapped open, and it took a moment for her tiny brain to register that she was safe in a place she knew and where kind people fed and cared for her.

She was about to go back to sleep when the strange energy she'd begun sensing when they first moved in, caused her to find her way to the laundry room as she'd done on numerous occasions.

Samantha squeezed between the drier and the wall and found the loose flap where a piece of drywall had cracked and partially deteriorated. She stepped through the opening and walked between the wall studs until she found the old stairway. The smell didn't bother her, though usually smoke caused most cats to experience immediate unrest.

The stairs ended at the beginnings of a tunnel that she knew led all the way to the lake. She slowly crept along the dark cavern, careful not to disturb the human bones that were scattered almost its entire length. Samantha had no way of knowing that they were the remains of the Sunny Meadows staff who had planned to use the tunnel as an escape route once they trapped the inmates and support staff in the basement and started the fire.

A heavy rain the day before they enacted the owner's plan had loosened the soil at the far end of the tunnel and caused the partial collapse of the hand-hewn dirt ceiling just as it met the lake. Unable to move the huge rocks that had come down with the earthen roof, the smoke from the fire that they themselves had set found its way into the dark shaft, suffocating them all where they lay.

Samantha had traversed the burrow-like escape path numerous times. The large rocks allowed her just enough room to squeeze past and emerge into the open air. She didn't like the journey, yet had, on each occurrence, felt obliged to make the pilgrimage. It wasn't a conscious decision. All she knew was that some dark energy willed her to do it.

Samantha had no concept of life or death, but each

time she found her way through the tunnel, she could sense that the energy within it was growing stronger. During her earlier visits, it had felt benign and if anything, a little curious.

Now she felt something different. Something that caused the hair along her spine to stand on end.

She sensed anger.